"Intensely humane and beautiful. Stronach's richly imagined world is never too heavy for itself: shot through with black humor at every turn, it is nonetheless tender and sympathetic while also being starkly unsentimental. Part police procedural, part queer fever dream, part love letter to a city that doesn't exist: Stronach makes the impossible look easy. Its distinctly Kiwi voice is a new salvo for New Zealand fantasy on an international stage. I loved it."

— Tamsyn Muir, *New York Times* bestselling author of *Gideon the Ninth*

"Fiercely queer. A strange and wondrous reimagining of noir that takes its cues from biopunk and SE Asian mythos to create something wholly different. There's real imagination at work here—I loved it."

— Rebecca Roanhorse, *New York Times* bestselling author of *Trail of Lightning* and *Black Sun*

"Worldbuilding at its peak. *The Dawnhounds* heaves with life, a tangible sense of cosmic power simmering from the waters around this port city and from the people trying to save it. Just don't call them heroes, aye."

— Chloe Gong, *New York Times* bestselling author of *These Violent Delights* and *Our Violent Ends*

"*The Dawnhounds* roots in the mind like a night garden, vital and voracious. I can't get it out of my head."

— Amal El-Mohtar, award-winning coauthor of *This Is How You Lose the Time War*

"*The Dawnhounds* packs hard-hitting, mind-bending weirdness into a story that's still touching and human. If you're looking for gritty queer spec fic that isn't unrelentingly grim, you've found it."

— Casey Lucas, award-winning author of *Into the Mire*

"The tones of Stronach and Pratchett are enormously similar. . . . Delightful."

— Octavia Cade, author of *The Mythology of Salt and Other Stories*

THE DAWNHOUNDS

THE ENDSONG
- BOOK ONE -

SASCHA STRONACH

SAGA PRESS

LONDON SYDNEY **NEW YORK** TORONTO NEW DELHI

SAGA PRESS

AN IMPRINT OF SIMON & SCHUSTER, INC.

1230 AVENUE OF THE AMERICAS, NEW YORK, NEW YORK 10020

First Saga Press trade paperback edition June 2022

SAGA PRESS and colophon are trademarks
of Simon & Schuster, Inc.

For information about special discounts for bulk purchases, please contact Simon & Schuster Special Sales at 1-866-506-1949 or business@simonandschuster.com.

The Simon & Schuster Speakers Bureau can bring authors to your live event. For more information or to book an event, contact the Simon & Schuster Speakers Bureau at 1-866-248-3049 or visit our website at www.simonspeakers.com.

Interior design by Michelle Marchese

Manufactured in the United States of America

1   3   5   7   9   10   8   6   4   2

Library of Congress Cataloging-in-Publication Data
has been applied for.

ISBN 978-1-9821-8705-7
ISBN 978-1-9821-8706-4 (ebook)

For Jay,
neither beast nor burden

AUTHOR'S NOTE

Dear Reader,

This novel may at times use New Zealand slang. This is, as I have assured my editor, intentional.

You may find a simile missing its final word and say to yourself, "Yeah nah, that's not on, mate, you dropped the bloody ball there," to which I must cordially respond, "Oh yeah nah, it's meant to do that aye, Kiwi slang is good as."

Yours faithfully,
Sascha Stronach

Tahu, I have made petition to the wind
and listened at the small places
but heard nothing in reply, save wind;
must all our stories end in death?

ONE

Nobody would meet Yadin's eye, but that was fine. They didn't understand what it meant to be a captain, to make hard choices. He paced the deck, hands in the pockets of his coat. He'd kept it on despite the muggy heat, because it made him look the part of captain and because the crew needed to know there was still somebody in charge. He *was* the captain now: the chain of command was clear. Some of the men weren't happy about the alchemist being at the helm, but they were scared and emotional. They'd thank him when he brought the ship home. The thrice-cursed coat made him sweat like a pig in a cook pot, though; he'd sell his soul to the birds for a bath filled with fresh ice.

They'd been hearing gull calls for almost a day: home was close, he knew it. They'd been in sight of the city itself before the fog rolled in, its lights like a constellation floating above the inky midnight waters. After two godsdamned years, he'd see his Betej again. (And his child—a son? He didn't know. They'd set sail before he knew.) He'd kiss her and call her "sugarcane," then have a nice long bath, then kiss her again, and they'd screw until the bed broke, then he'd have another damn bath. Then he'd put on his clothes, saunter straight through the great wooden gate at Heron Hill, hand in his resignation, have one last bath for good measure (salt, salt, the endless bloody salt . . . it was in his hair, his eyes, carving little white roads through the lines of his already sweating hands and the chiseled notches of his tattoos, making him itch), then start his own clinic, raise his kid right, and never think about going to sea ever again. Hells, he'd probably think twice about crossing a canal. Maybe move the family inland, to Nahaj Kral or one of the Garden Cities. Betej had always wanted to, but Yadin had worried about one of the old volcanoes blowing its top. This whole mess had left him less afraid of fire—there were worse ways to go.

The waters around Hainak Kuai were usually easy sailing, but the *Fantail* had suddenly hit a fogbank he hadn't seen coming, and the strong tailwind had fallen away to nothing. It had come upon them out of nowhere, and the weather wasn't right for it: too warm. You'd sometimes get whorls of mist over the surface of the water this time of year, but this was something else. It was dense and clinging, which made it hard to see much except shadowy silhouettes of the crew. They'd been in sight of the lighthouse when it came roiling up over the gunnels, but now the light was nowhere to be seen. The smart money was on waiting it out, but there were other concerns.

There was no water left, nor food. Well, that wasn't quite true: there *was* water, and there was food, but they were in the hold, and the hold was off-limits. The crew had nailed the hatch shut and piled barrels of grub food atop. A few men had protested, because they hadn't seen . . .

It.

They hadn't seen *it*. How quickly it had spread. A single broken vial of the stuff. Lots of food down there, of course. The rations, the water, and the . . .

The ship had set sail from Gostei with twenty men, and there were only nine left. Even with all those double shifts, sleeping no more than four hours a night, they struggled to make the cutter sail true. Exigencies of command: unavoidable, no sin in triage. The expedition's backers would understand, everybody would get hazard pay, and the crew would thank him for getting them out of a difficult situation in one piece. The admiralty had sent them deep into Suta looking for botanicals with "military applications," and by that metric, the journey was an unmitigated success. They'd found the vials in an overgrown ferro-tech lab, deep beneath a ruined city of white stone. Ancient electric lights had come on and the screens had spoken to them, but their translator had been less than useless. He was dead now. Well, not *dead*, but . . .

A moan came from belowdecks. By Luz of the Field, by Crane of the Sky, by Dorya of the Deep, this was a disaster. He toyed with the worry beads in his pocket.

Elvar, the bosun, shot Yadin an evil glare. Elvar was a big man, with a mop of sandy-blond hair, armor grafts on his forearms, and a mouth full of iron teeth. Northerner, from . . . well, the North. Geography had never been Yadin's strong suit. There wasn't much worth investigating up that way anyway: snow, cannibals, steel cults, *engineers*. Worthless stuff. The savages didn't even know alchemy, though they were always trying to crack it. Elvar's metal teeth'd gone to rust in the salt air, of course, but he didn't seem to care. He glared at Yadin. His hand wasn't on his knife yet, but there was something about his poise, pent and coiled like a snake.

Yadin took a step forward. He needed to assert authority, but violence would lead to violence, and the crew could ill afford more casualties. He needed to take a more subtle approach: he tapped his foot on the deck once, twice, then he began to sing. He'd been a choirboy when he was younger, but fear and decades out of practice left his voice stiff and crackling.

The lion prowls the seas,
me lads, his wicked teeth
I know, but I've no fear,
I've got youse here, so sing
for hell and sing for home.

There was meant to be a call-and-response after each verse: *Yeah nah yeah, sweet as, bro.* Such a colorful expression: it meant *Yes, no, maybe, we're brothers, I won't remember you tomorrow.* The crew stayed silent. Elvar took a step forward. They'd never got on, even when the ship had been riding high—Elvar didn't talk or dance or tell jokes. Elvar only watched and took notes in very neat handwriting in his little brown notebook and did exactly his duties and not one thing more.

A wet, choking cough reached out from somewhere below. Yadin could almost feel it in his own chest: thick, cancerous, oily. Pulmonary edema? Possible. No, no. This was no time for diagnostics. He brought his foot down harder on the deck, right on the beat. *One* two three, *one* two *three.*

The northern wind is cruel
and cold, she'll rip the skin
right off your bones, so haul
away, don't haul alone;

A voice cut through the muggy air behind him. Raspy, female: Ajat, the tall woman with the pale patches of vitiligo staining her dark skin. She spoke all the guttural island languages, plus a few more: Reo Tāngata, Torad, Dawgae, and, uh . . . Northern. For a moment he almost lost the beat, wary that she might move to hurt him, but her voice turned into a pleasing alto harmony as they hit the last few notes together.

haul a line, haul on home.

Another moment of silence, and then he heard it. Hardly enthusiastic, but a ragged chorus of perhaps half a dozen men.

Yeah nah yeah, sweet as, bro.

He and Ajat went into the third verse, and another voice joined them, then another. Surprisingly good pipes for ruffians and thugs. The evil moans from belowdecks got louder and more insistent. Something had wiped out the people of Suta so long ago their names were lost to history and so completely that nobody dared settle there ever again. Something had turned their cities into charnel houses and their memory into smoke. When Yadin was a kid, they'd played make-believe and pretended they were valiant explorers in the Ghost Cities, cutting through dense jungle and climbing cloud-piercing towers. They'd never stopped to ask why the whole continent was silent; Suta belonged solely to the dead. He was furious with himself and his superiors and every single soul who saw the marble-white spires emerge from the mountains and got so interested in the *whats* that they forgot to ask about the *whys*.

5

The crew's chant moved to match the awful groans of their colleagues. It was a song from the war, and most of them hadn't had reason to sing it in a long time. Yadin had cut his teeth as a medic during the siege of Syalong Cherta, where they finally broke the Lion's back. He'd hummed it to steady his hands while the bullets flew, and he hoped it would steady them now. Was it a trick of the mind, or did Yadin feel the wind in his hair? The fog hadn't moved, but a pleasant chill ran down his spine. He scrambled for another verse. Had it really been ten years? But of course, it was a sea shanty: simple, repetitive, vulgar enough to turn the wind blue. The words came to him.

> *Them lion cunts, we'll fuck*
> *'em all, we'll fuck 'em hard*
> *and slow, we'll fuck 'em up*
> *we'll fuck 'em down, we'll fuck*
> *the lion to and fro.*

The whole crew was singing now except Elvar. He had death in his eyes, but it wasn't the song. The North hadn't been in the war—they'd vultured around the edges, taking slaves and sacrifices for their great furnace, but never actually picked a side. No, it was that the ship had lost its captain, the chaplain, the lieutenant. Beneath them in the chain of command was the alchemist, then the bosun. They'd lost them because Yadin had the parliamentary warrant to oversee sample collection, and somebody had mishandled one of the flasks— somebody curious, maybe, or just clumsy. The incident still sat ill with some of the crew, festering in their minds. Yadin hadn't experienced quite this sort of hatred before, but he'd seen strains of it; he'd heard whispers. He couldn't mention Parliament without Elvar spitting out *"provisional"*—the war wasn't *over*, after all, it was just a decade since anybody had seen a Ladowain warship anywhere south of Dawgar, and they certainly weren't coming over land; Hainak forces controlled the great bastion at Syalong Cherta. The desert north of the ancient chain of mountain fortresses was strewn with rusted tanks and acid-eaten armored cars, its cave networks infested with the ravening offspring of early-model artillery shells that had failed to detonate on impact. Every so often somebody would spot a Ladowain scout car patrolling outside the guns' range and remember that the war wasn't technically over, that resentment between nations was still festering after ten long years.

Tonight's hatred was different: right before him, front and center. He could almost feel Elvar's dagger in his heart. He rubbed the tattoo on the back of his hand—a pig in a crate, an old sailor's charm to ward against drowning. Ajat had given it to him—they'd gotten exceedingly drunk about a year back, and he'd let her go to work with a whining electric device she'd managed to smuggle out of the Vault, which she powered by plugging it into her own scalp. When he'd asked why a pig in a crate, she'd shrugged and said, "Pigs float." It still itched on cold days, and he was worried the damage might be permanent. He'd get a proper fleshsmith to look at it back in Hainak. An electric needle? *Gods*, what strange things foreigners did.

> No kings no more, no gold,
> no thrones, no steel shackles
> cold, we sail through hell on
> frozen swell, and sing to
> warm our souls.

Elvar took another step forward, his hand perched on the hilt of his dirk. He was close enough to smell now: salt and shit and stale rum. The sounds from below ceased, and so did the singing. The scrape of drawn steel cut through the night—metal weapons. *Gods*— Yadin didn't know how to fight. He'd patched up a lot of men afterward, though, and he knew one thing: you got no winners when weapons came out, only the dead and the suffering. He drew his own pistol and raised it. It was long-expired, the grubs inside having starved weeks ago. He cleared his throat and—

"LIGHT!" shouted Ajat.

They'd almost missed it in the fog, to their port side. It was smaller than Yadin had imagined, its beacon struggling to pierce through the fog. He couldn't even make out the lighthouse, but he didn't care— just one little light changed the whole shape of the evening. It flashed on and off in short and long bursts. The codebook was with the captain, and talking to the captain wasn't an option right now. It didn't matter; the crew was hooting and hollering, cheering and crying.

In the midst of it all, Yadin made eye contact with Elvar. The homicidal intent remained, but then Elvar smiled. Slowly, with exaggerated care, he put the knife back in its sheath and looked toward the light. It would do, for now.

"Light the lamps! Drop anchor! Break out the oars!" said Yadin. He was the captain now, dammit. Well, acting captain. Same thing. The ship sprang to life around him. The *Fantail* itself was becalmed, but they could row the boats to the lighthouse and get their report in to Hainak. Somebody from Parliament could pick up the ship; somebody with quarantine experience, or failing that, a box of matches and as much liquid fire as they could carry. It was *done*. It was somebody else's problem.

The sails were already trim, but they dropped the anchor to be sure. They put red filters in the lamps to warn of danger and strapped them along the gunnels. There was a single yellow lamp on the starboard side that Yadin didn't remember hanging, but he had other things on his mind. When it was done, they dropped the boats. They only needed two, and Yadin made sure he wasn't in Elvar's.

Yadin was not a sailor: he hated the sea. He'd taken the job for his country, and because the little man with the parliamentary seal had offered a bigger number than he was willing to say no to. Nevertheless, the slap of oars on the glassy water filled him with immense pleasure. He hummed as he rowed and didn't even complain about what the crush of oars against waves would do to his flawless surgeon's hands (excepting the tattoo—wine could make men do strange things). He was going to go home, kiss his wife and call her "sugarcane," and never leave land again.

The first shot took him just below the clavicle, perhaps an inch above his heart. He dropped the oar and tried to cry out as the grub began to do its vile work under his skin. The neurotoxins hit his nervous system, and he screamed. He knew in an instant that it was fatal, but he wasn't dead yet. The thump-thump of borer fire came from the direction of the lighthouse—little wet blooms in the fog, glistening like morning dew, almost beautiful, if you could ignore the chattering of their sharp little teeth flying closer and closer. He drew his pistol and tried to return fire, but nothing came out. He fell backward into the dinghy. The other crew fell, or dived overboard, or reached for their own guns. The bottom of the boat was full of water, and Yadin realized that some of the grubs had hit their hull; the little bastards would go through wood just as happily as flesh. His mouth was full of blood. He rolled onto his stomach, then shrieked in pain as salt water rushed through the hole in his chest. The little lifeboat yawed, then broke in half. Yadin went under. Shots smashed through the surface of the water above him. His nerves burned, but his skin was so very cold.

As the red lanterns on the *Fantail* winked at him, they might as well have been a world away. The yellow lantern, too, blurry and indistinct through the surface of the water—odd, he still didn't remember hanging that one. Elvar sank beside him, eyes sightless and jawline a ragged mess of muscle and bone. Yadin slipped farther down into the water, and darkness took him.

TWO

Jyn Yat-Hok wiped sweat from her forehead. The weeks before the rains were the worst: climbing humidity, but not a drop of water from any of the Four Heavens. Even in the dead of night, it was too damn hot. A hawker grabbed at her arm and thrust a platter of bean cakes in her face. She flashed her badge at him, and suddenly he saw the boundless opportunities available in bothering somebody else.

Sergeant Yit Kanq-Sen walked beside her. He was a Garden City boy with an incomprehensible accent, who was wiry as an alley cat and infamously slippery in a fight. He whistled as they walked but didn't say much. She enjoyed his company immensely. Despite his insistence on calling everybody "mate" and about ten different things a "fuckeen' tinny," he possessed a perishingly rare ability on the force: knowing when to shut up. He swung his feet in little arcs when he walked, in a way she'd initially taken as sloppy and eventually come to realize was tremendously efficient—all momentum, no effort. It wasn't the way they'd trained her to march at the academy, and it didn't look professional, but she'd given up trying to talk him out of it.

The Tinker's Horn, growing from a nearby thatch of vinework, turned its petals up to face the moon. "Three a.m." it called, "Three a.m." It was an older model: its trilling voice didn't sound human. Nobody bothered to update the network in this part of the city—the older vines met and merged with the new ones beneath the titanic wall at Arnak-Vonaj. When she'd been a kid it was all ferro, just machines and steel. Amazing how fast alchemic botanicals had come up. They claimed it was a blessing from Luz himself, the right hand of heaven elevating the people of Hainak from field to greenhouse. Dad had believed that with his whole heart, had prayed to Luz in his little laboratory every evening. Prayer hadn't kept the fumes from eating his lungs. She could barely remember a world without the wonders of botany. The first prototypes had sprung up about fifteen years ago, a half decade before the revolution, and they'd been exactly what the city needed to throw off the crumbling remains of the Ladowain Empire. It was political now: you couldn't just cast aside the tools of the revolution, especially with the revolution refusing to fully revolve. If you could afford to go botanical, you owed it to the people, and if you couldn't, then they were happy to have you in their debt. An arm lost in an industrial accident could be regrown, and just as easily repossessed if you couldn't make the payments. She didn't even recognize Hainak as the place she'd grown up: the myths and songs might be the same, but the rapid change from iron to alchemy had filled the place with gaps. There were districts that had never caught up because they just didn't have the money. It was an explosive age, good for the well-heeled and the strong who could take advantage but awful for the slow, the sick, and the poor. The wonders of science didn't reach some corners of town until after the rich had bled their every drop. Not that the old order had been better, but at the end of the day, bootheels were bootheels. Hainak Kuai: the mismatched city, the ragtag city, the city of walls and gardens.

Yat took out her bell and rang it. "Three a.m. and all's well," she said. The end of her shift, finally.

"Shut up!" somebody shouted from a nearby rooftop. Male, cracking—a roof rat? Sounded like a teenager; his roof-running days were probably numbered. It was a life that didn't end in a lot of open doors or hot meals. She put her bell away—no need to make his night any worse. The officers' manual said that citizens would often become belligerent or even *bellicose*, but that this was not a crime in and of itself. Yat wasn't entirely clear what *bellicose* meant, but it had been double-underlined in the regulations, so she assumed it was pretty exciting. The manual was very clear on how to deal with these situations, and she didn't have the energy to do more than the bare minimum.

She saluted the space where she assumed he was standing and said in her loudest voice, "THANK YOU FOR YOUR INPUT ON THIS MATTER, SIR. THE CITY WATCH WOULD LIKE TO CON-GRATULATE YOU FOR ENGAGING IN FRUITFUL DIALOGUE WITH US AND WISHES YOU A MERRY EVENING."

Sergeant Kanq-Sen nodded and threw the kid a much lazier sa-lute. Yat did a neat about-face, then stomped off through the streets, muttering to herself, with the sergeant trailing behind her. This was hardly what she'd thought her job would be when she signed up for the academy. What else was she meant to do, though? She'd grown up on the south side of the city, but in the shadow of the wall—her father had been a botanist whose work was too strange to be popular and too useful to be fashionable. When Dad died, he'd left almost nothing. She hadn't expected much, but even so, it struck her how hard he must've worked to put food on the table and make it seem like everything was fine. The chemicals he'd worked with had burned so many holes in his lungs that it was a wonder he could breathe at all. Between his death and her joining the force, things had been difficult for a while. She felt for kids who'd suffered like she had and did what she could for them. Sometimes doing what she could meant following the letter of the law and not one letter more.

A few inquisitive faces poked out from nearby windows to investigate the shouting, then popped straight back in when they saw who was doing it; they didn't trust cops in the north side. They had their reasons, but it didn't make the job less difficult.

Arnak-kua-Vonaj loomed in the distance, one of the only old buildings in the city to survive the fall of the Ron-Yaj Ladowain—Radovan the Lion. The name was meant as an act of rebellion; as Radovan had become Ladowain, so had Arnak Cherta become Arnak-kua-Vonaj. By their seizing the name, it no longer belonged to the enemy. Nobody liked the word *cherta* much anyway—it called to mind grinding, endless battle in the mountains and veterans with acid burns, victims of their own poorly designed weaponry. The ugliest battle of the war so far, the moment of Hainak's triumph that had somehow dragged on and on until it started to taste bitter in their mouths. *Cherta* was the enemy's word, a reminder of something that was meant to be over. They said Arnak-Vonaj had been kept in place as a symbol of what Hainak could overcome, but Yat had lived rough too long to believe that. They were free from foreign occupation, but it didn't mean much unless you were in the right place to exploit it. Even overgrown with engineered vines, the wall looked alien and frightening. In Hainak, metal was still used all over the place—some things just didn't work in botanicals—but it was rare to see so much in one place. It was a great, monstrous thing. A cluster of amanita hovels clung to the side lower down; their gills heaved, and little faces peered down from their windows. The vines and a network of mycelium kept them solidly in place, but they still made Yat feel slightly ill. You didn't live that precariously unless you were really desperate.

She couldn't be bothered dealing with the guards at the wall—her demotion was the talk of every station in town, and she didn't want to deal with some pig-shit newbie deciding he needed to take her down another peg. She could probably lean on the sergeant to push them through, but it hurt her dignity less to just avoid going that way entirely. He was humming now, with his hands in his pockets. She didn't know how he did it—how he managed to care so little.

She made for the port. The walls there were modern, guarded by blanks—they certainly weren't smart enough to ask questions. Their empty stares made her uneasy, but nobody ever got blanked who didn't deserve it. They had failed the city, so they were remade to serve it. No steel out at the port, just low palisades of engineered hardwood: post-revolution tech. Ladowain built in steel and gold; the Vault in concrete and glass; Hainak in cellulose, mycelium, and stone.

She took a sip of tea from her hip flask. Tea was, as her father had taught her, the panacea for all ills. Too cold? Tea. Too hot? Tea. Feeling like your job is going nowhere, and your life is empty and hollow? Lots and lots of tea. Drown yourself in it; crawl into a towering fortress of teacups beneath the sweet sea and never leave.

The flask was steel, and she enjoyed its cool weight in her hand. Technically contraband, but it was one of the last things her dad had given her, and she knew Sergeant Sen wouldn't snitch on her. Steel wasn't dangerous, it was just . . . political. There was steel all over the city, even where it wasn't useful, because it was difficult to tear down and a lot of folks couldn't afford to replace it. She ran her thumb over the engravings: her family name in the center, and an old story around the edge—the one about the gods' golden peanut. It had been her favorite story when she was a kid—everybody was either good, clever, and strong, or bad, craven, and weak. Nobody was just scared or confused or trying their best in a difficult world. An ordinary cat could steal the secret of magic from the highest heavens; an ordinary girl could be anything. She put the flask back in her pocket.

No sooner had she done so than its weight wasn't there. She turned in time to see a small figure tearing off down the street with a chunk of dull steel in his hand. She was chasing him before she even realized what he'd stolen, her feet moving a half second ahead of her head. The streets in this part of town were alchemically treated teak, which flexed and creaked beneath her boots as she pounded after the thief.

Same kid from the roof? He was running north toward the Shambles. She knew that part of town better than most, but if he got into that rats' nest of alleyways and overgrown houses, she'd never catch him.

He turned right down Janekhai Street, and she followed. The last of the vendors were still there, packing up their carts—the night market stragglers must've finally run out of coin. She skidded around the corner and almost crashed into a man carrying a cauldron of hot soup. She apologized and pushed past him, trying to find the kid. She saw him leaning against a wall, cap low over his face, trying to look casual. A woman in a flax pōtae was trying to sell him something, but his eyes were on the two flatfoots who'd just rounded the corner. As soon as their eyes met, he was off running again.

"Stop!" shouted Sen. "Stop that bloody thief!"

There were too many people. A lot of them were carrying things, or elderly, or just tired: they were shuffling out of the way, but not quickly enough. Yat pushed through them, but the kid was escaping, tearing down the street straight toward a fruit stall. He shoved past a young soldier leaning on a crutch, his face a mess of scar tissue, then leapt up onto a crate. He leveraged that for another jump and grabbed ahold of the collapsible arm of the stall's awning, which barely budged under his slight frame. In one deft movement, he swung his body around and let the momentum carry him upward; he caught the guardrail of a second-floor balcony, then hauled himself over. Their eyes met again, and he stuck out his tongue at her, then clambered over the windowsill into the house.

She tried to calculate the jump as she ran. She could make it. Well, she could've a few years ago. Gods, she used to be quick. Back then, it was either be quick or dead. Cop life had softened her up—not a lot, but enough that she was starting to notice. She didn't have much time to hash out the angles of the jump, and at the last moment, she slowed. It was the wrong move: she stumbled, and it was all she could do to stop herself from going ass-over-teakettle. Sen skidded to a halt beside her, grabbed the cuff of her uniform, and yanked.

"Henhai Lane," he said. "We can cut him off at the Grand Canal—he'll need to go street-level. *C'mon.*"

She took one last look at the balcony, then ran after him.

He was trying to talk his way past a blank when they showed up. Bouncing up and down on the balls of his feet and looking at the other side of the canal while the half-man went through his papers. Must've been an older one: it took the city alchemists a couple of years to get the process right. They used to take too much consciousness away, which made them work slowly, stiffly. This was maybe an mk2, a pre-revolution conversion? Unless it was serving life, it would be coming up on the end of his sentence. She'd never met anybody who'd come back from being blanked, but apparently they were around. The process was good—if it worked correctly, an outside observer would never be able to tell.

The kid's papers would be fake, of course, but blanks were bad at figuring that out. They *were* smart enough to grab a runner, though, so the kid was playing it cool. He was too busy watching his front to hear them approach. Yat stumbled toward him and put a hand on his shoulder. She had her cuffs ready in the other hand: figure-eight vines that would constrict when the arresting officer tore the right stem away and only release again with the application of a special chemical broth back at the station.

"You're—" she gasped, "you're under a-arrest."

He slumped, and the blank responded to Yat's words by grabbing tightly onto the kid's shoulder. He spoke in an empty monotone, as if he were just making sounds and didn't understand their meaning.

"Do not resist, citizen," it said. "This is an ar—"

"Yeah nah, mate, I think he knows," Sen said.

"—rest. Compliance is its own reward. If you have any issues with the way your arrest has been handled, please contact—"

"Arse," said Sen. "Override: Jen-xat, 13186."

The blank slumped but didn't loosen its grip. Its eyes—already dull and empty—went milk-white, and it shuddered once, twice, then stopped speaking. The kid had gone the same color, like he was about to be sick.

"'m sorry, miss," he said. He couldn't be older than thirteen. He had what looked like his first crop of pimples covering his cheeks.

"Yeah, well," she said, "you can be sorry back at the station."

He looked at the blank, then back at her, and started to cry. Not the petulant tears of a kid caught with his hand in the cookie jar, but real panic sobbing in bursts between gulps. He was staring at the blank now, moaning.

"Please, miss," he said, "you can't."

He thought they were going to make him into a blank. It didn't happen like that anymore: back in the bad old days they'd snatch anybody, but now there were *rules*. The bridgeman had probably been a savage killer. If he wasn't, somebody would see him walking around and they would say something. The system worked. Yat had been where this kid was before, and they'd had her in a cell for a while, but she'd turned out fine—this would straighten him out. It would be good for him. She'd make sure the right papers got filed and he got some rice and a warm cot, and they'd chuck him out into the street in a few days when his belly was full.

Sen cleared his throat.

"Constable," he said, "a word."

She shot him a look, but he shot one right back: *I'm being nice, but I'll pull rank if I have to.*

The blank had the kid firmly in his grip. She turned reluctantly to Sen.

"You want to end up explaining to brass why you've got a pretty chunk of steel in your pocket? You're already on thin ice."

"I need to show them I'm good at this—"

He shook his head. "I'm invoking my discretion as senior officer, *Constable*," he said. "You can take your property back, and then we're leaving. Our patrol's nearly done anyway, and I'm sure there's some lovely paperwork to be filled out back at the station."

She sighed and spun on her heels. When she reached the kid, she stuck out her hand.

"My flask," she said.

He nodded and fished it out of his pocket. Once she had it safely back in her own jacket, she nodded at the blank.

"Mistaken identity," she said. "Release this man."

The blank let him go, and the kid's whole body twitched. Yat realized how hard the blank must've been squeezing his shoulder.

"Sorry for the inconvenience, sir," it monotoned. "If you wish to lay a complaint, you may—"

Sen cut it off again.

"Now sod off," he said.

The kid sod off.

Yat and Sen lived in the same part of town, so they walked home together. They passed through the Eitu Gate, nodded to the blanks on duty, and made their way down to the docks. There was a corner out beyond the bars and brothels where you could just see the beacon of the Hainak Lighthouse. All the lighthouses used clusters of bioluminescent fungi for the lamp itself but were otherwise old Lion structures of steel and stone. Yat sat down on the pier and passed her flask from hand to hand as she watched a winking light in the distance. Her feet dangled over the edge. No ships in the harbor this time of year: a sporadic outbreak of peace in Accenza had sent the merchants scrambling east, and the war fleet was patrolling up north and around the Sea of Teeth. She closed her eyes and let herself take in the gentle murmur of the water against the docks and the earthy smell of seaweed and salt water.

"Yep, that's water," said Sen. He sat down next to her and pointed at the lighthouse. "And light," he said. "Liiiiiiight."

Yat pushed her anger down. She'd made the right call with the kid, and he'd used her demotion against her. She considered the man a friend—perhaps her only one at the moment—but it had been rude of him to stop her, and he wouldn't even acknowledge it. Still, she could ill afford to chase him away: he was one of the few good men left on the force. The recent recruitment drive had come up short on good candidates, and it turned out "good" wasn't so important. They wanted more officers and guns, so they didn't seem to care much about the quality of the officers. She once told Sen he was a relic of a better force, and he'd laughed and shaken his head and asked how exactly she'd been keeping track of quality. He was a good guy, but he just didn't understand how it was for those street kids or why it was important to look out for them whether they wanted it or not. Her shoulders slumped: it wasn't the time for that fight. She pointed at the lighthouse and cocked her head to the side.

"Light?" she said in her best overenthusiastic rookie voice. "Like when it's night but it's not?"

"Exactly," said Sen. He drew himself up, waved a pontifical hand, and put on his best law enforcement bureaucrat impersonation. "You'll go far in this department, Constable Yat-Hok. Got a bright future ahead of you. Like a lighthouse, except it's meta-forrical instead of actual, and also it's in the future."

"Very good, sir," said Yat. She liked the sergeant, despite herself. His hair was always a mess, and the less said about his uniform, the better. He outranked her but had apparently never read the regulations. He told her once that he'd been in the army, and that rules were sometimes useful but always exhausting. It was fine, though—Sen only broke the ones that didn't matter.

They stared out to sea for a while.

21

"You forgot to sign in at the precinct when you got in—" he said.

Hells.

"—so I did it for you. Signed you out, too. You worked a full eight hours, as it turns out."

They sat in silence. The light winked at them again through the harbor fog.

"Thank you, sir," she said.

His mouth twisted a little. He looked like he was studying her. "Go home and get some sleep," he said. "Or, I dunno, go drink tinnies in a tinny. Just find yourself some peace."

"Tin?" she said. "Going hard on the contraband there, *mate.*"

"I'm a tinny bastard," he said. "They'll never catch me. Or you, for that matter. Do a little crime, just for you. You've earned yourself a couple of indiscretions. Steal a toff's watch or something, paint your name on the wall. I won't talk."

She turned to say something, then saw the concern in his eyes. She'd always struggled with that, how he seemed to crack jokes only when things got dark. Gods, she *was* tired. Three months of night shifts had thrown her body clock right out. She'd been up all night as a kid, but that was years ago, and she wasn't sure she liked going back to that life. She'd invested in heavy curtains to block out the daylight while she tried to sleep, but they didn't really work. She'd been having nightmares again—deep water, strange flowers, eyeless faces looming out of a grand and endless darkness.

"Sarge—"

"No more 'Sergeant,'" he said. "Your shift is over. It's 'Sen,' 'mate,' or nothing. 'Mr. Kanq,' if you're feeling polite, though I suspect you're always feeling polite. You ever get mad at people, Yat? Just let loose and call somebody a fuckwit?"

"No, S—no, I—" she stuttered.

"What do you do if they're being a fuckwit?" he said.

She thought about the kid. He needed a stronger hand, that was all. A role model, somebody to show him there was a way to break out and survive. Maybe her first instinct had been right.

"I tell them to have a nice day," she said.

"Damn," said Sen. "You kiss your mother with that mouth?"

She did not, in fact, kiss her mother with that mouth. She might've if she'd ever met the woman, but that was beside the point. She just shrugged. Sure, she liked the guy, but she didn't trust herself as a judge of character—she'd been frighteningly wrong in the past. Easier to just assume everybody was out to get you than assume otherwise and have them prove you wrong. If you accepted that the world would let you down, you could protect it without being surprised when it stung.

"Right," she said. "I'm going home."

When she leapt to her feet, Sen twitched just a little.

"You trust me, mate?" he said.

She shrugged again. "Sure," she said. She didn't, but she considered him a friend, so it seemed like the right thing to say.

"Sometimes," he said, "I feel like you've got shit going on that you don't admit to anybody, not even yourself. I worry about you, you know? You come out here all the time and stare at the sea, then come into work with bags under your eyes and fall asleep at your desk. Sometimes I worry you're not eating, but I've got no idea because you don't tell anybody shit. It's just 'yeah' and 'sure,' and if you keep refusing to really talk to people, one day you're gonna say 'I'm fine' and then fall down dead in the middle of a shift."

She didn't know what to say to that. Sarcasm seemed like a solid bet: her trusty shield against everything having to mean something.

She'd learned it from him. "C'mon, Sarge," she said, "tell me how you really feel."

He didn't smile, just pursed his lips and shook his head.

"Fine," he said, "don't talk about it. But you're gonna burst if you keep all that inside, and I can't be the one to sweep up all the pieces."

She should've known better than to use the man's own deflection trick on him. What was she supposed to say? That she broke everybody she touched? That her hands shook sometimes and she didn't know why? That staring at the ocean was the only thing that silenced the uncontrollable bickering of her own thoughts? But she couldn't keep her head down, of course. She had what the captain's report had called a *delicate issue.*

"Yeah, you will," she said, attempting a smile.

"Yeah," he said, "I am."

She sighed. It didn't seem right to complain: things had been far worse for her in the past. At twelve years old, she'd gone without eating for three weeks and passed out somewhere near the Grand Canal. She'd woken up to an old woman offering her a bowl of congee but barely had time to eat it before the guard came and arrested her for vagrancy. She'd been back on the street in a month or so, once somebody got around to doing the paperwork.

She sprang to her feet, her old reflexes still in place. She'd never been strong, but damned if she wasn't quick. And on the streets, that counted for a lot.

"A girl's gotta have her secrets," she said. Her head hurt and she badly needed a smoke, but she wouldn't tell the sergeant that. Better to pretend it was a game or a little mystery. Better to hide in familiar words than explore ones she'd never figured out how to say. She stared silently out to sea.

A ship had appeared on the horizon, just a dim impression of sails in the dark. Fog was rolling in from somewhere, thick and fast. *Really* fast, roiling like an avalanche. She'd never seen anything like it. It swallowed the little ship in mere seconds.

She turned to Sen. "This weather, huh?" she said.

He chuckled. "Yeah, mate," he said. "Feels like the end of the bloody world, doesn't it?"

That seemed to sum up the entirety of everything. She turned to leave, then heard a low, wet pop from deep in the fog and whirled around to face it.

"Gunshot?" she said.

He nodded. "Large-bore, organic. Ossifier, maybe," he said. "Can't see shit, though."

Voices were shouting, strangely muffled. Another salvo rang out.

"We need to help them," said Yat. Sen shook his head.

"I'd bet my last yan those guns are military-grade, and if they're loud enough to hear from here, the harbor patrol will be on it. Some situations are above our pay grade. Folks get shot every day in this town, and I'd prefer we weren't among them."

A puffball floated nearby, a trash collectors' punt with a pole long enough to reach the harbor floor but almost certainly not long enough to get deeper. She and Kiada had stolen one for a joyride more than once, and she knew if you jabbed one in the right place, the spore burst could get you a lot more distance than you might expect. Then, of course, you were on a deflating puffball and far from shore, but solving that problem was half the fun. She clambered onto it and picked up the punt pole. The puffball deformed beneath her, making a comfortable divot to sit in. She raised the pole, started working out the angle, and then—

25

Sen stood, eyes wide. Yat turned to follow his gaze. The fog had contracted into a plume almost as high as the lighthouse, centered on the point where the boat had been. She could *feel* its hatred—she didn't know how, but deep in her bones, she knew the fog hated her. It held its form for another few seconds, then collapsed in an instant, spreading out across the harbor until it vanished entirely. The harbor was empty and silent. No ships, no shooters. Yat balked. She knew she couldn't always trust her own senses, but this was different. Sen was staring out, too.

"Yat," he said, "get off of there."

She lowered the pole but didn't get down. She had a thousand questions, and she couldn't just leave them unanswered. She watched the impossibly empty ocean, watched it like it might attack her if she turned away. It was awful, profane somehow, an enemy silence.

"Constable," said Sen, "I'm giving you a direct order. Gods forgive me, I've never had to pull rank twice in the same day, but I'm not going to let your damned noble streak get anybody killed who isn't dead already. I saw some shit like that fog in the war, not *that* specifically, but I reckon I know what we just witnessed better than you do. Folks need to stop unearthing ancient weapons from abandoned bunkers deep inside the bloody earth. They blew up one civilization, and I'd rather we didn't bring them back around for another go. If this was above our pay grade when it started, it's *definitely* above our pay grade now. Let the spooks deal with it. I heard they just brought two new lads with officer-grade splices down from Syalong Cherta and gave them suspiciously vague desk jobs. It's their first week, and I'm not keen to be the first gumshoe to get in their way. They're probably looking to set examples."

Yat sighed. She'd had cases like this before, and they always got taken away from her before she could resolve anything. Placed with government agents. Always a man, always in a suit grown perfectly to his measurements—occasionally synth-skin but usually not so showy, more often the sort of dull lab-grown cotton that showed no stains—never carrying a badge, rolling in like they were the gods-damned Sparrows or something. She'd asked enough questions to learn it was pointless. She'd sometimes find the paperwork later, re-dacted with proprietary inks that couldn't be read without the right optical membrane—which she, of course, didn't have.

She climbed down off the puffball, letting it roll gently beneath her and tilt her back down onto the dock.

"We'll need to file a report," she said.

"I'll head back to the station and sort it out. You can sign it tomor-row. For now, go home and get some sleep."

She didn't know what else to say, so she just nodded and left, mak-ing her way northwest into the city. She hated feeling powerless, but half the job was observing things and pushing them up the chain. Especially now that there was a whole lot more chain above her than below. She couldn't afford to cause the brass any more problems than she already had. She strolled through the alleys of the Shambles and tried to put the incident out of her mind. She couldn't sleep yet; she was exhausted but still too wired. She needed to find a way to burn off the energy. The streets were mostly empty, with just stragglers going home from bars, Erzau priests in their feathered masks, the occasional hawker trying their luck.

She took off her helmet and badge and stowed them in her bag. She could be anybody in a beige uniform without them, a mercenary or a civic alchemist or any of the hundreds of private guards hired to watch over rich households.

She didn't put her nightstick away, though; with the cnidocyte asleep, it looked like any old piece of wood. But coiled inside it was a rubbery, whiplike vine; with a touch of a button, it would unfurl from a hole in the top. Its toxin was ostensibly nonlethal, but Yat had spent too long in her father's lab to trust that—anything could be lethal with the wrong dose, and a cnida was hardly a precise delivery mechanism. They were part of the new equipment rollout—it was important that the police were seen to uphold the principles of the revolution.

She remembered sitting on a high stool as a kid, watching him bent over a tray of cellulose cultures, leaves singing. Their patent had gone nowhere. He'd tried to argue with the parliamentary science committee that they'd been used as the basis for the early-model Tinker's Horn, but they laughed him off. Dad had died poor. He got through the last few years making fireworks—pretty, useless things. The chemicals he worked with burned a thousand microscopic holes in his lungs, and one day he just stopped breathing. The city ate him piece by piece: first his ideas, then his dignity, then whatever else was left. Yat had nobody else. It was a hard few years after that. But here she was, getting maudlin again.

Her hands shook, and she could feel a stabbing pain coming on from somewhere between her eyes. Today had been too much. Her edges were fraying at the best of times, and these certainly weren't the best of times. She took a moment to look around. In an alcove across the way was a statue of Siviss, goddess of thieves and secrets, inexplicably not headless, though her face was entirely covered in lichen. She should probably call it in and let the lads up at Heron Hill come down to take the head off, but she wasn't feeling especially generous toward the Cult of Crane. Siviss had been the go-to goddess on the streets.

Her worship was illegal, but what wasn't? Yat wasn't sure how safe Siviss had kept her but, well, she was still around, and that counted for something. She placed her thumb and forefinger against her eyelids and pulled them closed in a brief thieves' salute. *I swear on the Four Heavens, I didn't see shit.* The Cult of Crane controlled the damned government and had half the force kneeling to them; they could use all their money and manpower to hunt heresies on their own time.

A blank shuffled by, carrying a cask of palm wine. His glassy eyes made her uncomfortable, but she knew he wouldn't tell anybody. Blanks weren't smart enough to make conversation: they could follow orders, and that was about it. The city used to hang people, but now, well, it had found a use for them. A humane punishment, as far as those went.

She took out a kiro cigarette, lit it, and took a deep drag. The instant opiate wave crashed over her, and she staggered to the side. She had to lean against a wall to keep herself upright—this one was stronger than usual. Cut with something? Maybe yes, maybe no, who cared? Too much thinking. Too much . . .

—please, there's been a mistake. I was onl—

—please, I have a daughter. She's sick and she n—

. . . too much detail. She reeled under the weight of memories that weren't her own, pulled from whatever communal consciousness the kiro had tapped her into. Sometimes she even got them when she wasn't high: snatches of song from another frequency, little blaring bits of nonsense. The drugs made them clearer, but less sharp, as though clarity took away some of their bite.

She wasn't an addict, of course. Addicts were a blight on the city and belonged in the cells. She was a good . . .

—following orders. Just kept on firing like Mr. Ż—

. . . a good cop. Like the ones from the stories. The ones you needed to balance the bad cops out.

She finished the cigarette and stomped it out. Strongest stuff she'd had in a long time: she swore she could feel somebody else's breath coming up through her throat. The wall was soft, coated in a colored layer of mycelium. Cosmetic? Probably.

Yat yawned. She was tired, which was fine. Sleep didn't come easily, and it was no sin to get a little . . .

—I don't underst—

. . . a little help. Well, maybe it was, but not a big one, and it was okay because she did more good overall, unlike . . .

She wondered if there had once been magic in the world. Unreal, world-breaking magic. Every kid heard the old stories: all men had lived forever, until the goddess Night took the secret of immortality and ate it. When the trickster Hoihoi tried to sneak into her belly and steal it back, she caught him between her mighty thighs and broke him in half. Magic didn't exist here now; it belonged to the dead.

Music floated to her on the wind, a familiar melody she hadn't heard in years.

Kiada's song.

Could it really be? Kiada was gone, in the way so many street kids were—one day there with a clever smile and a bright, clear soprano, and the next, nowhere. Like she'd never existed. Taken by the city to the place poor kids went. She'd come here from the East: swung in one day on a merchantman, got left at the docks. She hadn't talked about it much, but they'd talked about everything else. She was pale, like all Easterners, with hair like flame and deep brown eyes. They'd been children, then older than that, sitting with one another and watching the moon rise and touching in quiet ways that never went anywhere. They were filthy and homeless, but somehow Kiada always smelled like home. Then one day the city ate her whole, without even having the courtesy to spit out her bones.

She used to sing that song, sitting on the rooftops looking out over the canals. She said it was from an opera they'd had back home in Accenza. There was more, but she didn't know the other songs. She knew that one song because they'd sung it on the ship, and so far as Yat knew, Kiada hadn't had a life before the ship. Just ocean, then Hainak.

Somebody was singing it now: not Kiada's bright soprano, but huskier, earthier. She stumbled after the music as though her heart and her legs were in accord and the rest of her just had to deal with it. There was a man in the gutter who was very conspicuously not meeting her eye. One of his arms was twisted backward at the elbow, withered and jaundiced. It smelled sharp and rancid, like old apples. Probably a cheap splice gone bad, stuck in a loop of replication and modification, some back-alley flesh doc making it up as they went along. Limb replacement in a real hospital cost . . . well, an arm and a leg. Regulation retrovirals were meant to burn out once the job was done, but the replication-limiting factor was one of the harder things to get right, and the people who needed cheap splices were rarely the sort of people with the power to do anything if it went wrong. Eventually the limb would run out of fuel; whether that meant eating itself and falling off or consuming the rest of him, it wouldn't be pleasant. That sort of work was very illegal, but she didn't have anything more than a hunch and wasn't interested in pursuing it. Poor bastard had enough problems. If she tried to take him to the hospital, they'd arrest him, then arrest her for not arresting him first. She reached into her pocket and found only a small handful of wooden coins, meant to keep her going for another week. She dropped one at his feet and kept walking, following the music.

It took her to a door in the Shambles, painted white. She knew the place well: a bar for folks with *delicate issues*. Folks unfit to be cops or citizens, folks the world tucked away where it didn't have to look at them. Folks the city swallowed sometimes. A wave of shame washed over her; she'd been caught doing this before. The police had a register of places like this. They didn't raid them unless the voices in Parliament got too loud: the men in bird masks still held control over Parliament with their tenuous minority coalition, but whenever it was threatened, they'd start shouting about sin, about the cycle of death and birth and how certain *delicate issues* could break the gods' perfect system. There was an election coming up; things looked bad for them, and as it got worse, the zealots' yelling got louder. They were already reliant on friends from other parties to get anything done, trying to appeal to the nationalists and the police union and the alchemists and the rich all at once.

She slumped against the door, it swung open, and she fell a short distance before she hit the bouncer's chest and he wrapped an arm around her. He was a broad-chested man in a half-mask shaped like a stylized buck. He held a big bit of wood in his free hand: something not clublike enough to count as an illegal weapon, but enough to crack a troublemaker's skull. His face softened when he saw her.

"Bakky," she said.

The bouncer smiled at her. It wasn't his real name, but they didn't use real names. The place was like a dream, its memory lost in the morning.

"Ezu," he said. He laid the wood against the doorframe and wrapped her in a hug. She hugged him weakly back but didn't smile. The drugs were making her head spin a little, and she felt nauseous as he pulled her in.

"Music?" she slurred.

He cast a suspicious eye down at her.

"I'm letting you in," he said, "but I'm telling the bar you're prematurely cut off? You're all right for a pig, but Shazza will kill us both if you puke on the floor again."

"Yeah," she said, nodding. "Music?" She wasn't planning to drink anyway: it usually just made her feel ill at the time and worse in the morning. She stumbled down the stairs into the bar. It was quieter than she'd expected; then she realized the crowd was just enraptured by the woman onstage. She wore a synthetic caul over her face like a mask, though her chin jutting out below was dark-skinned like a local's, not pale like an Easterner's. Her hair was red, but not red like Kiada's—dyed red with henna, running down her back in a single, strong plait. She *was* singing Kiada's song, though. Despite the difference in their voices, it was unmistakable. Yat had never known what the words meant, but it was clearly a song of sorrow. The crowd swayed back and forth, arms around each other, as the woman sang. Yat swayed with them, tottering through the crowd as though the ground were swaying beneath her feet like a ship in a storm.

A band stood at attention at their instruments. They didn't play, except for the percussionist, who beat a single immense timpani, each beat seeming to shake the world to pieces. Some of the instruments were traditional: a viol, the drum. She didn't recognize the rest: a clear sac embedded with wooden pipes, an array of flesh that hummed when squeezed. New instruments fresh from the labs. The drum's beat was beautiful, primal, and Yat let it wash over her, approaching the stage in a half trance. The song pitched upward, gaining in speed and intensity, and then . . .

. . . stopped. Yat hung in the moment, the sudden silence richer and more vibrant than any song could be, as though the world had drawn in a breath and she could do nothing but stand and wait for it to exhale a hurricane.

It hit as the band unleashed all at once: strings and pipes smashing the wall of silence, amplified by the Tinker's Horns on the walls. It annihilated thought and pain: for a moment, there was only music. It could've lasted forever. The crowd danced around her, but she just stood in front of the stage with her eyes closed. She felt safe here. She knew she wasn't, that this could be another night she got unlucky. Logically, she knew, but she didn't care. They couldn't take the music from her; they couldn't take the strong-chinned woman with the beautiful, husky voice or the way her body and her sound made Yat feel, the warmth and tension in her muscles and somewhere beyond. The woman finished the song and began another, one Yat vaguely recognized from street fairs. It was good, but the spell was broken: she pushed her way back through the crowd and found a wall to lean on. She watched the dancers warily: men with men, women with women. It was so exciting, but that excitement ashamed her. She watched them dance as she felt something she didn't want to give words to.

A man pushed another against the wall, and for a moment it looked like a fight. She stepped away. Her head spun, and again she could hear thoughts in her head that were not her own, snatches of kiro-talk echoing around inside her skull.

"Are you okay, sir?" she said.

The two men gawped at her, and the one against the wall laughed.

"I'm fine." He grinned. He had a spiral design painted on his face that seemed to dance in the light—Yat realized it was a temporary subdermal implant, probably built to stop blank patrolmen from identifying him. She couldn't call it illegal because she didn't think the law had even caught up with it. The other man pushed against him, put his chin against the base of the other man's neck, kissed up and up. His face was painted red, with white lines cutting through it. Yat's senses weren't quite keeping up: the drugs in her system made her words come out too late. She realized what was going on, but her mouth was already moving.

"Is he hurting you, sir?" she said.

They both laughed at that; then the kissing man pulled the other one close and stared into his eyes.

"Am I hurting you?" he said, with a big smile.

His partner shook his head, mock-coquettish.

"No, sir," he said in a piping imitation of Yat, "not at all, sir."

Red-Face grabbed him and kissed him fully on the mouth. He had one hand behind his partner's head, and another tilting his chin up. They kept going, and Yat blushed. When they pushed apart for only a moment, she saw Spiral-Face pull back his tongue.

"How about now?" said Red-Face. The other man was going a little red himself, and for a moment, everyone had red faces.

"No," he said, and smiled. "But if you want to try again, my place is up the road."

They pushed together, nose-to-nose, and Spiral ran a playful hand across Red's cheek. They stood there, swaying to the music, not looking at Yat, so very gentle together. She didn't know what to do, so she wandered back into the dance floor, closed her eyes, and let the music wash over her again. The band was finishing their second song and taking up a third: the percussionist had moved from the drum to an array of bone plates, hung by vines from the roof. He danced between them with a small hammer in one hand and a bundle of short vines in the other. Each plate played a different tone, and he beat out a hypnotic rhythm. He also wore a caul over his face, but was otherwise naked except for a loincloth. His movements were sinuous and beautiful, and a warmth moved up her. He was a small man, and dark, and he glistened with sweat as he danced. It occurred to her as she watched him that she did not find men beautiful by default, with women as a defect, nor did she move between men and women: the contours of the body mattered less than the *way* it moved, how gentle its arms looked, how it made her heartbeat quicken. She loved men and women, not men *or* women.

She stayed and watched the rest of the show as the night wore on. She burned through most of her kiro and weaved among the crowd, simply letting them exist around her. When it was done and they closed out, she returned to herself and remembered why she'd come: Kiada's song. The band went through a door at the back of the stage and disappeared. The crowd was going its separate ways, pairing off and wandering into the night. She clambered onto the stage. Bakky saw her, sighed, and shook his head, then turned to find something else to do. The door was still half-open, and she slipped through it into the greenroom. The percussionist was reclining on a long couch, smoking a pipe. He looked up when he saw her coming, then cleared his throat, stood up, and left. The rest of the band stood up, fidgeted, smiled, and went with him, filing out of the room, deeper into the guts of the bar.

For a moment, Yat was crestfallen. Then she saw the singer standing in the corner. She was even more beautiful without her caul: strong, oak-eyed, and solemn. She was perhaps thirty, but held herself like a wisewoman. She took a step forward.

"I saw you watching me," she said.

"I, uh . . ." said Yat. "Um." Smooth, as usual.

As the woman swept forward, Yat stepped back, almost stumbled, felt her back hit the wall of the greenroom. Her cheeks flushed hot. She had lain with women before, and with men, but her shame made her feel like a child. Her memory flashed back to those officers in the boardroom with their dead eyes and empty smiles.

The singer stepped back and held her hands up in front of her. "You don't need to be here, if you don't want," she said. There was a disappointment in her voice, but she stepped to the side to leave a clear path to the door. Yat shook her head.

"That song," she said, "the first one. It's beautiful. . . . You're beautiful. You're—"

She didn't know what else to say. She stared at the woman, almost defiantly, as if to say *I belong here, like you, with you.* She didn't step forward, so the woman did it for her. They came together, and Yat pushed her face into the woman's neck. She was such a perfect creature: something from another world, and yet here, just another one lost in the night.

Yat didn't know the woman's name, and she didn't want to: she was the Caul, and that was it. Yat pulled herself into the woman, let her warmth and her smell encompass her, become her. The Caul was strong, lean, well-muscled: when she pushed back, she did so with just enough force to send a shudder through Yat. A current, starting between her legs, spreading into her belly, moving up her back, making the hairs on her neck stand on end. She let the woman take her, push against her, slide a hand across her breasts, down her stomach, a trail of lightning. Both women stopped for a moment, negotiated her belt buckle, hand meeting hand, pulling back, startled, then moving in together in concert. The Caul's hand went down past the open belt, and Yat's body parted for her.

The Caul spoke, and Yat could hear her smile in her voice.

"You *do* find me beautiful, don't you?"

Yat couldn't speak; her chest was too tight. She let out a gentle moan as the woman's fingers opened her and entered her. If she could will herself to open more, she would have: open completely, let the Caul have all of her—the things that lived in places without names.

"Yes," whispered Yat. The word fell out of her. She didn't know what she was answering: yes to everything. Yes, it felt good; yes, this woman was beautiful; yes, she could have whatever she wanted. She felt the Caul's hands inside her and against her, steady yet urgent. Yat's breathing was heavy, and her chest rose and fell in time with the Caul's, the woman's breasts pressing against her own and making her feel warm even through the stiff cotton of her uniform, joining with the heat moving up from her legs, dancing together as her muscles tightened, starting somewhere behind her thighs and moving up through her until she cried out; it fell away, built again, and broke inside her, making her grunt; then it fell away again and sent ripples out across her hips and down the backs of her legs, a tightness building and building, reaching a crescendo until she was all fire before the wave broke and rolled over her, a spasm running down her body as she pushed her face deep into the Caul's shoulder. She bit down to stop herself from crying out again and heard the Caul's ecstatic moan fill the place instead, and then they slumped into each other, laughing between teeth.

Yat looked into the Caul's perfect dark eyes and breathed for what felt like the first time all day.

"Can we—" she said, "can we go somewhere else? Can I, uh, return the favor? Please?"

The Caul shook her head and smiled sadly.

"Go home, Constable," she said. "Or I might end up telling you my name, and we both know how that ends."

THREE

*M*ate, *mate,* maaate. *Thank gods, I've been trying to get a clear line to you for aaaaages—matey potatey, you've got no idea. Anyway, anyway, you know me. Or you don't. It's hard to follow the rivers these days: they run back and forth and back and forth and—*

Here's an old joke: a fisherman sits in his boat, hooks a fish. As he reels it up and up, his friends sit in the boat with him and laugh.

"Water's fine today," he says.

The fish hears this as it's hauled from the water and dumped inside the boat. The air here is wrong, and it chokes, its tiny lungs filling with fluid. As it drowns in the dry, it hears strange booming sounds, and it thinks, What's water?

Here's another joke: a fish goes down too deep, and suddenly the whole world is dark and crushing. The fish here are barely even fish. It's eaten by something with too many teeth.

Point is, there's a very narrow band of existence fish can survive in. Words like time *and* space *mean very little until you come to a place where they don't matter anymore. What's water, ay? Haha.*

Which is to say, it's all sort of, you know, a bit fucked down here. They call this place a lot of things. None of them fit—it's hard to find words for the wordless. Light doesn't exist here; neither does time. It's endlessly empty, except it ain't. The things that live here don't fit the description of anything you've ever seen or could ever hope to understand: they don't verb the way we verb. On the other side, we call them gods; *in the Big Barren, they just* are. *It's hard to describe them in words made for tongues and teeth, for a different Are and Is, but we've gotta try. What I see, it matters, mattered, will matter.*

Down in the darkness, something moves. It casts its shadow on the surface. A colossal eye snaps open. Synapses fire, and a sleeping titan wakes. It sees, on the other side, where things are small: a shifting of gears, a music so quiet it fights to be unheard. It looks from world to world and sees tall buildings of steel and glass, empty and burnt. It casts its eyes from one to the next and sees choking clouds of toxic ash, then emptiness. It sees world after world abandoned, until at last it comes to a place with life.

It stands, and the world around it dances away—flees from its bulk in great swathes of color and fire. It hears the rumble before an avalanche, a hiss of carbon monoxide, a blocked tailpipe. A single spark moving with purpose—the overture to an inferno. Do you know these words? I'm sorry, mate, but you will.

It sees a movement in the darkness, so cataclysmic it would rend Is from Is. It sees a wave, an irruption that will echo back through the ages and into the dreams of the mortals night after night, year after year until they awake screaming about a war in heaven.

There is silence, then a shadow, then . . . from everywhere and no-

where at all, a new music rises from the deep. No, not music, the very opposite of music—a darkness come to swallow the world. An unsound unspooling across heaven until nothing else remains, remained, will remain.

What's water? Mate, mate, that's a good one.

FOUR

Salt. Salt water and . . .

. . . mud? Peaty, boggy, salty, like the worst whisky Yat had ever tasted. She sat up in her bed, then went over to the window and spat, then closed the window. She couldn't remember leaving it open, and the humidity had done awful things to her hair. The sun hung in the sky over Hainak, and she sighed: she'd woken up early again. Still not adjusted to the night shift. Not the first time she'd had to reverse her body clock. She lay back down in her bed and closed her eyes. It did nothing. In her mind's eye, she saw that plume of fog rising over her, casting an impossibly long shadow. How could you just ignore something like that? But it was out of her hands, too big for her. Everything was too big, too much.

She rolled over and tried to curl up around her pillow. It was comfortable, but it didn't make her any more tired. Well, *tired* wasn't the word—she was always tired, she just couldn't sleep. Her head hurt, and her mouth tasted like an ashtray. Her clothes were a mess. Somewhere in the course of the night, she'd lost her belt: she'd forgotten to do it back up after her encounter with the Caul and then just lost the whole damned thing.

Of course, the night shift wasn't a *punishment*, no; the report said she had a "gentle, feminine bearing" that made her "unsuitable for certain environments," and that the night shift would be a more natural fit for her talents. Down at the bottom of the captain's report, there was a quiet note about her "degeneracy," almost as an afterthought. A less aggressive role was meant to help her deal with her *delicate issue*; it was all fine for a male officer to visit the brothels, of course. Boys with girls was how it had always been, but girls with girls needed male supervision to make sure the poor things didn't fall into sin. Hainak wasn't like the Vault, where they worshipped Dorya the Broken from a massive ferro factory deep beneath the island, or like one of the cities on the Eastern Shelf, where they just let *anything* happen. It was a mess over in the East: a warlord in each valley, a god on each street corner, and of course, no sense of decorum or chivalry or right way to love. Kiada had been Eastern, with pale skin and hair like fire. She'd had dark, sad eyes that were always searching for something. She'd loved to sing—she used to sit on the rooftops, belting out arias from home; they had a style of play over there called an opera, where the actors sang every single word and each song was a story. They'd shared some time together before Kiada went missing and Yat had been in no place to find out why.

Yat had just been unlucky: an undercover officer sitting at the bar. They didn't fire her: she liked men, too, and so she didn't count. It wasn't a broken soul to them—just a dalliance with sin, a poor little thing capable of redemption. She *could* be with a man and be happy; she had done so and enjoyed it, and even felt the stirrings in her heart that marked something deeper. After they'd caught her with a woman, there'd been a panel of senior officers who decided she was half a problem and worthy of half the punishment: demotion to the night shift, paperwork and passive aggression, and no hope of ever going anywhere.

Neither Ladowain nor Hainak had a tolerance for *delicate issues*. They shared a scripture, and the scripture was clear: Great Crane made men and women to carry out the great circle of birth and death. Those who did not fit the pattern did not count as people and could be ignored until it came time to remove them entirely.

Yat was in a strange position. She could follow the scripture if she needed to: she didn't *mind* boys. She even rather liked some of them. It was the path of least resistance, and she enjoyed it enough, but sometimes—

Shrik shrik shrik went claws on glass.

The cat. Of course. She opened one eye. The stray peered into her window. It was missing half an ear. Its fur had once been ginger, but now it was dull like rust. She hadn't given it a name—she liked it enough, but she thought naming it would make it *her cat*, and she wasn't ready to let anybody quite that far into her life. This way, it would remain a nameless street cat that came to her house sometimes.

"Cat . . ." she mumbled.

It pawed at the window again.

"Go 'way, cat," she said.

It did not go away. It went *mrrrrrow?*

"Mmmnnno food here, cat," she said. Yat rolled onto her back and opened her other eye. "No food," she muttered.

She lay on her back and tried to ignore it for a while. The scratching stopped. After what could've been minutes or hours, she sat back up. The cat was still there, staring pensively into the house. She wondered what cats thought of human houses. Did they understand what a house was, or did they think that humans were just sometimes found living inside giant fungal hollows filled with their stuff? Not that there was much in Yat's house: two uniforms, one soft cork patrol helmet—protection against bricks and bottles but not much else—one small bed, a book of stories, a single ferro electric lamp sitting on the floor. She barely had enough here to be messy, but she was close nonetheless—the uniforms hung over the footboard, because there was nowhere else for them to go. It was less of a house than a small room with a bathroom attached.

She picked up the book and passed it gently from hand to hand. It smelled like fertilizer and alchemical acid—like Dad. She flipped through the pages without reading them; she knew it back-to-front anyway. The stiff leather cover felt good in her hands. She stood for a moment, then put it down and smiled at the cat. Dad had loved cats. Or rather, hated having them in the lab but loved having them around the house. He'd said they were very tidy animals. His favorite story from the book was the one about the cat who stole the peanut— the same one Yat had come to love. It ended with the cat returning the peanut, because stealing was naughty and the gods would set him on fire if he didn't. Dad always did the voices: the sly cat, the haughty gods, the squeaky peanut. Nobody ever asked why the gods needed a golden peanut in the first place. It was a story and stories ran on different assumptions: magic flowed through the world, and kingdoms sat on clouds, and everything was simpler. She thought again of the fog, so thick you could probably balance a palace atop it. Probably not magic, though possibly another weapon ready to go critical and burn a hole in the sky. It happened on occasion, and you learned to live with it. It wasn't like you could stop it or move somewhere that it wasn't a threat—there was probably another one ready to go off in that city, too. Handling today was hard enough; that was tomorrow's problem.

Her window looked out onto somebody else's wall. Presumably, the cat bothered them, too. It was fat for an alley cat. Nothing like those south-of-wall alchemically engineered house cats with six legs and jewels in their collars, but doing all right for itself. Modifying pets was very fashionable among the wealthy, but it had always struck her as cruel.

She pulled the sheets off herself and wandered back to the window. She opened it and scratched the cat's head. It purred. The wooden wall outside belonged to an alchemical tea shop—the little old uncle who owned the place spent his days with a burette and a flask, inventing flavors not tasted anywhere else in the world. The business had been failing for years. Somewhere beyond the shop wall, the city roiled and heaved. The nicer houses had gills that absorbed and expelled moisture to keep the place temperature-controlled. They could live for years without fertilizer, feeding on just nutrients from the inhabitants' sweat. Some of her friends had lived in places like that when she was a kid, before things got bad. Yat's sheets reeked of sweat.

"No food," she said again.

The cat didn't seem to mind. It purred.

"Nice cat," she said. "Bye, cat."

She patted its head, then closed the window, slowly enough for it to get out of the way but quickly enough that it couldn't sneak on in. The cat pawed at the glass, then flicked its tail at her and jumped away and out of sight toward better dinner prospects. Her stomach grumbled, and she sighed. She had to let it go on complaining; pay wasn't coming for another two days. There were always generous officers in the station cafeteria, if you buttered them up right. She didn't have any butter, though—butter was only for rich folks. There weren't enough cows in the world to make it affordable, even with new grain cultivars keeping them fat and hormonal. Greased them up? Noodled them up? Didn't have the same ring.

She showered in cold water, then toweled herself off and put her uniform on. Her shift didn't start for hours, but it couldn't hurt to go in—it would make her look *keen*, and the brass loved keen. She might even get to see some of her old friends from the day shift. They hadn't stopped in to see her on the night shift, but they were probably busy with their own lives.

Shower, done. Uniform, on. Food, not a hope in the heavens. She opened her front door and stepped out into the street. An Erzau with an ibis mask stared at her. He had white feathers on his epaulettes. She made a quick sign of the sun at him and resisted the urge to call him *bin chicken*.

"Praises be," he said. He gave her a hand sign she didn't recognize.

"Yep," she said, "you too."

The Bird Cult made her uncomfortable, but she knew better than to challenge them. They held twenty-two seats in Parliament—almost a quarter—and more than enough to make life difficult for folks they didn't like. Fingers crossed, the election would change that. It would take place the day after the anniversary of the revolution: they'd sworn in a new government as quickly as they could, with the promise to find a more permanent solution when the war ended, and until then, an annual safety-election to keep the provisional government on its toes. Every year, hungover Hainak drifted its weary way to polling stations all over the city and put in its votes before going home to sleep it off. It was hardly a perfect system, but it was better than the Lion. At least they had a say, even if it often felt like they didn't. The Erzau Temple had always been able to push the levers of power, but the last decade had been something different—they'd gone from over half of Parliament to under a quarter, bleeding a few more seats every year. They'd gotten nastier in their rhetoric as they went down, and they particularly did not like folk with *delicate issues* that disrupted the great prime circle: women were given the sacred trust to create life, and those who refused were barely considered human in their eyes.

She couldn't bring herself to finish the priest's couplet—*Praises be/Long live death*. She'd seen it scrawled on walls as a child while the city burned. They said they worshipped a *metaphorical* death, but metaphors had a way of cutting into the real world. Men obsessed with metaphorical death often brought literal death along for the ride. She'd heard rumors from out east that they'd sabotaged the church's reactor in Featta on purpose, started a meltdown to get the gods' attention. Impossible to prove and heretical to say out loud, but that didn't make the thought itch any less. They'd been forced to dismantle the Hainak reactor after the revolution, and the power plant in Heron Hill had been converted into a great temple. She'd been there a few times as a child for services, and the thought of it still filled her with a sense of dread.

She edged past the priest as nicely as she could. She didn't make eye contact, but she swore she could feel him moving to follow her as she left: something about the way the chill from his shadow played out across her back. She pretended she didn't notice and did her best to get lost in the crowd.

The street was jam-packed with carts, all trying to sneak and jostle around each other. Some folks were heading home, others were heading to work, and nobody bothered to ask the other to clear the road. Same old beautiful mess as every day.

She forced her way through the press of people and tried to ignore the smells of food: sweet potato, smoked fish, new cultivars of alchemical fruit fresh from the Garden Cities. She almost knocked down a portly man carrying a barrel of fungal beer, and he glared at her. He had a good ten centimeters of height on Yat. She looked at her feet and ducked around him.

"Sorry, sir," she muttered. "Police business."

The journey to the station was busy, but she got there without falling asleep, so she counted it as a win. She arrived just before sundown. The station was pre-revolution: steel, stone, and red brick. They'd done their best to grow some vines along the walls to make it look less intimidating, but not so many that it wouldn't scare the shit out of any troublemakers. She'd never gotten used to the harsh glow of its halogen lamps. The last of the day shift were hitting up the punch clock, which had new tech for the same old jobs: a proprietary enzyme that left a little blue stain on the card. She waved at Varazzo, who shook his head at her and looked away; wouldn't do for a good cop to chat with the faggot, no sir. He pushed his punch card into the machine, muttered something, then slapped the side of the punch clock and smiled as the card came out with a little blue dot. Varazzo was from the East—Accenza? Degliano? She never could tell the cities apart—but he'd fit right in at the station. The ninth son of some minor noble house, he knew how to stomp and shout and get his way. Tall, skin the color of milk like all of them from out that way, a thatch of short, dark hair, a lantern jaw. She'd once seen him showing the other officers a rapier. *A toy from the old country*, he'd said. *Lets the plebs know you matter.* Right there in the mess hall with a fucking sword, and he hadn't even gotten a caution. Brass liked him. Varazzo was going places: he couldn't afford to be seen with the *wrong crowd.*

Sen sat at one of the tables where the public were meant to wait for assistance. He was drinking coffee from a porcelain-and-shellac mug and waved her over.

She sat down beside him. His coffee smelled rich and earthy— probably had some fancy new spores infused to make the flavors really pop. It made Yat's mouth water, but she knew better than to touch it: Sen was infamous for how hot he liked his coffee. A rookie had once tried to steal a sip and ended up unable to smell or taste anything for a week. He saw the look in her eye and pushed a small plate of rice and beans over to her.

"You sure?" she said.

He shrugged. "By accident," he said, "I got two. Already ate mine."

She picked up the fork and ate as slowly as she could—she didn't want to let anybody know how hungry she was.

Sen glared at Varazzo.

"Great white shark," he said, just loud enough for the other officers to hear but quiet enough to have plausible deniability. "Small white cock."

Yat tried to laugh while eating, but some rice went down the wrong pipe. She coughed, and the room went very quiet for about half a second. They weren't meant to have food outside the cafeteria. Nobody followed that rule, but somebody with a grudge could probably get her an infraction.

The murmur returned. That didn't mean it was over, but nobody wanted to make a scene in the foyer. Revenge would probably come in a blizzard of minor humiliations, spread out just enough to make them seem like coincidence. Cops were the pettiest people in the world sometimes, less inclined to throw the book at you so much as kill you with paper cuts.

She finished her plate and pushed it back to Sen, the porcelain scraping across their little table.

"Sorted out the paperwork from last night," he said, "and whaddaya know, it was gone by morning. We're still here, though."

She didn't say anything. *Gone by morning.* Cute euphemism. Half the paperwork in the station was gone by morning; some bloke in an expensive suit and dark glasses showed up from . . . somewhere and took it away. She didn't even want to speculate who they worked for. That sort of thing was above her pay grade.

"Your pay slips coming through properly?" he said. "Brass can fuck you around, but only within reason. If you're not getting paid on time, you've got a right to complain. We've got a union rep in Parliament— if somebody tries to fuck you, we can fuck 'em right back."

"Just tired," she said.

"Uh-huh," said Sen. His eyes said, *You didn't answer my question.*

And she couldn't. The pay slips were coming through fine, they just didn't cover expenses. Rent and food and paying down her father's debts plus her own, then getting her uniform cleaned, and kiro, and . . .

A blizzard of paper cuts.

"*Sen!*" a voice boomed.

The sergeant shrank back against the wall like he was trying to push himself through the cracks and disappear. Yat had never seen the man so rattled. The source of the shouting soon made himself known: Sergeant Wajet. His presence shook Yat from her thoughts in much the way a typhoon hits a shack on the beach.

To call Wajet fat would be true, but also a bald-faced lie. He was *big* in the sort of way that meant he'd once been pure muscle that had recently softened with age, but he still looked like he could punch through a door by accident. He didn't so much walk into a room as launch an invasion of it. His gray hair was trimmed short, and his mustache was exquisitely waxed in the Taangata style. Rumor had it that every time he was on cell duty, at least one person managed to slip out. That he'd intentionally tanked every single performance review since his promotion to sergeant to stop himself from being promoted into a desk job. He was a man of tremendous volume in more ways than one.

"Sen, mate," he expectorated, "I've got a job for you!"

As he stormed over, the floorboards trembled.

"'m busy," said Sen. "Got paperwork."

Wajet loomed over them now. His mustache twitched. It was like somebody had tied a cat to his upper lip.

"Sen, me old chum," he said, "are you saying that you'd rather sit at a desk and write about some drunk's home life than visit town with your old friend? I need a ride-along to assist me tonight. The criminal element is out and about, and it messes my wairua right the fuck up. The fiends must be stopped."

Sen did an excellent job of inspecting the tips of his shoes, and he shook his head. Wajet either didn't notice or didn't care. He leaned in with a great big grin.

"Who's your charming colleague?" he said. He snatched Yat's hand, then bowed and kissed it. His mustache was scratchy against her skin. Sen looked at her; she couldn't read his expression.

"This is Constable Yat," he said. "She's new to the night shift."

"Yat, Yat, Yat," said Wajet. He chewed the word like it was some new alchemical candy.

"Hmm," he said. "Yes. I read the report. Good to have you aboard. Good luck with your paperwork, Sen."

"You don't need somebody to come along?" he said.

"Well," said Wajet, "I've got the constable here to assist me. It's a very juicy case, Constable Yat; could look good to the lads up the chain. This case, you see, involves an informant who's tragically been stabbed quite a few times. The poor fellow seems to have been caught up with all the wrong people. I would very much appreciate any assistance or insight you could provide."

She resented being treated like a child, but she had to agree that it sounded juicy. Murders weren't part of her purview. She'd joined the force expecting people to call on her constantly as the ex-crook, to leverage her inside knowledge, but instead she mostly rounded up drunks and stood around at the occasional state function looking more important than she actually was. She'd been waiting for a break like this for a long time. Maybe, just maybe, she could climb the chain enough that she didn't need to sit by when shit went down on her patrol. She raised an eyebrow at Sen. He shook his head so slightly it almost could've been a random twitch, but his eyes held some emotion she couldn't read. Was it anger? Concern? She grimaced at him, then stood. She needed a good mark on her record, to prove she could work proper hours again—she needed a *win*. She was sick of feeling powerless, of standing under the shadow of the world, of turning the other way. This man had seen the report about her *delicate issue* and didn't care, so he couldn't be too bad. He was Tangata, and they were fine with folk like her up there. Besides, if there were real danger here, Sen would've let her know. He gave her one last plaintive look, and she turned away from him.

"All right, Constable," bellowed Wajet, "come along now."

He charged away toward the foyer's grand double doors—steel frames, golden lintel, polished hardwood panels, an insult to modernity with a certain unspeakable don't-fuck-with-us weight—and Yat found herself pulled along helplessly in his wake.

"You like heroes, Yat?"

"Heroes, sir?"

"Heroes," drawled Wajet. "You know—sword, armor, fight a taniwha and all that."

Wajet walked much more quickly than any of her other partners, though he wasn't even sweating. Yat knew it was hotter where he came from up near the Vault, though she could hardly imagine higher temperatures than the ones that had been keeping her up at night. Her father had told her about taniwha, Taangata sea dragons that lived in the ocean, presumably because of the heat. She struggled to keep pace.

"I like them," said Yat. "Taniwha gotta be fought."

"Do they now? What if the taniwha's nice?"

Yat was too out of breath to deal with Wajet's particular brand of pontifical bullshit. She stopped, hands against her knees, and tried to recover. After a few deep inhales and exhales, she straightened up.

"Monsters are never nice," she said. "They only exist in stories, so if a story says they're bad, then they're bad."

"Ooh, very good, Constable," said Wajet. He pulled a bean cake from somewhere within his coat and ate half of it in one bite. He chewed it, nodding thoughtfully, then swallowed with his whole jaw. With his lips pursed and mustache wiggling, he generally seemed to be enjoying himself very much.

"I suppose," he said, little bits of pulped black bean decorating his mustache bristles, "that stories've got to have good guys and bad guys. What if a taniwha were real, though? Couldn't it be nice? Or mean, but just because it's hungry? What if it's trying to protect its home?"

"Make your point, Sergeant," said Yat. *I'm the dragon here, right?* The moment the words left her mouth, she regretted them—she was already treated like garbage by half the force. She couldn't afford to alienate one of the few officers still on her side. Wajet just smiled, though.

"You'll find there are those in the city sympathetic to—what did the report call it? Your 'condition'?" he said.

"Issue," she said without thinking.

"Your 'issue,'" said Wajet. He stopped for a moment, and she took the opportunity to catch her breath. After a few seconds, she looked up at him.

"My *delicate issue*," she said, "is not an issue."

"Oh, I know," said Wajet, "and I think you'll find others who feel the same, if you only know where to look. Funny who manages to slip the cells when certain officers are on duty. Not just *anybody* does, of course. We run a tight ship down at the station. Some avuncular advice: pay attention, Constable Yat, and you'll go far."

Then, without warning, he turned and took off at a brisk trot.

Yat followed along as best she could. It seemed like half the city knew Wajet: beggars and prostitutes and the occasional back-alley lawyer all came up to shake hands with him, and many left with a few more coins than they'd started with. It didn't seem like bribery, but it didn't feel like charity, either. Between heaving breaths, Yat made a mental note to ask Sen about it. Ahead of her, Wajet had stopped to chat with a young woman in a very small dress. He said something, and she laughed, sudden and explosive. Wajet patted her on the shoulder, grinned, and then took off again. Yat caught up to him a block later, still trying to keep up.

"I saw something last night," she said. "I could use an officer's opinion on it."

"Ah, yes," he said. "I saw Sen's report. Well, that's a lie—what I saw was a lot of redacted material alongside your names. Can't say I'm not damned curious, but there's a time to discuss such things, Constable, and that time is never. Come and find me after my shift, and we definitely won't talk about it then, either."

She took the hint and didn't say any more. It felt like they'd been walking for hours, though it was probably closer to twenty minutes. Yat's lungs burned but she did her best not to show it. She almost didn't realize that Wajet had stopped. They were in a part of the harbor she didn't recognize: somewhere out in the south, near the Axakat Delta. Hainak was technically an island: the Axakat and Panjikora Rivers converged out west of the city, then split off again in opposite directions and arced around the city's edge, with their tributaries and channels redirected and built up into canals. Their slow-moving waters were a natural moat, and they gave sailors access to the heart of the continent. Yat and Wajet were in a strange part of town: too close to the toffs to be poor, but too close to the edge to be rich, mostly inhabited by the sort of well-heeled criminal who preferred implications of violence to the real thing. She got her breath back and looked up, then put two and two together.

"No way," she said.

"Yep," said Wajet, grinning.

A ship bobbed in the water in front of them. It was beautiful. Gold scrollwork along the gunnels, fancy cosmetic biowork all over the place, and a golden figurehead of a mermaid with a dog's head. Flowers covered every square inch of the deck: devil's pipes, orange-rose, a dozen others she didn't even recognize. The *Kopek*. She'd never seen it in real life, but she'd heard rumors from the other officers. The last Dawgar privateer ship and the most dangerous pub in the city. It came and went as it pleased, despite law enforcement's very best attempts to keep it bolted to the docks. If a scheme was happening in Hainak, you could bet good money it had started on the *Kopek*.

"*This* is our murder scene?" she said.

Wajet nodded. He'd pulled a cheroot from somewhere and put it behind his ear. He hadn't struck her as a smoker. He must've seen her looking at it.

"It's not for me, Constable," he said. He inclined a gracious hand toward the gangplank. Two guards leered down at her. They both wore scarves over their mouths. One was Hainak: dark-skinned and wiry with a shaved head. The other was a Northern-looking woman with ice-white skin and a shock of red hair. Yat found herself staring at it, lost for a moment in memory, and then something else caught her attention. The guards' skin looked rough, almost bark-like, and she gasped when she realized that they'd had biowork done on *themselves*. Totally illegal, of course, and they didn't seem to care who saw it. Folks on the other side of the wall got work done all the time, but it was different seeing it here: the ones there followed laws only if they pleased; the ones here couldn't afford the same luxury. The door between them had a layer of gold paint on it and strange runes carved into the lintel. Yat locked eyes with the Northern woman, and for a moment felt something strange in her head—a sort of push, gentle but insistent, urging her eyes to look away. It didn't matter, she knew it didn't. She was just tired. Yat composed herself as best she could, then stepped aboard.

To call the *Kopek* rowdy would be like calling the ocean wet. It was amazing—she'd heard nothing from the outside, but the interior of the ship was somewhere between a party and a full-fledged riot. She saw a man cut off his own finger, drop it in a glass of beer, then regrow another finger while his friends cheered him on. She could count the possible infractions: illegal biowork, assault on one's own person, and potentially poisoning, considering how dirty the finger looked. With all the relentless, violent merrymaking, it was amazing the ship hadn't simply broken in half. It took perhaps thirty seconds for the inhabitants to realize they had a pair of cops among them, and the room went quiet very quickly. Yat did her best to appear small.

Once they stopped moving, she got a better take on the place. Maybe a hundred people. Lots of visible biowork and tattoos. Flowers all over, just like the outside of the ship. She squinted at something attached to the back wall behind the bar—an ant colony? That seemed like a liability. There was a piece of sealing wax smeared along the middle of the glass.

"Wajet," said a voice. Yat didn't know what she'd been expecting from their host, but it wasn't this: a woman's warm, husky voice. The crowd parted to reveal the speaker.

She was a small woman with heavy-lidded eyes and light brown skin. Perhaps fifty, perhaps seventy. Her dark hair was tied back in a single braid; gray strands cut through it like rivers carving through stone. She wore hardy, practical clothes with leather patches sewn into lightweight cotton. Somebody had stitched little gold filigrees onto the cuffs and neckline, but they didn't make her outfit look any less like armor. She had rings on every finger, but not gold or platinum or hardwood: heavy iron ones without ornamentation. Her mud-stained boots lay on an incongruously plush footstool, soles pointed at Yat. Wajet whipped out the cheroot from behind his ear and bowed deeply.

"Sibbi, my dear," he said, "it is an honor to be aboard again."

Oh *gods*. Sibbi Tiryazan, of *course*. She was smaller than the stories said, but that wasn't hard; she could've been twenty feet tall and carved from pure granite and still not live up to the back-alley legends. She was infamous: a Dawgar pirate who'd taken a commission against the Lion during the war. They said she'd sunk more ships than the entire Hainak fleet. That the last country that had crossed her didn't exist anymore. Her service got her a lot of patience from Parliament, though patience wasn't the same as kindness. It had never been clear how involved she was in the ship's operations beyond the obvious work to keep it afloat, but that absence of evidence pointed more to skill than innocence.

She nodded to one of her men, who took the stogie and handed it to her. She put it into her mouth and . . .

. . . lit it? Without a match, though. She clicked her fingers, and it was lit. The ship's timbers seemed to groan, and the bioluminescent fungi in the lamps dimmed for a moment. A murmur of approval went around the room. Yat had never even heard of biowork like that: How could plants make *fire* out of thin air? People were coming up with mods like that all the time, but the gene-grafts never held properly and could take large patches of skin with them. This was bleeding-edge, but without the blood. *No flame, either, just ignition. Didn't even get ash on her cuff.* She looked for a wire—maybe some stolen Vault machine up Sibbi's sleeve—but her hand was empty. Gods above and below. Yat had grown up around an alchemy lab and had never even dreamed of that sort of work. She realized she was staring now, and that Sibbi was staring right back at her. She resisted the urge to shut her eyes, as though in prayer.

After an interminable minute where she sat gloomily puffing away, Sibbi snuffed the cheroot on the arm of her chair.

"Who is your friend?" she said. Her accent was light, with little grace notes on the ends of her words: *Who is² your friend¹?* She leaned forward in her chair, put her feet down from the stool, then stood up. It was a remarkably efficient movement: she was fast, yet smooth and careful. She put a single finger beneath Yat's chin and tilted her head back. After a short inspection, she gave a little *hmph*, and twin plumes of tobacco smoke coiled out of her nose.

"Wajet," she said, "come with me. There are matters we need to discuss privately." She turned on the balls of her feet like a hauhau dancer and made her way to the bar, then slipped through the beaded curtain behind it and vanished from sight. Wajet shrugged at Yat, then followed. Yat moved to go with him, but he shook his head and mouthed, *Wait here.* She tried to make the expression for *You're not leaving me alone with these lunatics*, but he gave her a sorry-not-sorry grin and disappeared behind the bar.

FIVE

They're fucking," said Ajat. "Do you know what fucking is, pig?"

She was a tall, muscular woman with a network of scars across her shoulders and patches of vitiligo staining her face. Her hair was a mess of vines grafted on the top of her scalp, running all the way down to her waist. She patted Yat on the back and laugh-roared. After introducing Yat to her keeper, Wajet had been gone an hour, and she had been adopted by what appeared to be a group of pirates.

"I know what fucking is," she said. It didn't sound as assured out of her mouth as it had in her head.

"I don't mean sex, little kurī. Not biology," said Ajat. "Do you know *fucking*?"

"Be nice," said one of the pirates, the one with the shaved head. Pity was even worse than insult. There was a tension in the room, a bowstring drawn taut beneath the big obvious emotions. Yat didn't know what it was, but she knew it was there. She was being observed.

"They're the same damned thing," she spat. This got a laugh, and

Yat blushed, ashamed. She balled up her fists a little beneath the table. If anybody noticed, nobody said so.

"Only technically," said Ajat, "and technically don't count for much."

That got an even bigger laugh. Once they'd figured out that Yat wasn't a threat, the crew of the *Kopek* had started treating her like a small cat or a pet bird: something adorable that would kill you if it could, but since it can't, it's hilarious. They were, as the common parlance went, effing with her. Yat had stopped trying to count infractions about ten minutes in, when she hit the triple figures. She didn't feel threatened by them, but she would rather be anywhere else. She decided to change the subject, but the *Kopek* was so utterly singular it made it hard to talk about anything else.

"What's with the footstool?" she said. "You steal it?"

"We didn't steal a single thing here, officer," said Ajat, "but least of all did we steal the 'orseman. He rode all the way here himself across an ancient desert. He's well over a thousand years old, and you'll treat him with respect, thank you very much. That stool has got more history and integrity than every cop in your department."

As Yat struggled to think of something to say, Wajet stepped out from behind the bar. He was a little red in the face, which summoned appreciative jeers from the crew. He shook a few hands as he strolled through the bar, then arrived in front of Yat.

"Right, Constable," he said, "that's our investigation sorted. Thank you for your assistance."

She'd had just about enough of this. Drawing herself up to her full height—a mighty five-foot-five—she took out her notebook. *Did he have that bag on his belt when we came in here? No matter. Focus.*

"And how was the matter resolved, *Sergeant*?" she said.

"Wouldn't you know it," said Wajet, "it was an accident. The poor fellow was moving a box of dinnerware down the stairs, and he tripped. Got a whole mess of knives into him. Very nasty. This is why you must always follow the rules, Yat: never move sharp objects without adhering to safety protocol."

"And the body, *sir*?"

"Oh no, Constable, he's not dead," said Wajet. He motioned to a sheepish man standing near the bar. "All those knives, and none of them anywhere vital. I hesitate to call him 'lucky' what with all the pain, but he'll live."

She sighed. The snitch didn't have any scars that she could see. He was shirtless, drinking a handle of some sort of honey wine. He shrugged.

"Fool that I am, always slipping over," he said, "but no harm, ay?"

She barely even realized it, but the crew was shuffling around— there was a clear path to the door now. The clumsy snitch looked at her with twinkling eyes. Yat got the message.

"I've noted that, sir," she said. "I'll be putting it in my report."

Wajet grinned at her. She didn't know the man well enough to be sure, but she'd seen the same look on cats with mice in their paws.

"Please do," he said. "Good to have everything aboveboard. I'm sure the brass will give your report the utmost attention."

Her *report*. Pointed word choice. He knew about the demotion. It had been no accident that he'd found her. Despite all the niceties, he'd only brought her along because you needed two officers on a job like this—and he knew nobody would take her seriously if she turned him in. He'd also brought her along to humiliate her in front of his friends, because who gave a shit about some little night-shift faggot? Maybe it was funny to them to make her hurt. The little bag on his belt jingled, and she realized it was newly filled with coins. That was the last straw. Wajet could dance the gallows-jig above the Grand Canal, for all she cared—maybe this arrogance would be the end of him. She *would* report it, and he could live with the consequences. The system worked sometimes.

She stood, breathing hard now, trying to keep her rage bottled up. Her hand moved to her cnida, just for a moment, and as her hand met the handle she felt the vine inside begin to come alive. But she stuffed it back in her pocket and hung her head low—her throat hurt like she was about to cry. She clenched her fists so hard her nails cut into her palms, but she refused to shed a tear.

"I'll see you back at the station, Sergeant," she said.

Wajet frowned a little. "Of course," he said. "And come talk to me after your shift."

Why the continued pretense of interest? It didn't matter; she wasn't playing his games. The exit was waiting: Yat took it without looking back.

Minutes later, she regretted her rashness. She pushed past a small cluster of sparrows pecking at crumbs in the gutter. They scattered as she stumbled by. She didn't know this part of town. The streets were all pre-revolution: cobble and brick, laid out in wild curves with no regard to order. They twisted and doubled back on themselves or led nowhere at all. The streets were lit by electric lights on top of steel poles, curved like the mournful arms of a willow. She kept close to the water's edge: she knew if she followed it far enough, she'd find her way back to the station. It wasn't that easy, though—parts of the waterfront were walled-off private property. Yat had to keep taking detours into the messy jumble of streets and slum houses, cutting through abandoned homes and clambering over piles of garbage and effluent. She hadn't been out this way for years, and she'd lost her old climber's instincts. They didn't even build with wood down here, just unadorned brickwork. Figures watched her from windows and rooftops. She could hear and feel her own heartbeat and taste copper. She tried to relax, but her breaths were quick and sharp—they hurt. *Oh fuck oh fuck, I'm going to die. I'm going to die. I'm so stupid, I'm so—*

"You changed," said the voice above her. She looked up to see a pair of legs dangling over a rooftop. Pale skin, red hair. Kiada, not a day older than the day they'd taken her in.

"You're a ghost," said Yat, drawing her clothes more tightly around herself and keeping her head down, trying not to look, "I saw you d—"

She stopped, and choked back the word. It wasn't quite right, either. She hadn't seen Kiada die. She'd seen her walking around with a broom, glass-eyed and empty. She hadn't had the courage to try to talk to her, so she'd left and pushed it down somewhere so deep that it looped around and came falling out of the sky with the evening thunder.

"Yep," said Kiada. "Funny, that. You saw, and you almost took that kid into the station anyway. You know what they do to us."

"It's *different*," said Yat. "I keep track of them. I make sure they get fed and released. Somebody needs to look after them, to make sure no more kids get lost in that system, and I'll put up with this shit for the rest of my fucking *life* if I can save even one."

"Mhm," said Kiada. She was standing in the street now, a girl of no more than fifteen staring up through the years. There was mud in her hair, but she didn't seem to mind.

"And how's that working out?" Kiada said. "The streets talk, and nobody is saying *shit*. The instant you turn your back, somebody tears open the floorboards and those kids go falling down. Just because you don't see it doesn't mean it's not there. After all, you can see me."

She winked and vanished. Yat swore and fumbled for her bag.

You've been here before. It's in your head. You've got tools for this.

She reached in and took out her last kiro cigarette. Payday tomorrow, and she could top up. She didn't like to smoke herself dry, but this felt like an emergency. She put it in her mouth and lit the match, hands shaking. She recalled how strange it had been that Sibbi had done it without even a flame, but no time for that now. She snapped it against the side of the matchbox, swore, found another. It lit, and she cupped it to the end of her kiro and took a drag. The warm smoke filled her lungs, and she felt her heart rate

slow.

She didn't know how much time was passing. The voices pulled her to and fro, and she followed them without question. There was something different about them this time, something directed. The random white noise had given way to a signal, and the signal had her in its grip. Kiro often induced a sort of dream logic: nothing made sense, but she followed it without question

—left here, closer, closer—

—that's right, luv, it's just this way—

until the streets spat her out at another patch of water, and she spotted the lighthouse in the distance. Finally, some good news. If she could see it, it meant she was in the northern half of the harbor district, and that meant she was on the right track. She didn't know exactly where she was, but it was better than being totally lost.

A puffball boat bobbed up and down in the water. A man in a flat cap stood on it, poking something in the water with the punt pole, trying to drag it toward himself. He saw her and waved. She waved back.

"Say," she said, "you know the way b-back to the station?"

—the sound of paper being gently torn, or boots through fresh snow—

—how do I know what snow sounds like? I've only read that word in books—

She walked closer to him and peered over into the water. She couldn't see what he was poking, probably a crab trap or something. He pointed vaguely north. Better than nothing. The voices in her head overlapped, jabbering, cajoling, screaming now. She couldn't make sense of them, but their sudden urgency frightened her.

"Thanks," she said. She took a step closer and noticed the cloudiness in his eyes: a blank.

Wait, blanks don't wave. Blanks don't—

She took another step forward, and the smell hit her. Rich, earthy, acrid. She'd smelled it once before, but it had stuck with her since: the smell from Dad's room the night his body had finally had enough.

The man in the water was dead. Normally, there were procedures for this to keep the cops from making a mistake and having someone buried alive. Yat didn't think they would be necessary: the man floated facedown, and the back of his head was a ragged cavity of bone and gray matter. A tattoo on the back of his hand: a pig. It looked cheaply done, not enhanced in any way—just needle and ink. She vaguely remembered some sailor's story about pigs being good luck at sea. The stench had fully surrounded her now, and she gagged and stumbled back. White-green fuzz had grown all over his skin and inside his wound; his skull looked like a peach gone bad. He was bloated from seawater, and there were two more wounds in his back where the digestive enzymes had burned their way through, and she could see a little halo of teeth, an awful little rictus grin from the dead grub still lodged inside his body. His right shoulder was a mess of torn flesh, and the veins in his neck were black and bulging. She reeled, and a voice began to etch a tattoo on the back of her consciousness:

Blanks don't wave blanks don't wave blanks don't wave—

—unless they're told to. Unless they've been given orders.

They weren't alone. Her hand sprang to her bell and she rang it. "Three a.m. and all's not well! Three a.m. and all's not well!"

The Tinker's Horns were meant to pick it up and broadcast it, but they weren't working. She screamed the words at the horns, but nothing happened. She screamed and screamed until her voice broke away and—

And she was alone, except for a blank and a dead body. She dropped her bell and turned to run and—

—two officers appeared from a nearby alleyway. A big guy and a little one, helmets tilted down with their brims covering their eyes. She didn't recognize either of them. She dropped her body low into a fighting stance.

—run girl run, he's a shark he's a crane he's a lion—

"Hold on," said the little guy, "hold on, backup's here."

His voice was gentle, almost convivial. Wiry body, telltale acidic scarring on his hands that marked him out as ex-military. Yat's hand moved away from her cnida as he approached. The panic and exhaustion hit her all at once, and she had to bite down on her lip to stop herself from sobbing. It was too much. It was all just too fucking much. The voices whirled inside her, pushing and pulling.

—no, he seems nice. I trust him—

—I'm just scared and I want somebody to make me not scared—

—RUN—

—I can't I can't, it's too much—

72

"Dead body in the water," she said. It took all the energy she had left. She felt faint. The voices had never spoken *to* her before. She didn't know which ones were hers and which were the kiro. Big guy was hanging back, watching the alleyway, hand on his holster. It was dark, and he was too far away for her to make out the details, but something about him looked wrong. She realized it was ferro: no feeder veins, no ammo sac, just stiff dark leather. The little man—a few feet away now, amazing how fast he'd closed the distance—smiled at her, and too late she noticed his teeth, filed down to sharp points. Ladowain officers were rumored to do that to strike fear in their enemies. She'd always assumed it was a myth or some sort of propaganda. He took something out of his jacket pocket, and time seemed to slow to a crawl, as if to say, *This is important; take in every detail, because you won't get a second chance.* A long metal tube attached to a cylinder. She'd seen one in training: a revolver. A fucking *gun.* Ferro, Lion-tech. Little bronze etchings along the barrel and a stink of sulfides as it came up and up—

The muzzle emerged from the mouth of a little golden lion. Her dad had told her stories about weapons like this—high-end Ladowain stuff. Could punch a hole in the thickest sheet of cellulose. *And now it's at my neck and now—*

—amazing, the strange things the mind chooses to focus on. How the whole world can move like treacle, and yet your arms stay pinned to your sides. Amazing how beautiful and clever and stupid the human mind is. Just amazing—

—just let him. If you had a problem with this, you never would've taken that scalpel from your dad's lab after he died and—

—RUN GIRL RUN—

—no, he seems nice—

The barrel was against her forehead now, and of course the blank hadn't been waving: he was signaling. Blanks were manual labor without the memories—the perfect accomplices. *Recover the body, wave for help if a stranger sees you.* Of course. Too late for revelations now. The cnida at her side might as well have been at the bottom of the ocean.

The lion roared, and night fell.

SIX

*C*ome here, little bird. Somebody has broken you, but I've a story to tell.

I remember a time when all this was ocean. I remember boiling seas, and new land emerging through fire. I remember jungles. I remember a woman who loved, and a woman who died and then loved again. I remember my daughter, and my daughter, and my daughter, and my daughter, and snowmelt, wingbeats, the great stained-glass roof of heaven. I remember stone and iron and cellulose. Above all, I remember silence, and I fear I will remember silence again.

I have seen many worlds, but this one is mine. I am the child of chapel and tree; I am twelve iron spears held up in the darkness. I was born here, deep beneath the earth, and I rose with the land. I left and found silence, then returned to find my home in diminuendo. I sing now against the silence. There is a pool at the roof of the world where the roots drink deep; the water has gone sour, and so the tree dreams in darkness. In the shadow of a mad iron god, my daughter lies dreaming.

Come here, little bird; somebody has broken you, but there is work to be done.

SEVEN

Down and down and down again. More water and darkness than a harbor could reasonably hold; more than the ocean could hold, than the world could hold. Yat fell, and a cacophony of voices tore through the hole in her head:

—I TOLD YOU TO RUN—

—PLEASE, I JUST WANT TO SEE MY DAUGHTER AGAIN—
—THE MONKEY LIES—

—THE LION ROARS—

—THE—

She left sense behind, and her body, and her name. There was no Yat, no woman, no fear or fury—just a soul hurtling down through the endless dark. The dead clung to her and billowed behind her like a grotesque dress. Their hands were warm, and their breath reeked of formalin. They whispered and shrieked at her, but their voices were lost to the same velocity that was tearing her to pieces.

Something dwelt in the dark; it was so large it defied reason, and she couldn't see it until its tectonic movement changed the shape of the world, and then she realized it was everywhere—a slab of meat and fur so monstrously tall it defied comprehension. She could scream, but there was nothing left to scream and nobody left to scream at. The titan stumbled, then put out a hand. Its palm was larger than Hainak, than the Ox, than the Sea of Teeth. She should've been scared, but she felt nothing. The new land rose up to meet her and she crashed into it at full speed, burning white-hot. The plateau roiled beneath her as she hit. She knew it should've hurt, should've killed her on impact. She looked up and realized she was sitting in the palm of a . . . monkey? Not quite: too many eyes, too little skin. Not even close, but as close a frame of reference as she had. It stared at her. Its head was the size of a moon, yet she could see something around the curve of it, half-hidden on the reverse side—another set of ears, another mouth split into a wide grin. It did not speak, but she knew what it said.

YOU DO NOT BELONG HERE.

Words punched into the surface of the world like nails going into a coffin. There was no malice in it. It seemed like an entity beyond malice, or indeed beyond any human emotion at all. Typhoons didn't get mad when they rolled through villages; plagues weren't personal. Men gave Death a face and made that face a skull, because that familiarity was easier to understand.

As the mouth on the dark side moved, the creature's entire neck twisted around. This new face was more familiar, identical except for the light in its eyes. A mad Death: a wailing, emotional, human one. The mother at her son's graveside, the killer in the alleyway, the frightened man who sold peace and order from the barrel of a gun. The voice came from everywhere, and it burned in her ears like sodium hydroxide.

NaOH, what's that? It's a base in alchemy. Dad used it in that protein broth. I spilled some on myself once, and he panicked and tried to scrub it off—there's still a little scar there.

Whose memory is this? Who am I?

I'm Y—

Oh, thank FUCK. Look, luv, I've been trying to get through to you for ages. I—

The beast clicked its neck and its head spun back around in a high-pitched concussion like a salvo of gunfire against a brick wall. She'd heard that sound when she was a child, in the streets below her house—she'd heard it on a day when she wondered whether the world was turning for the better.

FLY NOW, the forward face said. It moved its hand, and the world moved, too.

She was hurtling up and up and up again at terminal velocity—*haha terminal, nice one, mate*—a shooting star tearing through the fabric of the endless night. She hurtled back toward the world, and as she moved, she picked little pieces of herself back up. She found her fear first, then her anger—searing, unbridled by body or reason. She found her arms and legs, then her head—opened up and spilling gray meat out behind her like the plume of a comet, then stitching itself back together as she screamed. Lastly, within a breath of the surface, she found her name. Something glimmered through the surface of the water. It was close enough to touch, yet impossibly far and—

Sen knelt over her, his face red with exertion. His palms were one atop the other, flat against her solar plexus.

"Breathe, breathe, fucking *breathe, c'mon,*" he panted.

She sat up, knocking him back: it wasn't a particularly violent movement, but he'd thrown his whole body behind his resuscitation attempt. He scraped along the wood of the pier, then pushed himself back up onto his feet. They stared at one another for a moment before Yat vomited seawater all over the front of her uniform. Sen was babbling something, but she was barely processing it—his words arrived at her ears in pieces.

"Felt guilty . . . followed you . . . a fucking *gunshot*."

She didn't feel ready to form words again, but she did her best.

"'nother cop," she said. "W-where?"

She turned around: the puffball was gone. The dock beneath her feet was smeared with blood and flecks of gray matter. *Her* gray matter? She'd felt the bullet enter the bridge of her nose and shatter both her eye sockets; she'd felt her head cave in, her brains exploding outward and the warm wind rushing in. She couldn't think who else's it could be. Thinking—a thing that was hard to do when your skull was opened to the thrice-cursed sky. The thought almost brought up another torrent of vomit. She'd been working on the assumption that large parts of her night were some sort of kiro-induced hallucination. But she remembered the bullet, and then . . . *something*. Trying to take hold of the memory was like punching fog or piecing together a reflection in a broken mirror. All she had was darkness, falling, an immense sense of *scale*. She put a hand to the back of her head. Hair, skin, the reassuring hardness of bone beneath it all—and a conspicuous lack of exit wound.

"'s been a murder," she said.

"Well, yeah, I mean," said Sen. He pointed to the blood on the ground. Yat didn't know what to make of it. She'd felt the bullet tear its way through her skull and into her brain and right on through everything that made her human. She'd *died*. It hadn't been a near miss or an amazing recovery. It was—

"Got shot," she mumbled. She didn't have all her pieces back yet. "'m fine, though."

"Where?" he said. He leaned in and inspected her sodden uniform, sniffed, then frowned and glared at her. "Mate, are you *high*?" he said.

He sniffed again and screwed up his face. There was something strange about him, something she perceived only in her mind's eye, a writhing tangle of bright white fibers that moved with him, seemed to dance, jackknife, spell out words in a language she couldn't read.

"Gods, Yat, you're high again. You got high and fell in the harbor, apparently right on top of a murder scene! I'm not sure I can cover for you here. I've gotta report this. *What happened?*"

Big question. He wouldn't believe the truth, but pieces of the truth, that might work. Her world was in pieces anyway. She was soaking wet, covered in blood and vomit, grasping at memories as choking and ephemeral as smoke. Something unreal had come from the dream alongside her, these long, awful yellow-white worms that had infested Sen. She looked down at herself and realized she was infested with it, too, visible not through her eyes but some other sense on the edge of sense, like closing your eyes and knowing where your hands are. She needed to reassert reality, even when reality wasn't making that easy. Her father had taught her to think scientifically: *Go with the data you've got. If something doesn't add up, either file it away for later or dig deeper.* Slow, methodical. Piece by piece. She breathed in deeply and felt her heartbeat slow. How she'd survived was not a priority: she was alive, and she could figure out why and how later. For the first time since she'd left the *Kopek*, she felt like she was standing on solid ground.

"Saw a body floating in the water," she said. "Called for help. Somebody in a police uniform came up. Shot at me and uh, missed. We fought, he punched me in the head, I fell in the water. Had a revolver. Lion gun, unmistakable. Exactly like one of the forty-fives we saw in training." She couldn't manage more than short sentences, and each word fell out of her like stones into a pool.

"You get his face?" said Sen.

She shook her head. "Teeth," she said. "Teeth like a shark. Little guy, but he looked strong. He moved fast."

Sen's mouth hung open and he went pale. The worms inside him flashed a bruise-purple before returning to white. "That sounds like a Praetorian," he said. "I saw a few during the war. They're vanguard troops. They'd send 'em through first in a little squad with grenades and shotguns to make as much mess as possible, then the rest of the army shows up while you're still bandaging your wounds. Real Lion shit: 'Mercy is for the weak' and all that. Gods, Yat, this just got *political* in the way that's hard for the brass to sweep up quietly. Are you absolutely sure of what you saw? Tell me you're imagining things, Constable. Once this hits Parliament, it could mean war. Real war, not this sitting-around-twiddling-our-thumbs-and-occasionally-sailing-close-to-their-waters thing we've been doing."

"I'm sure," she said. She wasn't, though. It all seemed too obvious. What sort of spy would carry a weapon that said, *Why, hello, yes, I'm a spy and here's my nationality*? What assassin would let their target know who sent them? And what shock trooper snuck around in alleyways in the dead of night? *Go deeper.* It would be overconfident, sloppy, or a dangerous mix of the two. Who did she know who fit the profile, who'd been involved in covering up a murder, who had reason to need her gone?

The realization crept up on her. Her limbs were cold from the water, but something else filled them now, making them light and warm. Her rage was waking her up, and she'd been sleeping a long time.

"Wajet," she breathed. She could barely believe it. He must've panicked when he realized she was actually going to report him and sent friends to do the dirty work. Why bother bringing her along in the first place? She glared at Sen.

"You let me leave with Wajet," she said. His brow furrowed.

"What about him?" said Sen. "He's out on patrol."

"He tried to have me killed," she said. "Must've found a Ladowain veteran somewhere, armed him, send him out to find me."

"Wajet's not a killer," he said. "He's—"

"*Somebody* tried to kill me," she spat. Somebody *had* killed her. She was still putting that together with the reality of still being alive, but that part she was sure about. "You were all concerned then, and now you're saying he's a harmless little bean cake. You felt guilty and followed me. *Why?*"

Sen reeled back. "Look," he said, "you're in a vulnerable spot. You used to be a street kid. No, don't interrupt me—you used to be a roof rat and you need money. He's the dirtiest cop in the force; the man pretty much has a monopoly on bribes at this point. He's always looking for amoral or desperate officers to join his little posse. I thought he might try to turn you dirty, not *kill* you. Dead people can't earn him money."

A bell rang out in the distance, and the whole trumpet network sprang to life. *Officer down, officer down. Four a.m. and all's not well.* Footfalls in heavy boots, approaching their position. Maybe three men, maybe four. Yat wasn't going to wait to see their teeth. She turned to run, but Sen grabbed her wrist. The threads inside him concentrated around the connection point, linking up with hers, and she felt his touch resonate through her entire body.

"It's *backup*," he said. She tried to twist out of his grip, but he was strong and she hadn't eaten properly in days. She felt his emotions course through her in that moment, almost as though they were her own, and knew he believed what he was saying, which didn't help at all. She didn't know how to tell him how terrified she was: how an electric anxiety was charging down from her head to her hands and heart, shaking her to pieces. Men were coming here to kill her again, and her friend was going to help them out of the goodness of his heart. He hadn't been there or seen it, and she didn't have the words to explain it: they crowded in her throat and choked her. She could barely stand, and every movement made her head spin. Her hand slipped to her cnida, and she squeezed. The vine shot out, hit the ground, unrolled and then, in a programmed spasm of artificial muscle, wrapped around Sen's leg. He screamed and let go—she twisted out of his grip, then yanked at the whip and sent him sprawling to the ground. She heard the dull thud of skull against wood and turned to see him lying on the harbor boards, screaming.

"I'm sorry I'm sorry, *fuck* I'm so sorry," she yelled. She retracted the vine, but it had already done its work: he writhed in pain on the dock. That awful telltale discoloration of the veins around his neck let her know the toxin had reached his brain. The footfalls were closer now, close enough that she could hear voices. She recognized at least one, with its characteristic volume issues: Wajet. She took one last look at Sen, who shrieked as the venom ravaged his nervous system. His face was red and his eyes wild, the worms writhing, dark and angry.

Yat ran for her life.

EIGHT

She knew the rooftops. Every Hainak street kid did. You learned to climb, or you starved. In a city divided by high walls, climbing was everything. With the right set of skills, you could go anywhere: over walls, in through windows. She could barely stand up straight, and the wind rolling through the streets nearly knocked her over more than once. With the hounds at her tail, Yat turned to her old skill set—she went up.

Up across old brickwork, up through tangles of vines and hyphae, up stems and chimneys until the city lay spread out below her, steel towers like shrapnel piercing through a fungal canopy of white and pink. The whole city was packed with the same network of fibers she'd seen in Sen, a crammed weave of golden thread that seemed to connect every house to every other. The only places she couldn't see them were the old buildings of metal and brick. The climb was painful; she was out of practice and couldn't stop shaking. Her hands hurt, and the wind had nearly thrown her off the vines. Only her terror had kept her moving. She could see over Arnak Vonaj—anything tall near it had been cut down, but the farther reaches of the city grew dizzyingly high. She could see the Shambles in the north: the slum district that seemed to go on forever, into the foothills and jungle. She could see the House of Parliament in the south, high atop Heron Hill, decorated in absurdly flamboyant biowork. The old parliament houses had burned in the revolution—the new one was meant to *say something*, but she wasn't sure what.

As she climbed, a flock of kākā—night parrots—circled around her. Their screeching reminded her of Sen's shrieks when the cnida had wrapped around his leg, and the red feathers under their wings looked too much like his pain-mottled skin. They were modified with a second pair of wings: they must've once been pets or an exhibit. She tried to shoo them away and almost lost her grip. They seemed to glow, as if each of them had inside its little chest a tangled ball of golden threads. She knew now that she wasn't seeing these with her eyes: she was sensing them, her mind giving them form. They followed the lines of the bird's body, molten strands that seemed to paint a map of its nervous system, flow out through its bones, suffuse its form with skeins of hard white light from tail to wingtip to beak. She could see the same light inside her, and the stem she was climbing, and in the thousands and thousands of houses that stretched out below her. She knew she was sensing *life* somehow, in an impossible, pure form that was warm and inviting and seemed to sing to her to grab ahold of it.

A malnourished hypha broke off as she snatched at it—she cried out, threw her entire body forward into the mushroom's stem, and wrapped her arms around it. She was shivering; she realized that her freezing, wet clothes and the night wind were coming together in a way that could be lethal. Just her luck—she couldn't get a break from the heat without freezing to death.

The mushroom's gills heaved just above her head. It didn't look like the safest spot in the city, but it would have to do. She hauled her way, shivering, up the stem and onto the cap. The door was overgrown. She tore at it, and it came away in her hands in wisps of plant matter. This house had been abandoned for quite a while. The furniture was long gone, maybe absorbed into the walls for food. The floor was spongy, breathing in and out in a ragged staccato; the house was probably dying. Yat collapsed, and the instant her back hit the floor, she could feel it coming to life—eager for sweat, and hair, and flakes of skin. Houses were remarkably efficient creatures, but they still needed to eat. She lay on her back, panting, but she didn't cry. Something crackled in the distance far below, and she couldn't tell if it was fireworks or gunfire. The detonations rattled the overgrown windowpane and set her teeth on edge. She was too exhausted to even get up and look.

Yat collapsed into sleep. As far as she knew, she did not dream.

The kākā woke her up, their raw, chuckling cries cutting through her sleep. She wandered over to the window and pulled back the hyphae blocking the light. The city lay below her, and it wasn't on fire—the first good news in what felt like weeks. She looked out at a nearby ledge and saw two parrots, perched on a steel outcropping that had probably once been part of a trellis. She opened the window, and one flew over and alighted on the sill. It cocked its head at her. She moved to touch its beautiful feathered head and—

The smell before a fire. Something sparked through the air between them, and she realized that its threads had unspooled and cast themselves toward her hand. The parrot squawked and tried to fly away, but it was too late. Its feathers turned gray and began to fall out; its head twisted back as if in agony. Its nestmate screamed and took off. Yat tried to back away, but the connection was too strong, something elemental tying her to the dying bird. A river of fire ran between them, and she couldn't break away from it. Its little body fell sideways and hit the windowsill, then slid off and out of sight.

At the same time, a warmth filled her. Something had died in front of her, and it was . . . intoxicating. It had burned her guts like good chili peppers or bad whisky. It was so good, it threatened to light her whole body on fire. She staggered backward with a huge grin on her face. She laughed but didn't know where the laugh was coming from. There was no pain in her muscles. She looked down and saw that her clothes were dry. Had the house done that? She should've changed out of them—hypothermia was a very real danger, even in sweltering heat. She hadn't done anything, but they were dry. Nice houses could dehumidify themselves, but this was something else. Whatever it was, she felt amazing—more alive than she had in years.

She looked out the window and saw it.

Atop the old trellis, a small nest. The eggs were large and white, like a chicken's. She closed her eyes and felt the soft, glowing threads coiled inside them. Gods, she'd killed their mother. Left them alone just like she'd been left alone.

Dad's body hadn't even been cold yet when she'd found it. He'd gone out to his tiny greenhouse—the place he'd spent every waking hour—lain down in front of his little shrine to Luz, then curled up like a cat and died.

No money left, out on the street, climbing in through windows just to find food to hold off the pain in her stomach . . .

She fell to her knees and wept. She hadn't let herself cry in a very long time, but it all came out of her now, years of pain at once. The salt stung her throat, her eyes. She fell again onto her side and shrank into a ball. She didn't know what was happening or why. She knew that she'd slept in an abandoned house and hurt, possibly killed, her only friend, and that she'd died and was somehow here anyway. She was accustomed to the inevitable comedown from her panic, an endless grayness that carved hollows in her heart. This was something else.

The warmth that filled her body suddenly felt like a curse. She cried and cried. The house shuddered as her tears hit the floor—it must've been close to starving before she arrived. Her body shook, and the house shook. She cried until she was empty, then lay on her back and watched the mycelium on the ceiling grow.

NINE

It was hard to tell how much time had passed. She'd never seen a house grow like this, the windows and doors sealing over in front of her. There was no sunlight getting in, but when Yat closed her eyes, she could sense the whole house humming with the same golden threads she'd sensed in the parrot; a dense network of fibers, somewhere beyond sense, that ran through her body and into the floor, and up the walls. They weren't visible as such, but she knew they were there in the same way you can sense your own body when your eyes are closed. The house was drinking from her, or she was feeding it. The glow she'd gotten from the dying bird was gone now; she didn't know whether it was still a part of her or its energy had fled into the sky to join its family.

After what could have been an endless eon, when her revulsion finally overcame her exhaustion, she forced herself to stand up. She'd never felt so empty. She stumbled and made her way to the doorway, then tried to tear it open. It was properly grown over: trama and cuticle, real mushroom flesh. She tore at it with her fingernails. It came away in clumps. The house shook, and its threads fled away from her. It took some time, but she managed to rip open a gap big enough to crawl through. The golden threads came back together behind her and seemed to cling to her as she left, as if to coax her back in. She looked down and saw the parrots' nest—about ten feet below the lowest point of the house, and on the opposite side. The houses around her looked different, too—the place must've twisted and grown in the night.

The city looked tiny beneath her. She could see farther but make out less, so much higher above the city than she'd been when she went to sleep. She could see over the swamp and jungle to the south, and all the way across the Strait of Bitter Tea to Gostei, the gateway to great lost Suta. She could see tall, pale shapes of ferro towers behind Gostei, piercing the horizon like the skeletal fingers of some forgotten god reaching up into the sky—so huge she could make them out from five hundred leagues away.

She could see the Axakat River wending its lazy way through the city and out into the western jungles. She could see dilapidated and overgrown imperial factories, slums that seemed to stretch on forever, the great old wall cutting the city in half, the chaotic jumble of fungi and towers and minarets that impossibly came together to form Hainak Kuai Vitraj.

It was the same city she'd fled from—she felt like she'd been asleep for centuries, but it looked very much like only a day had passed. She breathed deeply: the air was clear up here, and sweet. For a moment, she wondered whether she could just live up here forever: eat and drink from the houses, keep company with the birds, answer to nobody but the sky. The thought didn't last long—her city lay beneath her, passed out like a drunk in an alley. It needed somebody to get it home in one piece. She'd had a hard life there, but it was still her home: it hurt to see how bad things were, even if she'd been trying her best to make it better.

She started making her way back down. The way up had been a war against the wind, the sky, and her own body. Climbing down shouldn't have been easier—it was too dangerous for her to be quick, but while it was slow work, she barely felt it. She felt strong, she felt *rested*, in a way she hadn't in years: her whole life had been one big hustle just to get by, with sleep being a luxury. She'd forgotten what a good night's sleep felt like.

The city didn't look so different up close, but there was something in the air—in the same way a good engineer can see a bridge under strain years before it collapses, Yat knew something wasn't right. Her feet touched the ground, and the stillness of it made her stumble: she'd seen sailors do the same thing when they came ashore after months at sea. A blank ambled past her, rolling along a barrel of something. She stepped around him in a wide arc—she could taste iron in the back of her throat and feel her own heart beating. Her head hurt. How long since she'd had a smoke? Too long.

And yet, she felt alive—like she'd been sleepwalking through the world for as long as she could remember, and now her whole *self* was waking up. She eyed the blank; he wandered away, not making eye contact. He was a short man with an owner's brand stained onto his shaved head: a stylized wing. She warily watched him go. She wasn't quite on the same street she'd ascended from, but she knew the district well enough. She could make her way to the station and let them know what happene—

It hit her: she couldn't go back to the station. They might be convinced to turn on Wajet, but Sen? He'd been her only friend on the force, and she didn't know if that was true anymore. Folks died from cnida stings sometimes, but she wasn't ready to face that thought yet, so she tucked it away in a quiet part of her soul where she wouldn't have to look at it. She'd hurt him, though—that was for sure.

Still, there'd been a murder. A body floating in the harbor. A man with a Ladowain gun. That was what the police were there for, right? To keep killers off the streets, to protect the little guy. To be on the side of the light, even if it meant getting a little dirty. They'd want to know what she'd seen, but . . . how would she ever explain it? Sen hadn't believed her. What hope was there that any of the higher-ups would take her seriously? She saw them in her head, sitting around a table and taking an inventory of all her failings. *Disgraced officer, degenerate tastes, looking to stir up trouble to get herself back in the department's good books. No body, no witnesses—just a mixed-up girl making up stories. Sad, really. I suppose we should've known; they're all like that.*

She couldn't go back to her own house; that was the first place they'd look. Fugitives almost always went home first: they all seemed to assume it was too obvious for the cops to actually follow up on. She'd been on hand for a lot of arrests where the poor bastard just wanted to grab a few sentimental things before skipping town. One guy'd had a barony set up for him somewhere in the Eastern Shelf, but he went home to grab his lucky coffee cup and ended up getting caught and turned into a blank. Her hand immediately shot to her flask; its comforting weight sat in her front pocket. She pulled it out and took a sip. The tea was cold, but it was better than nothing.

She didn't know what to do; she didn't have the data. She held her flask flush against her stomach and took a deep breath. Her dad's voice rang in her ears. *If you've got the time, get the data. If there's no time, make some.*

She still had her uniform, which would get her far. She didn't know whether they'd be looking for her yet, but she had to risk it. She put on her helmet, pulled the brim low over her face, and stepped out into a strange new day.

TEN

It had been, to put it lightly, a rough night. The roughest of Sen's life. The sort of night his old mum would've called *rough as guts* in that tobacco-scratched voice of hers. Even with a few days between him and his No Good Really Fucking Awful Night, it still felt fresh and raw. He couldn't remember much after grabbing Yat: a scuffle and then just pain coming on in waves, followed by a sudden floatiness and the thought that he couldn't breathe, his limbs too damned heavy to do anything about it. Anaphylactic shock, the medic said. Throat closed up, lost oxygen to his brain for a good forty seconds longer than he would've liked. They'd pushed an adrenaline needle straight into his heart, and he'd sat up and nearly punched out an orderly when it hit his bloodstream. His chest hurt where the needle had gone in, but it didn't hurt nearly so much as his damned leg.

It was an awful mix of hot and cold: blistered skin, deadened nerves. The toxins the cnida had shot into his system were resistant to biowork—they'd need to wait before they could fix the leg, and he'd gotten a very bashful answer when he asked how long that might take. It wouldn't move right, and he had to swing it in a tight arc, lean on a cane while he swung his good leg. They'd given him a department-issue cane, and it was a piece of shit. The handle made his palm hurt almost worse than his leg. They'd finally let him sit, but he wasn't celebrating. He drummed his fingers on the conference table while the Cap spoke. It had been a sleepless couple of days. He'd reopened the rash on his calf scratching at it, found himself in the station toilet wiping pus off his uniform. He'd already been through the entire station coffee tin and had resorted to bringing in his own. The steaming cup in front of him mingled with the reek of the room: cigarette smoke with a faint hint of piss. The piss was new. Most of the brass had been beat officers during the revolution—more than a few were missing fingers or eyes, but they'd all gotten fat and slow while the world turned under them. Their scars were healed over, but last night had torn them all open. The whole room stank like a fresh wound. They were all shouting, but nobody had a damned plan. Somebody had put food on the back table, but nobody was touching it. Twelve officers in all, though they'd had sergeants coming in and out. It was Sen's turn to face them. Captain Trezet stood at their center: a man with a face like a brick but with a gentle, lilting voice that felt wrong coming out of his scarred lips. Probably a conflict of interest that the parliamentary union rep was also a captain, but nobody cared because he got the job done.

A bin chicken—an Erzau priest, but Sen refused to call them that since, like real ibises, they belonged in the fucking trash—stood in the corner with his mask still on. Sen didn't like that, not being able to see his face. Part of being a good cop was knowing how to spot trouble before it happened, and reading faces was part of that—folks looking to make trouble usually let you know it with their eyes, and failing that, with their body language. The shifty bugger wore a red robe and a beaked mask that made it impossible to tell whether he was bored or angry or listening intently. Something in the tilt of his body made Sen think the latter, and that worried him more than the other options.

There weren't enough sergeants to have one per precinct, so they were bringing in a trainful of lads from out of town, from up in the desert marches near Syalong Cherta. Sen didn't like that, either. Border officers tended to have a certain swagger, a proclivity to go straight to violence and get condescending about *the things a city boy like you couldn't dream of.* They were the sort of cowards who didn't even have the decency to recognize their own bloody cowardice. There'd been lads like that in the army—good killers but awful soldiers. Put a man like that in a dark alley, and he'd end up putting a hole in an alley cat. Not that it was only country bumpkins who were like that; he scratched his leg again and grimaced. Gods knew the kid had her bloody demons, but he'd trained her better than that. One day on patrol with Wajet and she'd been a wreck. Something about the whole thing stank worse than a barracks latrine.

Wajet wasn't in the meeting, of course. He was meant to be there, second officer on the scene and all that. He'd swagger in late, and it would go in the report and be quietly forgotten. He was just *like that*, and the force put up with a certain amount of corruption if it didn't get in the way.

Sen had been too busy watching the priest to follow the conversation, but a certain name pulled him back into the world.

"Constable Jyn Yat-Hok, the subject of our present discussion, is a person of interest in the attacks last night," said Captain Trezet. "She has previously been given a citation and censure for certain moral infractions—"

"She is degenerate," said the priest. Despite the mask, the words came out with perfect clarity. Some sort of integrated speaker system? Hard to say. The church got all the new tech. "She should've been censured the moment you caught her. Sin is cancerous, Captain. It metastasized tonight, and we are all its host. Your inaction is noted."

"With respect, Brother, she *was* censured," said the captain. "She's good at her job; we thought it was worth a course correction, so we put her on the night shift to limit her movements. Put her on the clock during the hours of sin. To keep her hands full, so to speak."

"Then you failed," said the priest. "The correct censure for her crime is death. She refuses to partake in the sacred circle of life. The book is clear on this matter: burn the cancer before it spreads. The police force is beyond hope at this point, and one need only look at the girl to see it."

Big talk for an election year—somebody was *very* confident they weren't about to alienate a key ally. Sen wondered what sort of promises Trezet had been made. He couldn't take it anymore. They were both wrong, and he knew it: Trezet and his mealymouthed half defense and the bin chicken with his bloody clichés. They'd both taken it on faith that Yat was broken, but the only folks he'd seen trying to break her were folks like them. Sen tried to stand, but his leg wouldn't allow it. He tottered a little, then stabilized himself against the table. His leg screamed in agony, and he spoke through gritted teeth.

"Look, *mate*—"

"Ah yes," said the priest. "Officer Kanq-Sen. I was wondering when we'd hear your contribution. Perhaps we should be looking into *your* records. Sin begets sin, does it not? You are forty-five next year, and yet you live without a wife. Very suspicious."

It wasn't that, it was just that the job left no time for family. He was working all day, then hanging around late to look out for the rookies. He'd had women in his life, but they never stuck around—always got tired of him coming home late. He was married to the job, and his rookies were his kids, and he'd come to terms with that. The pain from his leg made his head spin. He tried to throw out a riposte.

"Nah, mate, I don't need a missus," he said, "what when I've got yours."

It wasn't a smart thing to say, but he was done playing nice with bin chickens. They didn't run this place. Or at least, he hoped they didn't. He turned to Captain Trezet, who sighed.

"I think it's probably best if Sergeant Kanq-Sen is placed on light duty. Macaque's Furrow is quiet: nowhere in the south was attacked last night. I hear there are some lovely gardens out that way. It'll be good for you, Sergeant."

"Is this a censure, Captain?" said Sen.

"It is not, Sergeant," said Trezet.

The bin chicken said nothing. He'd retreated back into his corner and gone a little too still, as though he were a waxwork. Sen took a peanut out of one of the bowls and chucked it at his head. It dinked off his mask, and the room went very quiet. Sen turned back to the captain.

"Is it a censure now, *mate*?" he spat.

"Sergeant," said Trezet, hissing through clenched teeth, "I think it's best if you remove yourself from this room and spend the next few days keeping your name from coming across my desk. The train from the north will be arriving shortly with our reinforcements, and it's best you be on the other side of town when it gets here. Are we understood?"

"Yes, sah," said Sen. "Of course, sah. Staying Out of Trouble's my middle name, sah; Sen Yit Grace Kanq Lok-aj-Wen Staying-Out-of-Trouble Sen III; Mum was a bit funny like that, sah. Will, with full respect to her cherished memory, gladly remove myself from the present company, *sah*."

Despite the pain, he stood up straight and snapped off a drill-parade-perfect salute, then picked up his coffee and limped out of the room as fast as his wounded leg would carry him. Something stank, and it wasn't the piss. He was gonna find Yat if it killed him, and then, well, he had a few damn questions.

ELEVEN

Yat noticed the changes immediately. The streets would normally be filled with merchants by this time, but they were near empty. Some of the banners were torn, and she passed a man with a broom sweeping up glass from a broken window. Armed officers roamed the streets, and more than once she had to step around a fully loaded paddy wagon. The last time she'd seen this many guns in the street, she'd been a child and the city had burned. She saw a face peering out from the paddy wagon and recognized the soup-seller she'd almost bumped into the day before, Mr. Ot. He lived somewhere near her, and she'd seen him out with his daughter from time to time. He looked very tired.

Folks were avoiding eye contact and moving out of her way a little too quickly. The man with the broom stumbled to get out of her path. She tried to act casual, but her hands were shaking. Despite everything, this was still home. Good food and kind faces and bars with white-painted doors. It was a place she served in her own way, even when it hurt.

"Morning, sir," she said to the sweeper.

He was already gone, disappeared off down an alley. She sensed the dancing fire in him as he left, brimming with agitation.

Shit. They know. There's been a blast on the horns.

She was so wrapped up in her anxious thoughts that she nearly walked into Varazzo. His eyes went wide.

"Yat," he said. Her hand flew to her cnida, and she was halfway to hitting the button before she realized he wasn't attacking her. There was a fresh cut on his face—not life-threatening, but definitely something they'd want the medics to look at. The blood was dry and crusty; it had probably been unattended for a few hours at least. Where were the medics? If they could regrow a limb, they could certainly heal a cut.

"You're out of your zone," he said. "You're—what's your zone? You're Sen's, right? He's over in Macaque's Furrow, I heard. They set off a bomb in a café over there, but it was mostly empty. The lads are pretty much just sweeping up debris out that way. You w-want me to walk you?"

He didn't normally stutter. Hell, he didn't normally do much except sneer. She could sense the threads inside him: red-hot, whipped into a frenzy, striking out in all directions.

"They?" she said. It seemed like an important thing to know.

"Gods, Yat, have you been under a rock all night? You queer *and* thick? Radovan. The fucking Lion. It's gonna be war, everybody says so. Real war, blood in the streets. They're back. We would've seen them if they'd come through the mountains; their navy must've slipped the blockade near Dawgar and dropped a squad off up the coast somewhere. There could be hundreds of them."

Great. Now, aside from the . . . well, Varazzo-ness of Varazzo, she had one more thing to worry about. "Just how many attacks are we looking at?" she said.

Varazzo shook his head. "Too many," he said, "but we'll get 'em back. We'll make ten dead of theirs for every one of ours. W-won't we?"

His breath was shallow, and his words had a nasal whine to them. She'd never heard a single patriotic thing come from his mouth. He only ever mentioned Hainak to complain about how the women were too dusky and the food tasted like shit. He talked about Accenza like it was heaven on earth, and about Hainak like it was a pile of mud and sticks.

She realized then that by grazing his threads with her own as they thrashed around him, she could feel a little of what he felt. She didn't fully understand it—more white noise, chaos. But buried beneath all that, something else, a little seed of contentment, like he *thought* he was upset but really he was vindicated. He didn't care about what had happened, but caring about it was useful to him, so in that moment, he cared with his entire being, twisting it a weapon he could use. He had barely been scratched, but he would take the pain she knew and twist it into his own just to magnify it and inflict it on people like her. She had never hated him more.

"Varazzo," she said, trying to keep her voice under control, "how many are we looking at?"

It was hardly the most inspiring show of control, but it seemed to bring him down to earth. He'd always been a servile little shit who kicked those below him and kissed the shoes of those above. A backbone like a piece of straw. She didn't feel like she was in control of much these days, but it didn't surprise her how quickly he folded.

"Uh," he said, "about twenty bombs. Mostly grenades, maybe a few shaped charges. A couple of folks got shot, mostly if they were in the way, it looks like. We don't have a pattern yet. I heard about this shit from Sen—they did it during the war. There's no pattern, and that's the point. They get you working on a puzzle with no answer. Keep you busy so you don't see them getting ready to hit you again. They're . . . we'll . . . the *bastards*."

One detail struck her: Sen was alive. That could mean a lot of things, but at the very least, a weight was lifted from her shoulders. Macaque's Furrow was a nice district up near Heron Hill, all swells in fancy silk cloaks and boutique biowork. Other side of the wall, and she wouldn't be getting through security alone, especially if the city was in lockdown. Varazzo was a fucking worm, but he was just the man she needed. She could lose him once they'd cleared the checkpoint, maybe find a way to blame it on him. She needed to see Sen, but he did *not* need to see her. Not until she knew what was going on, and where she stood.

There was something very wrong in her home. It had been brewing for a long time, and she'd chosen to ignore it—because she was too tired, always busy, so hungry it made her stomach hurt. She kept telling herself that the little things she did around the edges over and over again were enough, but now the crisis had spilled over in a way she couldn't ignore. She knew she could run: she could just get on a boat and change her name and be a merchant in Accenza and never worry about any of this again. She wouldn't, though, not while a cancer took root in her home. Dad had died piece by piece, too, pretending it was fine until the little holes added up and killed him. He'd been breathing funny in the days before he died: too much fluid in his speech, too little air in his cough. She'd noticed it, but it was easier to pretend it wasn't happening, that if they could ignore the problem long enough it would just go away, until one day

Dad had gone out into his little laboratory and never come back. Luz hadn't helped him, but then again, nothing had. Yat rubbed her wrist out of habit—the scar she'd given herself that night had never quite healed. This sickness threatened to turn her home into another gaping wound, and she wasn't about to sit back and let it. She had already waited too long.

"Let's go see the sergeant," she said. She motioned with her free hand toward the Arnak Vonaj and tried not to let her fear show.

TWELVE

The kid was lurking around the Janekhai Market when Sen found him. Thieves were rarely creative. Cops all over the show, watching with wary eyes. The locals had cleaned up the alley remarkably quickly. If not for the temporary membranes stretched over some of the windows, you'd never know anything had happened.

The standard watchman's approach would be to clap the kid in irons, drag him around a bit, dangle freedom in front of him if he talked, actually let him go if you'd already met your quota. Nobody cared about street kids. He'd done it before and couldn't deny it got results. He told himself it kept them off the streets, and it was true: he sure as shit never saw any of them again. He didn't know what had changed, but he couldn't do it anymore. He leaned against a wall behind the kid, happy to have a reprieve from walking.

"Psst," he said.

The kid turned and sniffed.

"You sure did, mister."

Sen sniffed his own uniform and realized how ripe he smelled. He hadn't changed it. He only had two, and the medics had cut the first one to pieces getting him out of it. He shrugged. Fair enough.

"Would you believe a big boy did it and ran away?" he said.

The kid gave him an incredibly world-weary look for a thirteen-year-old, then nodded.

Sen pulled out a silver coin and held it up. "You wanna make a half-yan?" he said.

The kid crossed his arms and puffed out his chest. "I don't snitch," he said. He'd obviously never said the word aloud before.

"I'm not asking you to snitch," said Sen. He paused. "Well," he said, "not on your mates. I'm looking for the lady I was with a few nights ago. The cop. Short, fast. Remember her?"

The kid screwed up his face. "You her husband or something?"

"Nah, mate, just a friend. I'm worried she's in trouble."

"Full yan or nothing."

"I did say my friend was in trouble, right?"

"Yep. You're police, she's police. It's police tax."

Sen sighed. It was fairer than most of his taxes. At least he knew this one would actually go to somebody who needed it. He bounced the tip of his cane off the cobbles and regretted it instantly as his leg sang out in pain.

An Erzau priest walked past them. He wasn't looking at them, but Sen knew better than to trust that. He let the bin chicken sweep by in his dusty red robes, then turned back to the kid.

"Sure," he said. His leg gave him another jab, and he winced and leaned back against the wall. "But half now, half on delivery."

The kid nodded, then stuck out his hand.

"Deal, mister."

Sen shook it with as much vigor as he could muster. Gods, he needed to sleep. It was barely midday and he felt like he was about to pass out.

"You gonna tell me your name?" he said.

"Nah, mate, I'm not telling a copper nothing."

Smart kid. Reminded Sen of another roof rat, in a way.

"Except what I pay you for, right?" he said.

"Yeah," said the kid without a name, "except that. Permission to sod off, copper?"

"Permission granted, ya fuckin' sprog."

He watched the kid go and wondered—not for the first time—whether he was doing right by the city. Not for the politicians or priests and certainly not for the police, but for Hainak. He'd spent a lot of his life in muddy wars, patrolling marches and walls that belonged to nobody, standing at the end of the world and giving it a shrug. The force had offered him an opportunity to change that: to be somebody, to *do* something. 'Course, the army had offered the same. He leaned against the wall as the market moved around him—even with the world in pieces, bread needed selling before it went stale, fish needed eating before it went bad. People were people: you could build as many bloody walls around them as you wanted, and it didn't make them less.

He waved at another cop, a man he didn't recognize. Pockmarked skin and military enhancements: probably one of the new lads. He scowled at Sen. He couldn't be older than twenty, meaning he hadn't even been born when the war started. They got 'em young, of course, when they were more malleable. He'd been a mad young thing himself once, desperate for order in a world that refused to provide it. Now he was a tired old man, and he wasn't even that old. One day it was gonna crush him, and he'd be one of those old men who hung around in bars with swollen knuckles, shitty combat splices, and a lifetime of nightmares he drank to forget.

The soldier-cop started chatting to a bin chicken, smiling and doing all the hand signs. Of bloody course. It had seemed, as little as a year ago, that the Bird Cult was on its way out, losing ground in Parliament and favor in the streets. You could go days without seeing a red robe. Now they were everywhere, like actual ibises, rooting around in the garbage, spilling trash everywhere. At least with the election coming up, he could help give them the boot, if only a little. The priest gave the cop a hand signal that didn't seem right—not part of the usual liturgy. Then he noticed the little smudge on the priest's mask: a little dark scrape in the midst of all that nice white fabric, like somebody had bounced a dirty peanut off it. Could be that he was just at a bad angle, but Sen hadn't gotten somewhere just north of the middle by letting things slide. He heaved himself off the wall and limped after the bin chicken.

THIRTEEN

It didn't take long for Yat to realize they were being followed. Whoever it was, they were good at maneuvering unnoticed—she wouldn't have known they were there at all if the light inside them didn't glow white-hot. They were so bright, she could follow them through walls. Everybody else she'd encountered had a similar glow, but this was something else: their pursuer's threads were dense, thick, and blinding. It was like being stalked by a lighthouse.

They were a climber, too, not just moving along the ground. She wasn't sure how they were moving so swiftly, though. She knew this part of town, and they were moving too quickly between floors, up onto rooftops and back down. Somebody fast and silent. She tried not to let her apprehension show. She knew she was failing, but Varazzo didn't seem to notice. He was talking to himself, his eyes darting back and forth across alleyways.

Varazzo had begun spewing rude commentary as he chattered away, and she tried not to let any of it in: *I reckon it's because we're plagued by degenerates, 'cause we let our standards slip. They hit that*

113

fag bar of yours—pity it was a weeknight. He'd never been a talker, but now he couldn't shut up. The shadow of Arnak fell over them: they were probably about five minutes away, but it could darken half the city when the sun hit it wrong. It was immense. Of course, it was the north that often found itself in darkness—that had been an intentional part of the design, to make sure the south didn't have to deal with stolen daylight. Only the very shabbiest parts of the south ever found themselves in darkness.

They stopped while Varazzo had a chat with the gate guards. Yat loitered around maybe a hundred feet away, trying to keep their stalker within her periphery. Whoever it was had stopped moving, though their threads were fanned out—they were drawing light from the world, pulling it into the host. *Hells, it's another . . . well, someone like me.*

She turned back to the wall. Varazzo was staring at her, though he was too far away for her to read his expression properly. He turned back to the guards, said something else, then wandered back and put a hand on her shoulder. His grip was a little too tight and friendly. The threads in him had calmed down and gone golden like everybody else's. They still twitched and writhed, almost seemed to tug him toward her. She smiled at him, hoping her disgust showed in her eyes.

"We can go through," he said. "The sergeant wants to talk to you."

He had a shit-eating grin on his face, and she knew they had her. They'd sent a runner to report that she'd shown up; of course they had. Standard protocol if an officer went missing on patrol: they probably had eyes everywhere, if the night was even half as bad as Varazzo seemed to think it was. They must've sent somebody as soon as they saw her coming. She should've known, but the last twenty-four hours had thrown her.

If she tried to leave, they'd know in an instant. There were men on the wall with borer rifles, long guns that could launch a carnivorous larva half a league. New stuff, straight from the front. The older models of grub usually died in the air before they got too far. These were smaller and lighter, with more efficient metabolisms but less bite power—to compensate, the army alchemists had spiked their toxin load through the roof. You weren't meant to handle the grubs without protective gear. They had one tucked away somewhere at the station. She'd heard officers salivating at the thought of using it, but they'd never had the opportunity.

Yat followed Varazzo through the gate and into the other city. She looked imploringly toward her luminous follower, but they stayed where they were—they might as well have been a world away.

It wasn't Yat's first time south of the wall—she'd grown up here, after all—but the stark difference still struck her. The streets were clean. There were police officers everywhere, but they looked different on this side: no uniforms, no side-eye, no cuffs. A detective she didn't recognize was talking to a woman in an absurdly large crinoline skirt made of iridescent pink vat-skin that wobbled as she swayed nervously back and forth. While the pink looked like an extension of her, its sheen was more synthetic. You couldn't grow something like that without a very, *very* large cell culture, and people didn't just give skin away.

Less visible brickwork now, too: they'd made leaps and bounds in covering the old-world structures in new growth. Tall trees and mushrooms lined the streets; their internal cooling systems—a series of gill networks that chilled and purified stale air—kept everything a comfortable temperature. She could sense the magic in them penetrating deep into the ground, linking up with the mycelial networks beneath the street. They drank deeply from it, and she realized that their systems weren't as efficient as she'd been told when she was young, that they stole their strength from the city and gave back only a trickle. A great golden tide flowed beneath the wall, pulling magic greedily into the south.

The farther they got from the wall, the thicker and more intricate the biowork became. Some of the structures weren't even recognizable as plants anymore, proprietary breeds whose alchemical designs were closely guarded secrets. The people she saw flaunted decorative biowork that made the rowdy crew of the *Kopek* look as somber and clean as Old Faith priests. They passed a man whose eyes appeared to be tiny beehives: insects crawled out of their holes and over his face. He stuck out a long tongue and peeled one honeycomb off, then swallowed it in a single gulp. He saw Yat staring and waved with no fear whatsoever that he'd be taken in.

In an ornate public garden, totally empty except for murmuring foliage, Varazzo got distracted by a trellis of chattering snapdragons. Yat took the opportunity to slip away between the maddening, twisted tree trunks. Everything here thrummed with the same golden threads as the north side, but these seemed to possess more *intent* somehow. It was as if they followed her as she walked.

Yat heard Varazzo's cry of alarm somewhere behind her and ducked behind the cover of a hanging curtain of vines.

Two officers swiftly met him from the opposite direction. They had rifles and weren't in uniform, but she knew they were cops. It was something in the way they carried themselves, like they were accustomed to getting their way and would get violent if they didn't. They had heavy gloves on, and one had a borer hive strapped to his back, encased in glass. A pale grub emerged from its damp, papery hive. It opened and shut its maw against the casing, its stubby sharp teeth making an awful scrape-scraping noise. An umbilical cord led from the hive to a device in the officer's hands: a tangle of cartilage for plugging into the gun. She'd seen a prototype in training, and the wet sound of the cord's muscles contracting as it pushed the grubs through still haunted her. The cops were arguing with Varazzo.

They put a tail on me. Not so friendly after all.

Yat could make out only a few words of their whispered argument. One stuck out: *Wajet*. They weren't taking her to see Sen after all. She was worried about him, but Wajet was another matter entirely.

A hot breath on her neck.

She spun around, but nobody was there. Yat paused for a few moments.

And the golden light reappeared. The stalker was hiding among the stems, but the glow gave her away. A familiar woman with dark skin, a dense network of tattoos on her face and shoulders—whorls that looked half ferro circuitry, half road map—and vines for hair. Vitiligo on her shoulders and chin, carved up by lines of ink. Big, Tangata, rough-looking but handsome in her own way. Where had Yat seen her before? She remembered the woman's voice before she remembered her name: *I don't mean sex, little kurī. Not biology. Do you know* fucking?

Of course. Ajat, Sibbi's muscle. She couldn't have been the one who called ahead to Wajet, though—she'd been following Yat for hours. One of the plainclothes officers shouted at Varazzo, and Ajat turned to watch them. It took only a second for Yat to slip back through the vines. She jumped and grabbed ahold of a tangle of vine-canes, then hauled herself on top of the trellis. Ajat turned back to where Yat had been. She muttered something in Reo Taangata. Yat didn't recognize the word, but she knew swearing when she heard it. Ajat took a step back, singled out a lock of her own hair, held it up to a nearby tree, and . . . pressed. The strand seemed to merge with the bark. Ajat's eyes went white like a blank's, and her golden light . . .

Every plant in the garden turned itself toward Yat. A vine snaked up and wrapped around her ankle, and she barely managed to jump back fast enough—it tore apart, but the end of it still clung to her leg. She fell from the trellis and hit the ground awkwardly, on her shoulder. She tried to roll but just ended up falling a second time. At the same time, her head exploded with pain. She could hear the wind whistling through the hole in her skull and feel her gray matter pouring out, and suddenly the ocean was pressing in from all sides and—

She was writhing on the grass as two shadows loomed over her. Their presence was so immense, it seemed impossible to fit into a mere body. Male voices shouted from somewhere nearby, and Sibbi waved a lazy hand toward them. Yat couldn't see what happened, but she heard glass breaking and awful, awful screams. Sibbi clicked her tongue.

"Looks like we've got a live one," she said. Waves of pain rolled over Yat, worse than a cnida, worse than being shot, worse than the time she got Dad's experimental protein broth on her skin and had spent the afternoon incapacitated by waves of agony. Sibbi took her by the forearm, gentle yet strong, and began to drag her. Yat tried to fight, but the pain was too much. She didn't know what the woman wanted or who she worked for, and the fact that she didn't understand was what terrified her—Wajet's friend, taking her away from Wajet's men? She was paralyzed, and a prisoner of the most infamous pirate to ever sail the Sea of Teeth.

Ajat walked alongside them. The pain receded, but Yat felt empty and lifeless. She looked at her own chest and saw her golden threads unraveling, glowing only dimly like fireplace embers in the morning. She knew the feeling well; she'd spent a lot of time living in the gray. It was that, but a thousandfold: a total void that made her old anxiety feel like a street fair.

Both women roiled with golden energy: a walking pair of hurricanes. Their threads drank deeply from her—whenever a spark rose up, they stole it away before it could kindle fire. They were muttering to each other in Dawgae. She didn't speak the language very well, though she caught a few words in her own tongue: Heron Hill, *Fantail*, Hainak . . . lamp? She recognized the switch back into Dawgae and could no longer follow.

She struggled again, but the two women seemed so much more powerful than their bodies, she might as well have been fighting the tide.

FOURTEEN

The little hairs on Sen's arms stood up as he lurked in the shadow of a factory out near Xineng. The priest was dressed like a lower-ranking member of the order, but the guards barely even looked at his papers before ushering him through. Even at a distance, there was something about their body language that Sen recognized immediately: cops desperately pretending they hadn't noticed something above their pay grade. Despite everything, it felt good to be right. If he wanted to be sure he wasn't seen, he should've hung back. It wasn't an option: he was straining to keep up already. Every step felt like it cost him five. He was going to need to cash in all his sick days when this was done. The priest wasn't even through the gate when Sen stepped out and made his way across the road, cane clicking on the ground with each step. It made him very conscious of how many steps he took: it was like Sen was being stalked by a metronome. No point trying to be subtle with it. He walked as quickly as his leg would allow, trying to minimize the time he spent in motion. A body lay in the street—looked like the poor bastard had been too close to a window when a bomb went off and had gotten cut to shit by flying glass. He stepped around the man, reached the wall, and saluted.

"Papers," said the guard.

Sen held them up. "Officer assigned to Macaque's Furrow," he said. Somewhere he wouldn't get into trouble. The junior of the two gave Sen's dirty clothes a side-eye, but the papers checked out, and that was what mattered. They waved him through, and he emerged into the other city: a place still called Hainak, but another world entirely. Different clothes, different names, different houses. They even stood their own way, as though they'd never had to worry that the way they stood could be used against them; as though they'd never been deemed *too proud* and in need of humbling.

They let common folks through, sometimes. The occasional scholarship kid going to the university, the occasional clergyman in need of special training they wouldn't get on the other side. An upjumped alchemist or two. They'd open the gates for religious ceremonies and pat each other on the back about how beneficent they were being. He'd been called in more than once to chuck somebody back onto the right side after they'd overstayed their welcome. He hated it, but he'd done it anyway.

He was so caught up in his thoughts, he didn't notice the medical alchemists running up behind him. They shoved past him, almost sending him sprawling. They didn't even stop. There were two of them and two sets of stretcher-bearers hauling ass down the street. He wanted to curse enough to turn their hair white and the air blue, but he barely had the energy to stay upright. He watched them go, then set off again.

He couldn't keep up with the priest, but he had a good idea where he'd go—the grand temple on Heron Hill. It wasn't far, but it took him almost an hour, and he was shaking by the time he got there. The temple was one of the only stone buildings left in the south: a proud symbol of traditionalism rather than just a sign that somebody couldn't afford the upgrades. Parts of the old reactor building remained, patches of concrete and rebar that had been repaired with stone and mortar, mostly sandstone. You didn't get any from the quarries near Hainak. It would've come from Ladowain, built in the old days and shipped down at great expense. Statues of each of the gods lined the boulevard leading up to it: Crane, obviously privileged, stood the highest, decorated with flowers, with her sons, Luz and Hekat, at her side; poor Dorya the Forgeborn was farther down the path with her hammer and pickaxe, her face in a snarl of rage and pain; the beasts Monkey and Tiger and all the rest lining most of the path now headless; the old statue of thieving Siviss removed entirely. It had been there when he was a kid, until one day it simply wasn't, and nobody ever said why. His mother had kept a small shrine to Siviss in the house, even after worshipping her had been declared heretical, after *criminals* and *secrets* were pushed to the front of her portfolio and *singers* and *stories* quietly pushed back; after that, Sen's mum never used the name, just talked about "She Who Bears History" in a way that wasn't *technically* heretical, but everybody got the gist.

Erzau priests moved back and forth, filling bird feeders and cleaning up all the pigeon shit. Sen sat on one of the benches and watched them for a while. No smudges on any masks that he could see. Not that it meant anything; the big feathery lad could have cleaned it off at any point. He wasn't sure what he was watching for, but he'd know it when he saw it.

While he waited, he turned the cane over in his hands. He'd spent time training with sticks when he was younger, before he'd joined the army. He'd loved stories about men who practiced the old arts, who could kill a horse with a single kick. Hadn't been half-bad at fighting in his day, though he suspected his days of hand-to-hand were over.

This was a beautiful place. Well-made, well-tended, serene. The only sounds were birds and brooms. They hadn't managed to sort out the humidity, but it was as close to heaven as Sen had been in a long time. After about ten minutes, a priest came out of the temple and stormed over to him.

"Sergeant," he said. "Don't you have an assignment elsewhere?"

Sen shrugged. "Can't a man meditate on the great divine mysteries?"

"A man can do that elsewhere, surely. You're frightening the birds. If you won't remove yourself, our friends will have to remove you."

The birds, as if by magic, took off all at once. A shadow fell over Sen. He turned to see a giant of a man with scarred hands and a distinctly unpriestly bearing looming over him. Another man was with him—lithe, smiley, eyes a little too wide. You saw a man with eyes like that, and you did your best to hide all the good silverware, but especially the knives.

"Źu, charmed," said the smaller man. "And you must be Sergeant Kanq-Sen." He grabbed Sen's hand and shook it with a tad too much vigor. The meathead said nothing, but Sen caught a flicker of intelligence in his eyes. He was doing the same thing Sen always did: assessing the level of danger. Big men were a yan a dozen, but big *smart* men? Deeply worrying. Źu clearly saw him notice and led Sen over as though presenting a debutante at a ball.

"This is my associate, Mister Źao."

Sen shook his hand. He'd expected a bone-crunching squeeze, but it was gentle, almost limp.

"Wasn't aware 'mister' was a rank," said Sen.

"It's not," said Żu. "I'll also take 'doctor,' though for our purposes today, 'mister' will do just fine." He winked, and a chill ran down Sen's spine. These men looked like soldiers and stood like cops and were in a very fancy part of town with obviously fake names, and the godsdamned priesthood were apparently fine with it. He'd been in the force too long to miss what they were. Fucking Sparrows. Worse, they knew he knew, and they were loving it.

"I'll just—" said Sen. "I'll just go, ay?"

Żu grabbed his arm and squeezed. It was in just the wrong place, sending a spasm up Sen's arm that almost made him cry out.

"But you were so close, Sergeant!" he said. "You were onto something, I'm sure. We could have a chat about it, if you'd like."

A "chat" that would involve flesh-eating acids, batteries, and a special place at the bottom of the river if he was lucky. He'd seen what happened to folks they sent to chat with the Sparrows. It was one of the things he drank to forget.

"I was wrong," muttered Sen.

"Hmm," said Żu. "What was that?" He grinned. It was the same look you saw on a tiger about to pounce. His grip tightened, and he turned his wrist slightly. It shifted Sen's balance just enough for his leg to scream at him. It was a clear signal: Żu could inflict a good amount of pain with almost no effort—almost like it was his job.

"I was wrong," repeated Sen through gritted teeth.

"Wrong about?" said Żu. His tone was jovial, like a schoolmaster helping a not-so-bright student finish a math problem. His beady eyes reminded Sen of a shark's.

"*I don't know*," said Sen.

Żu let him go and stepped back. "Very good, Sergeant," he said.

"Before you go, something to ponder: silkworms destroy their co-coons when they break out of them. They make something beauti-ful, then destroy it because they're obsessed with moving on. Do you know how we stop them, Sergeant? We boil them alive inside their cocoons. It seems cruel, but the results are so very beautiful. We pre-serve their art. In a way, it's a kindness, and it won't stop me wearing silk. Do you follow, Yit Kanq-Sen?" He twisted Sen's wrist again, and the searing pain nearly brought him to his knees. Źu winked again. *Tohoho, we're friends ain't we? Friends sharing a little joke.*

The two men stood there. The priest cleared his throat. Sen had gotten the message. They'd revealed something to him, even if they hadn't meant to. If the Sparrows were involved, this was political. *Really* political—not police-department office politics or the priest-hood clawing at the edges of parliamentary relevance, but top-level bloodshed political. Sen had found exactly what he'd come here for: assurance that he was onto something. Problem was, it was onto him, too. He hobbled away, shaking with pain, as all three men watched him go.

FIFTEEN

When the cold and numbness rolled back, Yat found herself strapped to a chair with thick cellulose bindings. The room was lavishly decorated with biowork, planters, and ant farms over every spare piece of wall or floor.

The chair was very heavy. She didn't remember sitting in it. She tried to shift her weight, but it didn't budge. The whole floor rocked gently back and forth—she'd bet good money she was somewhere belowdecks on the *Kopek*.

"It's bolted to the floor," said Ajat. "Good lu—"

Sibbi raised a single finger, and her bodyguard fell immediately silent. The older woman was smoking another cheroot. The blue-green smoke had an acrid chemical reek. Not kiro, but something adjacent—maybe a proprietary blend? A difficult thing to wrangle, but a pirate legend would have good alchemists at her disposal, so it wasn't a crazy thought. Being tied to a chair by a pair of pirates you'd barely met once, now *that* was crazy.

Yat had been anxious and tired for days: now she was *pissed*.

Pissed at crooked cops and hateful cops and damned impossible criminals. Pissed at her father for going off into the sky, at her city for not having her back, at the hateful pillar of fog that seemed to have kicked all this off. The room crawled with gold threads—she knew now that every living thing had them, and here they floated from place to place, chasing down other threads and merging with them as though the whole room were networked. She grabbed a nexus of gold from a cactus flower and pulled it into herself. All the room was linked up, and she pulled on every leaf, seed, ant. A surge of energy filled her, and the flowers began to wilt, as if . . .

But then it stopped. The threads withdrew to their homes, and Sibbi shone like a beacon. Captain Tiryazan took a deep drag, blew it out, and smiled. Her canine teeth were sharp as a dog's. Yat had seen enough sharp teeth in the past day to last the rest of her life, though these were very different from Ladowain sharpening: just the canines, done with some sort of bone growth stimulant. That was a Dawgar thing, though you didn't hear much about them anymore—Ladowain had stripped and salted the islands for their part in the war, and Hainak had been too new and fragile to help.

"Very good," said Sibbi. "A little rough, but workable."

She waved the stogie at Ajat and laughed. It was a surprisingly warm sound, accompanied by a network of laugh lines around her mouth and almost grandmotherly eyes.

"And you said she couldn't even grow a potted plant," Sibbi said.

"She couldn't," said Ajat. She leaned against the side of an ant farm and waved a lazy hand. "Gods' honest truth, yesterday she was as magical as goat shit. Maybe a twinge here and there, but it was mostly kiro."

Sibbi tilted her head to the side. Her wide brown eyes shone with intelligence and curiosity. There was something else in them that Yat barely recognized because it had been so long: compassion, perhaps. She hadn't expected it from the woman at all, and it made her angry, but she wasn't sure why.

"So," Sibbi said, "we know what that means. Rough night?"

All Yat's fear had transmuted into rage boiling up inside her. It felt good in a way that fear didn't, a rush to spit fire instead of letting it burn her up from within.

"You know the answer to that, you *bitch*," somebody said. "Your friend sent a man to shoot me. Your little pocket policeman had me shot in the fucking head because you two couldn't bother being discreet. Save me the whole act: shut up or kill me. I get the feeling it won't stick."

She realized with horror that the words were coming from *her*. These angry, reckless words were spilling out of her like pus from an open wound, and to her surprise, Sibbi just laughed again. The sound wasn't charming anymore; it was infuriating. *Jad ah lah, child, calm down and stop your fussing.*

"Well," Sibbi said, "it seems like you've got me. I surely got where I am today by being that sloppy. I'll save you the speech, clever one, since you've figured it all out."

She took something out of her pocket and turned it over a few times, and Yat realized it was her father's engraved hip flask.

"Steel," she said. "Quite illegal. Pity: it's useful stuff. It's everywhere, of course. They only arrest you for it if they don't like you." She held it up to the light. "Ah, yes. Fea the cat, stealing from the gods? They hang thieves, you know." She sniffed it. "Stinks of kiro, too. You keep your roaches in the same pocket? I thought cops were smarter than that." She twirled it around between her thumb and forefinger, just once.

"What's your point?" said Yat. "Are you threatening me?"

"My point," said Sibbi, "is that this little piece of metal is illegal on illegal on illegal. And yet, you keep it. You carry a thief not just in your pocket, but in front of your heart, next to your old dog-ends. It sounds like you've got more compassion for storybook thieves than real ones."

"He had a *reason*," said Yat.

"Oh, a *reason*," said Sibbi. "Well, that's different. No criminal has ever had a reason. They've done a bad thing and gone off to suffer for it. They've broken the *law*, and the law is never malicious or clumsy or just plain wrong. You don't break laws, do you, Constable? You're a good cop, after all; that's what everybody says. Pretty engraving, by the way—must've cost a mint."

She sounded . . . angry? No, less sharp than that. Resigned. The woman might be tough as old boots, but she seemed, just in that moment, small and tired. After some time, she looked up at Yat.

"I'm going to let you out of that chair," she said, "as a show of good faith. I want you to know that my people had nothing to do with what happened to you—I've got enough problems right now. You got yourself caught up in something I don't have all the answers to."

"Not for lack of trying," added Ajat.

"Aye," said Sibbi, "we're getting there. Or at least we were, until last night. Now we're sifting through the rubble and trying to figure out where up and down are. The last thing we need is some vlakas cop blundering into it, which is why you're tied up until we can figure out where you stand. So before I let you up out of that chair, I need you to tell me we're on the same side."

The same side? They weren't even playing the same game, as far as Yat was concerned. The woman had attacked her, tied her up, humiliated her, taken her godsdamned *flask*. Still, being untied would be nice. If this madwoman was going to help her out, she wasn't about to stop her. She swallowed her pride and nodded.

"We're on the same side," she said, hoping she sounded sincere. It was apparently enough, because the vines holding her down wilted and fell away.

"Now," said Ajat, "let's talk ab—"

Yat was already out the door, pounding along a hallway somewhere in the belly of the ship. The whole hall rocked back and forth, and she stumbled, barely managing to stay on her feet. She kept running and shoved past a sailor who seemed just as confused as she was, slammed open a door that led out into the bar (which was empty—why? No time), out through the main doors onto the deck and—

The ocean stretched out in all directions. It was early evening. Off in the distance, more than a few miles away, she saw the shape of Hainak's lighthouse with the city laid out behind it. The occasional firework went off—fewer than Yat expected at this time of year, but you couldn't stop some people from having a good time. She stared over the side.

"It's a ship," said Sibbi. "They do that."

Yat hadn't heard her approach. The woman wasn't even out of breath. A few men working on deck paused to peer at them, but their captain glared at them, and they returned to their work.

"B-but," said Yat, "your ship is grounded, and every cop in the city knows it. *Especially* right now. You shouldn't be able to so much as change the sails without being boarded by authorities."

Sibbi shrugged. Ajat strolled up behind her; she cleaned under her nails with a curved knife.

"I'd be a poor smuggler if I couldn't slip past a blockade," said Sibbi, "and a worse one if I told the how of it to a cop. We'll take you home, but I've got some things I need to do first, and I'd like to have a talk with you about your uh, *situation*."

"So, I'm a prisoner, then," said Yat, "just without the chains."

Sibbi laughed her warm, maddening chuckle. "What else is new?" she said. Something pushed against Yat's arm, and she realized that Sibbi was handing back her flask. She took it and rubbed her thumb over the engraving, which calmed her a little. She could feel the golden threads all over the strange ship tug at her. She could sense that the sea was cold, but not empty. It had a very different energy that set her teeth on edge.

"Come inside," said Sibbi. "We have a lot to talk about. How do you take your tea?"

It was a lot to take in, but Yat was done running. She was done being treated like a child. She was done being taken for a ride. But this woman knew something, and data was data.

"Black, two sugars," she said.

Sibbi turned and walked back inside.

Yat leaned against the side of the ship and stared out at Hainak, so close in her mind's eye and so far in practical reality. The air was warm and pleasant. She stayed out there for a few minutes, listening to the cries of gulls.

Ajat came out and put a hand on her shoulder, much more gently than Yat would've expected. "Tea's getting cold," she said. She smelled good: oak and citrus.

Yat turned and followed, though—at last—on her own terms.

The bar was different in the soft evening light. It was completely empty except for Sibbi, Ajat, and a beat-up porcelain tea set. It wasn't a large room. The plants on the walls seemed to turn toward them, the whole ship alive and interconnected.

The tea was delicious. It was smoky and fragrant—jasmine, licorice, and some lighter notes unfamiliar to her. The cups were sturdy, yet surprisingly beautiful: they looked like some sort of proprietary shellac with gold filigree. After taking a swig, Yat opened her flask and set it on the table. Then, without breaking eye contact, she picked up the teacup and carefully poured its entire contents into the flask. It took about thirty full seconds, and during that time nobody spoke. The only sound was the creaking of the ship, and the gentle murmur of tea flowing into the flask. If this breach of tea protocol upset the pirates, they didn't let it show. She put the cup down then, but as she moved to close the flask, it nearly slipped from her grasp and fell onto the table. She caught it just in time.

"Tremors," said Sibbi. "They'll get worse. When did you last smoke?"

"I don't—"

"Girl, don't lie to me. I've seen what you keep in your pockets. Everybody on my ship better have a clear head, whether they're working for me or not. I'm not having you fall overboard because you thought the moon was singing to you. Besides, you don't need it: you're a Weaver now. You need a certain thread, you ask. You need a smoke? Tough."

The word *Weaver* was new, but Yat understood it immediately. It wasn't a perfect analogy for magic, but it was closer than anything else. She grumbled a wordless response, which seemed to be enough for Sibbi.

"Now," she continued, "there's something else we need to talk about: blanks. Do you know what a blank is?

"A blank," said Sibbi, charging ahead without waiting for an answer, "is a criminal or a homeless man or an academic who asks the wrong questions, so they strap him down on a gurney and feed him a special drink, and then his mind drips out his ears. At first it was a special punishment, only for the worst. These days . . . well, factories need workers, labs need people to work with dangerous chemicals, armies need soldiers who aren't smart enough to run but are j*uuuu*st smart enough to take orders. They'll take anyone who won't be missed, and there are a lot of people in Hainak who won't be missed, or at the very least not by the sort of person with the power to do anything about it. You knew this, of course—I'm telling you because you managed to convince yourself that you didn't. Part of life is learning inconvenient things, then forgetting them if they hurt too much."

It was impossible. If it were true, somebody would've told her, right? Her dad or someone at the pub or her sergeant. Sen wouldn't have beat around the bush, he'd have *said* it; she'd never known him to be afraid to speak his mind. She would *know*. The government or the police or some brave scientist wouldn't let it happen; the gods would call down lightning or locusts; the families of those taken would burn factories to the ground. Blanks were criminals who had committed unforgivable crimes and been remade for service to the state, rapists and killers and . . .

There were a lot of blanks, she knew that. Thousands, maybe tens of thousands; they were the white blood cells of the city, hauling and cleaning and patrolling. Hainak had its troubles, but it had always struck her as hard to believe that even a city as large as Hainak had that many truly evil men. How many murderers could there be? And blanks died often: they blundered into the wrong alley carrying something expensive; somebody forgot to tell them to stop working and they starved; sometimes, they just plain stopped functioning and had to be decommissioned. Yat had always assumed Kiada had been taken because she'd stolen something *very* valuable—gotten overconfident, snuck into some rich man's house and taken something neither of them could hope to pay off in a lifetime. They didn't blank people just to add a few extra street sweepers to the mix.

Yat groaned inwardly. She knew blanks didn't just carry things: there were blank soldiers, blank miners, blank prostitutes. Wealthy alchemical botanists liked to use them as test subjects or walking advertisements: stuff you couldn't legally do to a human, but blanks weren't considered human. Yat and Sen had once worked security for an art exhibit where the artist had used blanks as canvases: living tattoos, extra limbs, spines and heads twisted all the way around, dead-eyed blanks fused entirely to the wall with a flesh-and-cellulose mesh. The audience had walked among them, drinking date-plum wine and tittering to each other. Nobody batted an eye: it was understood that they must've been horrible men, and it was almost better than they deserved to make them into art. Hells, she heard they used them in the medical college to teach anatomy, specially engineered ones with open chest cavities and very short lifespans. The blanks' feelings certainly hadn't been a concern: they'd failed as people, so they weren't allowed to be people anymore.

Everybody knew that blanks *deserved* to be blanked, but nobody had ever stopped to ask how they knew. It was just a truth you didn't question.

When Yat spoke next, she was very quiet. "Why are you telling me this?" she said. She wanted to go back to sleep. She was still half-drained from their fight in the park earlier, and this was too much to take in.

"Because," said Sibbi, "I want you to see what the city thinks of people like me—people like *us*."

"Us?" countered Yat. "What do you mean, *us*?"

As the words left her mouth, she saw it: the way Sibbi and Ajat stood with each other, the way they touched so casually.

"But—but you and Wajet . . ." she said.

Sibbi snorted. "That old goat," she said, "wouldn't have any interest in *me*. The man's a force of nature: he came here from the Vault and they told him he needed to change his ways, so he brought his husband to church and nobody even tried to stop him. He's crazy, you know. I'd rather have him on my side than a thousand good cops. That's why he's never got beyond sergeant, but I don't think he cares. He's our eye on the force—looks after certain, well, *vulnerable* officers. Gods know the police won't. He brings them to me, in time. I told him to find you, but, well, something changed. He and I needed to speak privately; you'll forgive the little ruse. The crew didn't know what to do about you, so I let Ajat entertain you while Wajet and I hashed things out."

Something changed. Between the station and the ship? Maybe he'd been warming her up but it hadn't taken. Had she been too quiet or pushed back too much, so that they'd held off on bringing her aboard until they could figure out what to do?

Then another thought dawned on her. "Does he—is he—do we all have magic powers?"

It was Ajat's turn to laugh. Yat was getting sick of her condescension.

"No, girl," she said, "we don't." She paused. "Well," she said, "it's complicated. You've got to die poorly for the gods to decide to stitch you back together, and this city isn't kind to us; this *world* isn't kind to us. It ain't right that our *delicate condition* gets us treated like shit. The transformation doesn't happen nearly so often to the powerful, who already get to choose what the world is about. They die soft and old. And if it doesn't happen to them, it doesn't exist to them, which is why you'll never hear about it. But the gods need soldiers, ones fit for duty. Folks like us? We die often, in the quiet places, and nobody talks about it because to those who decide things, we barely even count as people. We only matter when we're keeping their factories running, when we're filling their pockets. If we stopped working for them, we would hold no value in their eyes."

It was true. The hate wasn't usually as *direct* as it used to be, but that didn't make things square. Kiada—scrappy little fire-haired Kiada, who knew the filthiest jokes and sung arias on the rooftops—had gone out one night and never come back. Yat wished the last time she'd seen Kia hadn't been her pushing a broom, glassy eyes holding no recognition. Never mentioned it to the other kids, just grieved quietly as though Kia were dead. But what if . . .

Too many what-ifs. Too many injustices overlooked as Just the Way Things Are. She looked down and realized that her own threads were febrile, jittery, pale now—could the women see it? Most likely. She'd seen Varazzo's distress and that vile little seed beneath it.

She gripped her flask and drank the dregs of her now-cold tea. She didn't speak, and the two women across from her refused to fill the silence. They sat and listened to the outside sounds: the creaking of wood, the stamping of boots, the cries of gulls. It felt like a year passed before she spoke again.

"I need some time," she said, "to . . . think."

"Take it," said Sibbi. "You're welcome anywhere on the ship. Ask my people questions. Nothing is off-limits."

"Can I go home?"

Sibbi pursed her lips, then shook her head.

"I'm afraid *that* is off-limits," she said. "We have places to be."

She'd been so caught up in the conversation that she hadn't been paying attention to all the threads on the ship. There were so many here, it was hard to make out where one thing ended and another began. She hadn't noticed the large man lurking in the hallway.

Sibbi must've noticed her looking. "Wajet," she said, "come in."

The door opened, and the threads in Yat's body seemed to move on their own, reacting to a threat: they grabbed at the plants and the ants and the wooden walls and the hemp fibers in the rigging. She'd been told he was innocent, but something inside her wasn't ready to believe it. She could feel her skin going red, her heart beating faster, her body turning *force* toward him to smash something vital and—

Sibbi grabbed her, and the threads of their magic flowed together. Sibbi's own power was immense, beyond understanding; contending with it was like emptying a cup of water into the ocean. Yat's mind screamed at her, but she wasn't controlling the flow of power anymore. Sibbi took both their threads and twisted them into a rough braid, directing it toward a planter in the corner.

The mushroom in the planter exploded outward at the same time a cluster of orange roses around it shriveled. It was two feet high, then four, then seven, pushing up against the roof. And then it withered. The threads left it, dispersing back to where they'd come from. Sibbi had taken control of the flow, and the dead plants stuttered back to life.

It was done. If not for the gigantic dead mushroom in the corner of the room, no one would've been any the wiser. Sibbi breathed out loudly, then swore in Dawgae. Wajet stood in the doorway, looking baffled. It wasn't an expression he seemed accustomed to wearing.

"Constable Yat," he said, "I hear we've got some catching up to do."

SIXTEEN

Yat tried to sleep. They'd cleared out a small storeroom in the hold for her and put a mattress down. It wasn't comfortable, but it was a bed. And her own room, which seemed like a luxury on the ship: most of the crew slept together in a communal bunk area. The sailors were very careful around her. They didn't speak much or get too close to her. They didn't seem to want to make eye contact.

Her body thrummed with energy—she couldn't stop it. Her world had been shattered, and now she was putting it back together in strange new shapes. The ship seemed to toss and turn with her. After a few hours, she got up and left her room.

Most of the crew was asleep. She passed the occasional sailor on the graveyard shift but didn't talk to anyone.

The ship had three main levels: the belly was dominated by the hold and general storage. The kitchens, crew bunks, and carpenter's shop were above that, just belowdecks. The bar was raised above deck; it seemed like a later addition, not intended for life at sea, the mainmast punching straight through its middle. She'd overheard one woman complaining to another about how it fucked up the positions of all the ropes. Sibbi's private cabin was behind the bar, underneath the raised portion of the rear deck.

Yat moved quietly. That, she'd always been good at. She did it without even trying, but when she was, she was nearly undetectable. The trick wasn't to dart from shadow to shadow; it was to look like you belonged exactly where you were. Nobody challenged her as she explored the ship. She found a small grow room attached to the kitchen, filled with fragrant mushrooms. There was a room with a single large Tinker's Horn in it; the space smelled of Ajat's perfume. In the hold, she found what looked like a giant green heart, so bright with magical power that it hurt to look at, but she stopped and stared at for a minute or so—there was something hypnotic about it, a sort of hungry pull she had to work to tear herself away from. It looked like a human heart but it wasn't quite right, like somebody had taken a pile of moss, trama, and strange green flesh and tried to sculpt a heart from memory.

She found her way back to the bar. The tea service was gone, as was the giant dead mushroom.

She could sense four people in the room behind the bar: the twin beacons of Sibbi and Ajat, plus two men whose glows were smaller. She crept over to the door and put her ear to it. The voices were muffled, but she had no trouble understanding them. She heard the rattle of metal against wood, and then Wajet made a sound that could only be described as a *harrumph*.

"Nifty," he said. "I'll get it to him. Anyway, back to the issue at hand—this *intel* we've collected." The way he drawled the word *intel* wasn't quite sarcastic, but it came close.

"Don't talk to me like that, Wajet," said Ajat. "I died for this information. You ever drowned before? I don't recommend it."

"And?" he said. "You drowned for nothing. It's worthless. The crew got taken apart by sniper fire from a league away. You get a name? A face? Anything at all?"

"We got nothing," said Ajat, "and that's something. Ships don't just disappear."

A moment of silence, broken only by the tapping of fingers against paper. Sibbi's voice now, tired and irritated.

"Not ships with that sort of funding," she said, "and definitely not right out of a thrice-cursed harbor. They were in range of the lighthouse—closer to home than we are now. The *Fantail* had parliamentary backing. It had the army *and* the university behind it, and it just vanished. It's been two days, and nothing in the papers, nothing from our contacts. Nobody saw or heard a thing."

"It had us behind it, too," said Wajet. "Don't forget that. And the Lion, apparently, if they knew exactly where to hit it."

"It was Elvar," said Ajat. "He sold us out. I think he was probably expecting to be paid in silver, not in lead."

Yat swore she could hear a smirk.

"Right," said Wajet. "So where are we? The Ladowain have a mushroom. If they're trying to kick the war off again, they've got a thousand other ways to make it happen, and we saw a few last night. They don't need mushrooms, they have grenades. That's what I care about. They've shot people in the streets and set off bombs, but no follow-up fleet in the harbor. They don't *do* mercy, so this silence is making me nervous. We need to figure out what they're planning before we make our next move."

Sibbi now. She was pacing back and forth, her threads jumpy and agitated. "The university knows something," she said. "They've canceled classes, locked the gates, cut off outside communication. They had a man aboard the *Fantail*; maybe they had back channels, too. We need to find out what information they have."

"Yadin," said Ajat. "His name was Yadin."

There was a pain in her voice that left the room silent for too long. The fourth man spoke up, and she did not recognize his voice: heavily accented Taangata, rough but sweet—like honey and sandpaper. He spoke slowly, cautiously, changing the subject.

"You say the girl was killed with a revolver?" he said. "This is what her memories tell you?"

"What's that got to do with anything?" said Wajet. "They used them during the war. I *seen* 'em."

A pause, then the mystery man spoke again.

"Cousin, you've been away too long. The Lion hasn't used revolvers for quite some time. They were already outdated during the war, though some officers held on to them for their sentimental value. The last time they came over the Oxhead Channel, they had machine pistols, gas rockets, armored cars. We've been running low on ammunition ever since we lost the Forge. That was perhaps four years ago—a revolver really is a relic. I simply cannot see an enlisted Ladowain officer using one of these guns, but there are plenty floating around in Hainak. They are, after all, from the war. As sure as my koro is my koro, your assassin was a mercenary or a fake. If I had to guess, I'd say he was local. Probably a veteran."

"Noted," said Sibbi. "I have a few theories, but they're still coming together. It wasn't random, I know that. Somebody knew we'd tried to pick the girl up, and they wanted to remove her from the picture, send us a message. We're lucky Monkey got her—haven't seen him bring anybody back in a while. As far as we knew, he was gone like the others. We last heard from Tiger what, five years ago? Monkey, maybe three? Not even a resurrection, just a few of us hearing him hollering in a dream. Seems like he's running on fumes, but good to know he's still got the gift. There's hope for us yet."

"Hope," said the fourth speaker. His voice was so low, everything he said sent a tingle down her body. "Yes, there is hope."

She couldn't be sure, but was there a smile in his voice?

Wajet, never a man to let a pleasant moment remain unshaken, stood up and thumped his hands on the table. She could hear his chair shoot back across the wood and the twin slaps of his palms. "Shake down an egghead," he said. "Got it."

"We have a few days," said Sibbi. "We've got a supply run to do, then we'll swing back around to Hainak and drop you off at the docks. There're patrols everywhere, but I know a few spots we won't be noticed. I don't want to linger; once you're off, you're off until we can arrange another pickup. You know what to do if you need to talk to us."

A moment of silence, then something Yat couldn't make out, then a mumbled protest from Ajat. A shuffling of heavy boots on wood: the familiar *clomp clomp clomp* of Wajet moving toward the door. She could feel her heart beating in her chest—that familiar urge to flee. There was no time, though. She took a step back, just enough to avoid being hit by the door, then straightened up.

The door flew open. Even during surreptitious nighttime meetings, Wajet moved like a typhoon. He almost walked into her, then stopped dead.

"Constable," he said.

"Sergeant," she said.

Silence hung between them, but she didn't feel like it was out of her control this time; she let it hang for a few more moments.

"How much of that did you hear?" he said.

She shrugged. "Enough," she said. She wasn't sure exactly what she'd just heard, but she was starting to put the pieces together, so it couldn't hurt to make him think she knew what was going on.

He seemed to chew on this thought. Sibbi was leaning on the doorframe, watching them, her gaze shifting quickly back and forth. There was something almost birdlike about the way she moved, the way she stood, the way she held herself. She stood with Ajat, and a slim Tangata man in a pair of golden wire-rimmed glasses with lenses so dark they resembled obsidian.

"Looks like we've caught a spy," Sibbi drawled. There wasn't much force behind it—she didn't even seem surprised. Then it hit Yat: if she could see Sibbi through the wall, Sibbi could certainly see her, too, even if she glowed less brightly. And she'd never even let on that she knew they were being observed. Fear was bubbling up in Yat now, but she rode the wave, letting its energy make her bold.

"You said I could go anywhere," she said. "I came here."

Sibbi waved a hand, almost parentally, as if to cut her off. "You—"

"I saw it," said Yat. The words were tumbling out of her again, and she didn't seem to have much control over it: her fear had turned to anger. "I mean, I heard it. There was too much fog to see."

Was it Yat's imagination, or had Sibbi gone a little pale? She seemed to choose her next words very carefully.

"You were where, exactly?"

"Corner of Satek and Old Ox, out by the water. I go there after my shift is over. I like to watch the lighthouse."

"You and Sen," breathed Wajet. "The redacted report, of course. Between three and four?" he said. Yat nodded.

"And you saw . . . ?" said Sibbi.

"Well, nothing," said Yat. "Sort of. Fog came in out of nowhere, I heard shots inside it, like crossfire between ships, but then it rolled away and there was nobody there. The fog . . . moved wrong. Like it was alive." Her anger was subsiding now. She felt a little self-conscious as the four of them studied her appraisingly: Wajet, pacing back and forth; Ajat, who'd slunk out of the room and was pouring herself something sweet-smelling behind the bar; Sibbi, standing in the doorway and glowing with magical light, brighter than any light-house. She couldn't read the fourth man's expression at all.

Ajat stopped drinking. The glass was halfway to her mouth, and her eyes were wide. Sibbi was looking at her.

"Tahu, dearest," she said, "is it possible?"

Ajat nodded and downed her entire drink at once. She slammed the glass down on the bar.

"You don't get fog at this time of year," she said. "It's too damned hot for it. I don't know how I missed it at the time. Guess I was worrying about more immediate problems. Hard to tell what's going on from the inside, but, I just—I should've known. Somebody jumped the ship, and we both know how much power that takes. Outside of Sibbi, there's only one person who could pull that off, and he's dead. Well, not dead, but, y'know, *out of action*."

Sibbi walked over to Ajat and laid a gentle hand on her forearm. A look passed between them, but Yat couldn't read it. She turned to Wajet, but he seemed as lost as she was. Then his eyes went wide.

"The Sparrows," he said. "There are two active in town, and they're brothers. I didn't get much from the redacted paperwork, but I got that. I didn't make the connection because you said those lads were somewhere in Suta, spread out across the wallpaper. I thought they weren't a problem anymore."

Sparrows? There'd been rumors about their existence for years, of course—that they had a secret station north or south of the wall or out somewhere in the thrice-cursed jungle. Orders from the top, no oversight. Responsible for a mix of well-timed accidents and suicides. They had supposedly existed before the revolution; the Lion took local boys from bad homes and paid off the families to pretend they'd never existed. Sometimes, officers would take command of an innocuous operation, then disappear when it came time to write it up. Every case where the details seemed a little off, somebody would joke that the Sparrows had been pecking at it. Nonsense, of course: generally speaking, the force could barely shit and wipe in the right order. You couldn't hide something like that, not with the kind of paperwork the force required. But Yat could spot at least one problem with that theory. They didn't need a thousand officers and a mountain of paperwork, not if they had the blokes she'd met.

"There's a big one and a small one," she said.

Everybody turned to her.

"What the *fuck* did you just say?" said Ajat. "How could you know that?"

"I met them," she said. "And I'm not too keen to meet them again." She rubbed the center of her forehead where the bullet had gone in.

"If they are who I think they are, that's a very good policy," said Sibbi. "If you see them, run. You got lucky the first time. *Very* lucky. They weren't expecting Monkey to bring you back, or they'd have stuck around, and if they see you out and about without a scratch on you, they're going to know exactly what happened to you, and they'll sort out a more permanent solution. You're a loose end. For your own sake, stay on the ship. I need some time to think about this, but come talk to me in the morning. You might be useful to us after all."

"I was always useful," said Yat, the fear and anger twisting together like a lance of fire to her heart, then fleeing as quickly as it had come, leaving her sick and exhausted.

"Aye," said Wajet. "That you were. And with that, I'm off to bed." He yawned a little too loudly, then stomped out of the bar. Yat still didn't trust the man. She'd been told he was smarter than he let on, and braver, and kinder. But she'd seen none of that herself. When she looked at him, she could still taste gun smoke.

The fourth man followed. He didn't say anything but gave Yat a slight downward nod that almost looked like the beginning of a bow, then trotted out after Wajet.

Yat stayed for a few moments longer, drumming her fingers against her thigh. This felt like a victory—she didn't know over whom, or what it meant for her, but it didn't matter. She'd needed the win.

"Good night," she said. "And please don't invade anybody's mind. If you want to know something, just ask."

Sibbi was pouring herself and Ajat another drink. She nodded at Yat—no condescending laugh this time, just eye contact and a wary trust. It was good enough for now.

SEVENTEEN

The station at Macaque's Furrow was some noble's second house that he didn't use. The force had graciously been lent the property, on the condition that they kept it clean and didn't sleep in the beds. Sen had set up a hammock in the garden. You'd be mad to sleep anywhere outdoors in the less salubrious parts of town, but the perk of being around toffs was never needing to worry. No wonder they got so much done; money could buy you a lot less stress. It could buy sleep. Perhaps the folks who said money couldn't buy happiness were still right, but it could sure as shit obviate misery.

In a hammock in a yard whose upkeep cost more than he earned in a year, Sen slept fitfully. He dreamed he was being pecked at by sparrows, then that he *was* a sparrow with a sharp beak, peck-peck-pecking all the little crumbs until a dog arrived and chased him away and he flew up north, up beyond the wall, and into the silent city of . . .

He woke to dawn's light, the chattering of monkeys in the trees, and the gentle murmur of the house's breathing. This part of town had been a Monkey temple in the old days. Generations of monkeys had come and gone, but they must've still told each other the same stories: this is our place, this is where we belong, this is where food is plentiful and the humans are kind and slow.

Sen rolled out of the hammock and stretched out a little. His leg still hurt, but not as severely as yesterday. The cane was probably slowing his recovery down, making his arm as weak as his leg. What had the old penny manual said? *The body is a watch, an instrument where each part works in harmony with the rest. If one part is untrained, so are the rest.* Shit advice, but that's what you got for a quarter-yan.

"Oi," said Sen. A monkey peered down at him. He'd never been a praying man, but he'd liked that old monkey manual. He'd been awkward and gangly, and his dream had been to be a damned hero. He used to read about the monkey who stole fire from the gods. Yat's book said it was a cat, but that was bullshit. Everybody who read the real stuff—the stuff you got for a quarter-yan from some bloke in an alley that had pictures for all the punches—knew it was Monkey.

He stared up at the monkey and made a sign he could only half remember, one they used to do in secret on the playground when they were playing martial arts master.

"You see Yat," he said, "you tell her to come home. You tell her something's changing, and I need her more than ever. You tell her she fucked up and didn't see it, and I fucked up and didn't see it, either, and that there's none so blind as a cop who's got other problems."

The monkey bared its teeth at him in a frightened little smile.

"Failing that," he said, "send a typhoon. Send an earthquake. Send fire, send fog, send me old mum with a bag of razor-sharp knitting needles. Everything is so fucked. I just . . . I just want to know I'm not alone. I'm lost and I'm scared, and I feel like I'm the only one. I was always so sure I was doing the right thing, but now I just—"

The monkey bounced on its branch, then leapt up and scurried off. Sen sighed. That seemed right: a prayer interrupted . There were two other officers assigned to the temporary station, but they wouldn't be awake before noon. He couldn't go back to the temple or the docks ward station. If he left his post, he'd wind up feeding crayfish on the bottom of the Axakat. The Sparrows had him trapped. They were stronger than him, and higher up on the chain, and a dozen steps ahead.

Sen had survived two military tours and a revolution. He'd survived them by being young, strong, quick, and ruthless. He'd survived them by not caring—by looking out for himself and letting everything else burn. He'd tried to put it behind him, and now he was stuck in a fancy garden with a bamboo fountain and too many monkeys. He got onto his knees and continued to pray for the gods to send him somebody, anybody at all. Alone in the garden, Sen wept.

EIGHTEEN

Morning came. It was strange to sleep in a bed again, after however long on the run. It hadn't been a great night's sleep, but considering the run Yat had had in the last few days, it could definitely have been worse. She wandered up to the bar and found the crew eating breakfast. Rice and fish, nothing fancy, but the serving was generous and it filled her up. She was given a cup of tea before she even thought to ask for one. She sat with the sailors and saw them for the first time in the light of day.

There was a lot of biowork on display, much of it practical—a set of talon-like fingernails, acid burns on the hands and forearms (the telltale sign of early-model military splices, probably for endurance or metabolic efficiency), a pair of yellow marksman's eyes with those strange boxy pupils like a goat's—but a lot of it was cosmetic, too. She'd assumed most of them would be men, but there were a lot of women—she hadn't remembered there being so many—and in quite a few cases she couldn't tell. She knew of people like that, of course: if alchemical botany was good for anything, it was good

153

for changing bodies. Civilians weren't permitted that sort of bio-work, but it happened anyway. They'd be arrested for it sometimes, if they looked poor enough and the cop hadn't hit their quota. Or sometimes they *had* hit their quota, but they didn't understand what they were seeing and didn't take well to not understanding, so they twisted it around until it fit the shape of something they knew. You didn't see a lot of folk like that because the police worked hard to make sure you didn't.

Ajat sat with her and watched her eat. Yat went at the bowl hammer and tongs, practically daring somebody to challenge her on it. Sleep had refreshed her, and there were still traces of last night's anger.

"Right," said Ajat, spooning herself some rice porridge from the big bowl in the middle of the table, "so you've got the art. Here're the basics: every living thing has got life force in it, a sort of vital spark, and you put all those sparks together in one place and you get fire. My people talk about mauri, which is, well . . . the soul within the body, the vital spark. The energy that keeps your heart beating. It's not quite the same, but it's close enough, and calling it that helps me make sense of it. It's the difference between life and death. That's power, a power that can be hard to control. One that needs to be treated with respect. You want to stay sane and healthy, here's the tikanga—the rules, so to speak. First rule is, Don't get caught. They kill you, you'll pop right back up again. They change you? You're done for. They can only extend your lifespan so far, but trust me: a century as a blank is more than enough. Blanks haven't been around long enough for us to see what that does to the mind, but I don't think we want to."

The chatter and the clink of cutlery didn't exactly die down, but there was a definite shift of attention toward them—this seemed to be news to a lot of the crew, too. Their threads were mostly ordinary, though some of their biowork seemed to channel and move their life force in odd ways. Unsurprisingly, few of them glowed like Sibbi.

"Which leads," said Ajat, "to rule number two: don't let them know where you first died. You're gonna show up in the same place, in the same shape, every damn time you die. If they know where you're gonna be, then you're as good as caught, 'cept killing yourself isn't an option. Some folks will tell you there are ways to shift your anchor, but I've never seen it work. Seen it fail, though, and I'm not keen to see it again."

"Wait," said Yat. She didn't like interrupting, but she needed to know. "Does that mean people *know*? Who's sending people to pick us up? The police?"

"The authorities, sometimes, yes," Ajat said. "Individual officers don't seem to know, but they don't *need* to know in order to do what they're told. You've heard about the Sparrows, of course. Sometimes we go to pick a new Weaver up, and they're just not there anymore.

"Number three," she went on, spearing a piece of fish with her fork just a touch too hard and shifting the plate, "is that all power comes from somewhere. You can move it around, but you can't make more. If you *do* try to push without pulling from somewhere, it's going to come from *you*, and that's a good way to really, actually die. You get hollowed out, you're gone. Not even the gods can weave without a thread.

"Number four," she said, "is respect. If you're going to take life from somewhere and put it somewhere else, then you need to do it responsibly. You're fucking with souls, so to speak, and if you don't take it seriously, very bad things can happen. You need to think in ecosystems. Before you pull from something, know why you're pulling, and be a hundred percent sure it's worth it. You pull out the wrong brick, you bring down the tower. That's why we tend to use plants and the like, and we grow 'em like batteries—less messy. Then there's the City, which is . . . complicated. Don't worry about that for now."

"The City? You mean Hainak?"

Ajat froze for a half second, the sort of thing only a cop would notice, panic disguised as nonchalance, then shook her head.

"No, the heart, the big heart down below. It's just what Sibbi calls it. She made it, so she can call it whatever she likes."

Made it. Yat noted how precisely imprecise the word choice was, but chose not to push it.

Ajat chewed on her fish, staring at nothing. After a moment, her eyes snapped back to Yat and she nodded.

"The fifth and final rule is this," she said. "Don't die. Don't die permanently, but don't die temporarily, either. Every time you come back, you lose a little more of yourself. You get closer to the other side: stronger, less human. There are some like us who are thousands of years old, and you don't want to meet them—it takes a lot of force of will to hold on to yourself through all that. It's something you *can* do, but never something you should seek out. We're not about death on this ship. Captain's orders."

A call came out from somewhere above, then somebody rang a bell. Ajat groaned. "We're moving," she said. "I need to be downstairs. You want to learn something? Come with me. I'll show you how to use the heart."

She pulled her hair back, and for a moment it seemed to be almost moving on its own. She motioned toward the staircase, toward the lower decks. The room was clearing fast, sailors leaping to their feet and running off in all directions.

"C'mon," called Ajat. "It's going to be a big jump. Sibbi wants to hit up one of our stashes in Dawgar. Not the biggest jump we've ever done, but not one I look forward to, either. There used to be a mountain of lead down there we could use to lock in our vector, but it's all been mined away now, so we're basically flying blind. Sibbi hasn't even told me why we're moving, but if she's gonna do a stupid thing, then I'm gonna make sure she doesn't hurt herself."

Another cry from above, and the ship rolled so hard Yat lost her balance. Her hand shot out to her cup, and she just managed to stop it from spilling. Ajat's glow had turned almost white. The big woman extended a hand.

Yat hesitated, only for a moment. Then she took the hand and hauled herself to her feet. Their threads seem to mingle, and that strange warmth filled her again. Not overpowering her this time, but merging with her own, making her stronger. The energy was a lot to take in, but she had braced herself and managed to ride the wave. Her body had taken her halfway down the stairs by the time she realized she was moving.

They found their way to the glowing green heart in the bowels of the ship. It shone so brightly, it made her head hurt. The whole room around it seemed to ripple and dance. There was so much life in it: thousands of sparks, millions pressed together in one place.

Ajat sighed and ran a gentle hand across the surface of the heart. A vinelike tendril unfurled from its surface, then darted out and ensnared her palm.

It had hurt when Yat had killed the parrot: an awful heat, like she'd grabbed a handful of network wiring. This was worse: the bird had gone into Yat, but now Yat was going into the heart and becoming less.

Then Ajat spoke. "Focus," she said.

Yat could feel her somewhere inside the heart. She was part of the system, sending its energy up through the walls, up through the mast, and onto the deck, where a tremendous weight stood: Sibbi. She was pulling from the whole ship, tying it together inside herself. Yat was part of their network: power was flowing from her, but not enough to hurt her. She was just helping to guide the heart's energy to where it needed to be.

Yat realized she was still standing belowdecks, but now she was *seeing* from the crow's nest. Warmth filled her. She was part of the whole ship, a beautiful and dense organic system all turned to a single purpose. It was exhilarating. It was . . .

Focus. There's part of your soul that wants to live only for you, and it'll destroy you if you let it. Your goals, your wants, the wind at your back: you live like that, and reaching out with this power will tear you in half. It's a liar: it dresses your selfishness up and tells you it's virtue. This is not a place for the selfish, nor pretense. Focus. To give and receive life force is not destruction or sacrifice: it is an act of creation. Life exists in the places between us. We make it together. Focus.

She was inside Sibbi, feeling the monstrous energy build and build. Sibbi fashioned it into a harpoon and threw.

Across the waves, seeking, but something was wrong

Across the stone, seeking, but something was wrong

Across the reef and into the mouth of a cave where—

The harpoon struck something. Mist poured over the gunnels, an impossible mist for a warm summer evening. It came on fast, covered the deck. The crew vanished inside it, and Yat could sense only Sibbi and a terrifying white heat that could char timber and melt stone. In her network now, it was as though Yat could reach out and catch a passing memory, or—

"Good work," said Ajat. She was smiling, but there was something else to it. Yat had been in Ajat's head only moments before, inside Sibbi's head, inside the ship, inside . . . something else. Something in a cave that wasn't what it was supposed to be. The memory was gone, though, like trying to remember when she died: it just wasn't there. Yat pushed her unease aside. She'd accomplished something, though she didn't fully understand what, and it made her feel strong. It had been both her and Ajat doing everything—she'd felt the woman's thoughts inside her own head, guiding but not steering her. She'd heard her thoughts in Ajat's own language and understood them perfectly.

There was a small Tinker's Horn built into the wall, and Ajat was talking on it.

"Did we jump?" she said.

A tinny voice said something Yat couldn't make out.

"Shit," said Ajat. She turned to Yat. "I need to check on Sibbi. Sometimes she's a little too brave for her own good. Jumping takes a lot—I can get *myself* around without ending up inside a wall, but gods forbid I try to move anybody else. I guess that's lesson six: know your limits. I need to see my wife: she's tried to swallow an ox again. Jumping a ship without preparing a circle—*gods*, that impossible woman."

It was strange to hear the word *wife* so openly. Yat's curiosity about *jumping* was flattened beneath a more grounded concern; Yat was hardly ignorant about the intimacies of the thing, but folks in Hainak tended to bury it ten layers deep in euphemism: *Oh, they're such close friends; they're inseparable; she doesn't have a husband, but she's well attended.* The nakedness of their relationship stung her a little. She looked at her feet and pushed her lips together.

Ajat left. Yat rubbed the vine between her thumb and forefinger and felt it pulling at her, the entire weight of the ship calling out to her. Tentatively, she let her consciousness travel up it again.

It was harder alone: she was being pulled in all directions. She could feel the sea below her, filled with life, but devoid of magic. It had an almost expectant emptiness, like a monstrous rumbling stomach. There was life down there, but it didn't feel the same, something that reminded her of the dark place she'd seen in a dream, just before all this started. It pulled at her even more than the ship. She focused and went back up the vine to the crow's nest. She looked down at the quarterdeck and saw Sibbi slumped over the ship's wheel. Her threads weren't glowing the same way they had been; they seemed faded, frayed. Ajat rushed out to her across the deck and put her arms around her, and magic flowed between them. Sibbi lit up—less so than when Yat had seen her glow but still something strange and fearsome. Ajat shouted an order, and another sailor took over the wheel. The wives stumbled down the quarterdeck together, leaning on each other like drunks in the earliest light of dawn. Nobody sneered at them or made snide comments—the crew respectfully let them pass while they went about their work.

Yat didn't want to look at them anymore. It made her furious, but *fury* wasn't quite the word. She wasn't furious at them, she was furious that nothing else was like this. She was furious at everything except them—they were like a pair of stars that curved the empty night around them. She was furious that her own love had to be temporary: dying embers of nights she couldn't afford to remember. It was a lot to take in. There was only one thing for it: tea.

She stumbled up the stairs, running her hands along the ship's wooden sides and feeling all the little threads roil and tug.

The bar was halfway full of sailors returning to their abandoned breakfasts and cleaning up the messes they'd made when they scrambled to their feet. There were still a lot of empty seats. Yat didn't know how many crew they needed to keep the ship going, but it seemed to take about a third of them at any one time just to stop it tipping over.

When Sibbi and Ajat came through the doors, appreciative whistles and claps rang out. Sibbi was pale and a little shaky, but she was standing on her own. She made her way to the front end of the bar, where there was a small stage.

"First order of business: we're in Dawgar, but this isn't a social call. I'm taking a small crew ashore, but the rest of you stay here. We've got work to do, and I'm not losing a single sailor to the pub."

The sailors were too amped up to boo, but that definitely brought the mood down. Yat reached out with her new golden sense, then recoiled; something outside the ship was very wrong. She looked at Ajat; the woman's threads writhed around her, tight and controlled but still agitated. The original plan had been to let the crew have some shore leave, but something had changed. There was life outside the ship, but it was unusual. Familiar lines, but the shapes were all wrong. Dawgar was the pirate isles, populated by raiders and lowlifes, but very much populated by *people.* Whatever was outside the ship wasn't quite people, and that not-quiteness was the most frightening part.

"We'll get you some wine, you reprobates." *Ray-PRO-bah-tees,* Sibbi said it, as though she'd never heard the word aloud. It still got an appreciative murmur. Yat was trying to read her threads but she wasn't giving much away. Yat felt a tiny flicker of emotion but couldn't name it.

"And duqqa!" said one of the crew.

"And feta!" said another.

"And olive oil!" said another again.

Sibbi waved them down, nodding and smiling despite her threads coiling up inside her like a rattlesnake.

"Yes, yes," she said, "the usual. I know a man at the floating market. We've still got friends in the isles. I can get us the good stuff. Anyway, before we head out, there's something that needs doing. We have a new crew member, so it's time to tell an old story. Let's talk about the Old War."

A hush fell over the room. It didn't seem forced, but almost religious. A few sailors bowed their heads and closed their eyes. Some made signs she didn't recognize. Ajat picked up the 'orseman and put it down in front of Sibbi, who stepped up onto it.

"In a time before time," said Sibbi, "there was a god for every star in the sky. You know their names."

"Fierce Tiger," said a woman with braided red hair. It was the first time Yat had seen her without a mask on. She was squat and heavily muscled, covered in tattoos and scars.

"Stout Ox," said a sailor with dark skin and a shaved head: the other guard from her first day. They were small and androgynous, with a large, heavy ring pierced through the bridge of their nose.

"Clever Monkey," said Yat. The words came to her from nowhere, but she knew they were right. There was a murmur of approval.

"Noble Crane," said Ajat. That got a response, too: a certain tension that was as much absence as action as the whole room seemed to stop breathing.

"And on and on," said Sibbi. "If we sat here telling all their names, we'd waste the rest of our days."

Her words felt rehearsed, but they got a laugh. You got people wound up enough and they'd laugh at anything. Tension, release.

"In the time before Hainak, before the men of Suta, when the Sea of Teeth was calm and all people lived with fear, there was no death. The gods gave their gifts freely. Crane taught flight, Ox taught strength, Tiger taught silence."

The lights dimmed a little, and Yat noticed Ajat fiddling with a vine on the wall.

"But then men grew greedy," said Sibbi. "The land gave enough for each man, but that wasn't enough. They used their magic to wage war and left great scars in the land. The gods saw this and wept: their gifts were never meant to be weapons. They came together and made a new place. They tore magic from the world of men and moved it into this new world, placing the doors deep beneath the ocean and at the top of the sky. Both are empty and endless, and if you fly high or dive deep enough, you'll find yourself going from one to the other.

"But magic is life," she said. "It is the thing that animates. As sure as rivers flow to the ocean, life flowed into the new place—a place of pure magic, a magic over which men have no control. And as magic left the world, men's threads left them, too, and they died. In time, the new place became the place of the dead. Every soul is pulled there, in time. They scrounge for scraps of magic to keep themselves together, and then they run out and fade and become part of the great fabric.

"The shearing of world from world left great wounds: In our world, in the world of the dead, and in the flesh of the gods. The gods became caught in the madness of men and went to war with each other. In the lands of the dead—infinite and filled with the endless possibility of pure magic—they began to devour each other. The war has ground on for an endless eon, but at last it is coming to an end. Tiger wasn't fierce enough, Ox not stout enough, Elephant not wise enough. They exist only as shards now, twisting in Crane's belly and driving him mad. Only Monkey escaped, and despite all his cleverness, it was all he could do to survive. Now Crane rules the place of the dead, driven mad by his own family."

Well, shit. It all hit Yat at once: the Erzau priest outside her house with his leering bird mask, the sparrows on the road when she'd first fled the *Kopek*, the parrots peering in through the windows of the abandoned house where she'd collapsed. Birds everywhere, keeping an eye on her. She felt a little less guilty about killing that damned parrot.

"But Monkey ain't done," said Ajat. That got a cheer. "Monkey ain't the fiercest, or the wisest, or the strongest. Monkey is a fuckup; he was always the odd one out, just like us. Monkey is quick and clever and the only one still fighting, and sometimes that's enough. A thousand on a thousand on a thousand years have passed, more years than we have numbers for, more than our minds can hold, and Crane has never caught him. So Crane sure as shit ain't gonna catch *us*. The stars are in their houses, the seas are drawing back—the walls are coming down, and magic is back in the world. There's a fire in heaven, and somebody's gotta put it out."

A cheer rang out, a slamming of cups against tables. Ajat turned to Sibbi, and an indecipherable look passed between them.

"We fight the Old War," she said, "no matter which land we came from, and no matter who it was that threw us back."

Another cheer. *For Camel. For Snake. For Boar. For Scorpion. For Elephant.*

Whatever spell had bound them seemed to break, and the crew went back to their breakfasts as if it had never happened. Ajat was leaving with Sibbi, and Yat took a moment to step alongside her.

"What about Luz?" she said. "And Hekat, Dorya, Siviss?" The gods she knew.

Ajat laughed. "I've got a soft spot for Auntie Tori, but they barely count," she said. "Especially the last one, though I'm sure she'd love to think otherwise."

Sibbi rolled her eyes.

"Enough," she said. "That whole situation, my dear, is another story for another day. For now, I'm going to bed. Eventually, I shall get to sleep. I can't tell you what will happen in the interim, but there's not a lot of space for more stories. Not in all the damned worlds."

"But," said Yat, "wait, why are you sleeping? It's breakfast, and who's Tori? And—"

By then they'd reached the door to their cabin, and Yat found it firmly closed in her face. She turned back to the mess hall. Whatever magic had suffused the room was gone, and it was a perfectly ordinary breakfast on the *Kopek*. For that, Yat was grateful. She didn't have words for the subtle wrongness beginning to press in from all sides at Dawgar, but she knew she didn't want to face it. She sat in silence with her tea and thought about the way Sibbi and Ajat stood together. They reminded her of two mountains casting long shadows over the plain; perfect, serene, alone and together.

NINETEEN

The crates clearly weren't meant for Macaque's Furrow. There were eight of them in a neat stack, glued shut with engineered beeswax. Sen didn't recognize the officers who dumped them off, but they had that army look to them. A whole squad of newcomers; he didn't like it at all. He'd tried to get a message to the docks ward station about his concerns with the new recruits but had received no response.

Somebody would figure out they'd misdelivered the crates within a few hours, and he'd be in trouble if they found out he'd tampered with them. The officers-not-officers had moved them into a storeroom out behind the house. He shooed away a monkey that had snuck in, then checked the tags. The delivery address was a storehouse in the Xineng district; the return address was the university. HAZARDOUS, DO NOT DROP in large letters in four languages. Big police department seal on 'em. Machinery, maybe? Xineng was a stalwart of the old world, a place so polluted that any living technology wilted and died overnight. It pumped out old-world goods: guns and explosives, steel, gold. All strictly for export, of course—it would be horribly gauche to sell them at home, but exchanging antiquated metal parts for metal coin was just good business.

He tilted one of the crates and listened. He'd expected clanking, or for the thing to shift its center of gravity as he tipped it. It stayed solid. He heard a gentle hiss, like rain on cobblestones. Powder, maybe? Sand? He lowered the crate back down. From inside, there came the gentle clinking of glass.

If he had an afternoon, he could probably crack it open and re-seal it without causing a mess. He didn't have an afternoon: he had maybe two hours. The house was being watched. It occurred to him that this might be a trap, but if that was the case, then yeah, they'd got him. He needed to know what was in those bloody crates. He'd been going insane in half captivity, and this was something tangible he could work with. Somebody had delivered him evidence, and damned if he wasn't going to investigate.

White wax, alchemically treated. You saw it all the time, especially on ships. Waterproof, airtight, but easy to work with. Probably heat-resistant to a degree—enough that you could make it malleable, but not so much that it would break apart in warm water.

The house had a small chapel with a box of votive candles in the sept. They were more yellow than white, but they'd do the trick if he was careful. The place had a huge kitchen, too, with more knives than any sensible chef had use for. One of them might be sharp enough. Cut the wax, then reseal with a candle. Easy as.

It took him about fifteen minutes of rooting around in the kitchen to find a vegetable knife whose blade still held an edge. It wasn't perfect, but it could break the skin on his fingertip, so it would have to do; the rest of the knives hadn't started to rust yet, but they were headed that way.

Moving the crates at all was harder than expected: he couldn't lift with his legs, so he had to slide one against the wall with his upper body, then let it collapse along with him. It sent a spasm up his leg and his side into his neck. The crate jangled as it hit the ground, and he wondered whether he'd broken something inside.

The wax wouldn't split cleanly beneath his blade: he had to saw at it. Whole chunks of wax broke away as he worked, and by the time he was done there was a ring of it on the floor. His hands shook while he sawed, and left a mess of hairline cracks in the wax spiderwebbing out from where the knife had bit in. Turning the crate was the hardest part: it squashed the little pieces of wax into the floorboards and scratched the wood. His leg hurt too much for him to stand; he had to kneel while he pushed it around.

Grunting like he was trying to pass a kidney stone, he pulled off the top of the crate and peered inside. Glass tubes the size of his forearm, maybe twenty of them, each one filled with black powder. He picked one up and sniffed it but couldn't smell anything. It looked like gunpowder, but if there was one thing he'd learned about gunpowder, it was that it stank and nothing you could do would get the smell out. Hermetic seal? Who could even make one of those out of metal? He considered shaking it, but thought better of it: gunpowder could blow when you pushed it tightly together. Had Yat told him that? Maybe his old sergeant. He turned the tube over on his hands, trying to find a way to get it open. The top and bottom of the tube each had a heavy mechanical apparatus on them. The top one had a lever. He pulled it, but it was stuck and wouldn't budge. Why glass? Not membrane, but actual blown glass. He checked the tube twice over and couldn't find a single organic component.

He was shaking from pain. As he turned the tube over in his

hands, it slipped from his grasp. He'd always had quick hands, but they were moving a half second behind his brain. He snatched at it as it fell. He'd meant to grab it around the middle, but only managed to get a few fingers around the lever at the top. It hit the bottom of its arc a centimeter above the wooden floor and flipped back up. He fumbled for it and managed to grab it in both hands, pressed tightly to his chest. It looked like gunpowder, but somebody had done a lot of work to keep it inside this tube, and he wasn't about to ruin their day; he rather suspected he had almost ruined *his* day, too. Thank the gods he still had his old boxer's reflexes: it hurt to use them now, but they hadn't gone anywhere.

The tube shook in his hands. It looked different than when he'd picked it up. The powder was lighter now, flakes of salt mixed in with the pepper. As he watched, one of the pieces of white pushed itself against the glass, spread out hungrily, seeking the heat of his hand. The movement had awoken something. It matched his handprint, and he could feel a frightening warmth coming off it. Finding no food, it shrank back and vanished into the gunpowder.

The stuff in the tubes was alive. He knew it with absolute certainty. There were no organic components because whatever it was would eat through those faster than they could grow back. He'd heard about shit like this, usually from drunk biowarfare officers at four a.m. Why *gunpowder*, though? Very little actual powder traveled on with the bullet: it would be more dangerous to the shooter than the target. Unless they were sending rigged ammunition to the Lion, but who would buy bullets from their enemy? It made no sense. Gingerly, he lowered the tube back into the crate and laid it down with the rest.

The house's ancient grandfather clock tolled out midday, and Sen swore under his breath. He'd been at it for almost ninety minutes.

Cutting the wax had taken longer than expected, and he'd gotten lost in it.

He'd planned to light the candle and run it gently along the seal, but he didn't have time for that. He took out his lighter, held it right up to the candle's body, and held the candle over the crate seal. The *drip-drip-drip* took agonizingly long. The wax kept going cold before he could put the lid back on. He pressed it as flat as he dared, then held the lighter up to the side of the crate. It softened the wax, but darkened the wood. He ran the flat of his knife along the soft, warm wax to smooth it out. It looked . . . fine. If nobody was paying attention, they definitely wouldn't notice it had been tampered with. Pushing his back against the wall and sweating bullets, Sen hoisted it back onto the pile, then went and had himself a bloody cigarette.

When he came back in an hour and his hands had stopped shaking, the crates were gone.

TWENTY

"I t's a shitshow, I know," said Sibbi.

Ajat didn't say anything. They walked through the olive grove, and the trees stared at them. There were more than last time. Sibbi cursed herself: she'd left it too long again. She'd meant to make the time to come out, but then time had gotten away from her. One of the trees mewled as she passed it, and she felt its pain right in her sinuses. She was a good ten feet away from it, but its root network must've spread, tangled up with the mycelium somewhere. No-good, godsdamned awful nature at work again.

Dergula loomed in the distance, the tottering wooden pirate palace towering over the city beneath it. It had been built piece by piece over the centuries, in a dozen different styles. It was one of the only buildings that had withstood the burning, mostly because the dense root network woven into its structure refused to let it fall. In Hainak, they would've had an alchemist running the show, but here it just . . . happened. Even the memory of it hurt—she'd let the Tiger girl pull it out of her head, but its empty silhouette still kept her up at night. She didn't have the details anymore, but she got the gist: no more shifting anchor points. The bruised, flesh-pink roots started growing one day and any attempt to remove them failed, until they became a part of the structure and removing them would do more harm than good.

A man came out to meet them as they walked. Richly dressed, but not *too* richly: the sort of palace attendant who worked out in the streets. Nice clothes and hair, but no jewelry that could be easily snatched. The one exception was the golden pin in his hat, the symbol of the Fezaken. Nobody would steal it: it would be impossible to fence, and wearing it was a life sentence. He had been training his whole life for this moment, for the *Kopek* to appear on the horizon. She didn't recognize him, but he looked almost fifty. Gods, it had been a long time since she'd come back.

"Mighty Eternal Empress," he said, "it is with great hon—"

"Uh-huh," she said, and waved him away. He froze as though he'd been slapped.

"The uh," he said, stammering, "the uh, the king wishes to speak with you before you go to the great tree. It has been many years since we've been graced by your august presence, and—"

"Look," said Sibbi. Her head hurt, and it wasn't just from the trees. Something about this place made mist rise up inside her, made her dream of locked doors and ancient cities. "I quit that job. Never really earned it in the first place. Some jobs you can stumble into without blood on your hands, but god ain't one of them. I'm not destined to come back and save the islands. If you've gotta call me something nice, call me Captain. I run a boat these days, and it does me fine. Who's king these days, anyway?"

"The serene and powerful King Razakat IV of the Golden—"

"*Enough,*" said Sibbi. She didn't mean to cast, but all the threads of the olive grove moved toward her. The trees cried out and rolled their eyes and gnashed their teeth. It was an awful racket, but it was better than the sound they made when they were quiet: the sound the wind made when it rustled through their branches. The attendant cried out and took a step back, stumbled, and fell. Ajat grabbed Sibbi by the arm and squeezed, and it brought her back into herself. She didn't have time to treat with kings, but it didn't seem like she had a lot of other options. She sighed.

"What is your name, Fezaken?"

"Eshat," he said. He'd fallen on his arse and gotten his nice uniform covered in dust from the road.

"Rise, Eshat of the Fezaken," she said. "You have done your duty."

He rose and dusted off his bum.

"A thousand thanks, Eternal Em—Eternal Captain, Great Siviss. You honor us with your presence."

They set off down the road. Sibbi looked at Ajat, who was trying not to smirk and doing an awful job of it. They performed a quick eyebrow semaphore while Eshat led them down the road, unspoken but understood.

Is he serious?

Don't ask.

Okay, but . . . She mouthed the word *Empress.*

Oh hush.

I love you.

I love you, too.

It was comforting, but Sibbi could tell the trees unnerved Ajat. She'd been told about them, of course. It was another thing entirely to see them up close. The crew didn't know, and that was fine: their presence was kept a secret, mostly by being too outlandish to talk about.

It was a ghost story sailors spun when deep in their cups—with such unreliable narrators, of course, it couldn't be real. The thousand-year plague, a sickness that stubbornly refused to kill its victims or let them die. She'd once known its origins, but the memory wasn't there anymore, and it itched like a missing tooth. They'd kept the plague under wraps from their own people for centuries, but there were too many of the infected now to keep in the royal conservatory, and they'd spilled out into the olive groves. Farmers moved among them, picking olives from the actual trees, careful to stay out of grabbing range. Many of the farmers wore masks over their nose and mouth, though that wasn't the danger. It was proximity that did it: called to you in your sleep, made you go out into the forest, sink your feet down into the dirt, spread your toes and become one with nature. Folk could pull you out if they were quick about it, but once the changes set in, you were done for—you belonged to the great tree. If Sibbi didn't drain the great psychic cyst, it got swollen and septic and started to infect more and more of the land, and she had not been back in a long time. She'd been pretending for too long: she had forgotten her obligations, and her past. She had wanted desperately to forget them, to stop them from pulling her back. There hadn't been this many trees last time.

"I hear they make good coffee here," said Ajat, a slight tremor in her voice. It wasn't clear to whom she was speaking. She was looking ahead at the spire of Dergula and very intently *not* at the olive grove on either side of the road.

"The very best!" said Eshat. "And of course, the servants of the God-Empress Tiryazan may drink as much as they'd like. More coffee than you've ever seen! More than exists!"

"That much, huh?" said Ajat, raising an eyebrow.

"Even more than that!" said Eshat.

Ajat didn't even pick a fight about being called *servant*—she must be terrified, though she was doing a good job of not showing it. It almost made Sibbi want to reach into her, share a memory, calm her down. But no, they had a deal. It was hard enough to get privacy without living in somebody else's head. She wished she could just put her arms around the woman, to love her as easily as she loved. Instead, she canted her head slightly, leaned in, and pushed herself against Ajat's side. Ajat didn't recoil, but she didn't accept it, either— she kept walking, not looking at the trees, as the shadow of Dergula fell over them.

The top level was a ship, improbably speared by the central stone pillar of the tower. Its guts had been emptied out and filled with a plush audience chamber. Every inch of the place was gold furnishings or deep red carpet. There was no wood visible, presumably to cover the awful pink it would be stained by the vines holding it in place.

King Razakat lounged on his throne, surrounded by a gaggle of his most sycophantic advisors. He looked like an echo of a pirate: somebody who had been hearing stories about pirates all his life but had never actually met one. It must've taken the Ladowain miners months just to decorate his fingers. They used to just steal it, but the lead from the island's mines made a good insulator, and it could buy a lot of Lion gold. It also made bullets, and gods knew the Lion had use for those. Razakat looked strong—he could probably chop a training dummy clean in half. His great-grandfather had been a hell of a Weaver and the worst man Sibbi had ever loved. Those days were behind her—and certainly behind everybody else.

The Lion had burnt the whole island to the ground in living memory, but Razakat had forgiven them and moved on, because palaces didn't burn as well as fields. War had rules, if you could afford them. A good price on lead, an agreement not to raid the wrong coast. What's a few thousand homes in the scheme of things? There was more money in the assembled court than in the rest of the country put together. They'd been a council once: bright-eyed, talking about spreading the responsibility, working for the good of the islands. And year by year, they'd slid back to a king and made themselves comfortable nobles.

"Empress," said Razakat. He gave a mock bow from his throne. He did not say *witch*, but it was written on the back of his tongue, in the way he stood, in the fire between his neurons. People gave themselves up in a million ways, if you knew where to look.

"King," said Sibbi. Her knees were in no state to curtsy, nor was she in the mood. She gave him a bow in return: deep, respectful, and filled with as much venom as she could give it.

"You're smaller than I expected," he drawled, "though less ugly. Are we sure it's her?" That got a titter from his attendants. They had been hearing stories for their whole lives about the Witch Empress who'd torn the world in half and stitched it back together poorly. They were starting to realize, perhaps, that they were only dealing with a woman. In the bad old days, she'd have disabused them of that notion by spreading one of them over the wall. There were stains in this room they'd never managed to get out, covered now by banners and carpets. She bit back her rage and smiled.

"Many expect a monster," said Sibbi. "I aim to disappoint."

"Then you have exceeded yourself," said Razakat. Another titter. The vines around the building tightened, and it groaned. She didn't realize she'd been pulling on them. The king's entourage didn't even notice. She breathed in deeply, inhaling Ajat's perfume. Her wife's presence had a way of calming her down. Sibbi hadn't wanted her to see this place but was grateful she'd asked to come.

"Why have you called me here?" she said. "I could do the ritual on my own."

Razakat laughed and stood. He filled the audience chamber. The gold and furs added another forty pounds, but he wasn't a small man to begin with.

"I hear strange stories, dear Empress. The North has fallen: a spider-city roams the taiga; our own land springs forth new poison every day; there are lights in the sky over Radovan, and we haven't had a new shipment from them in weeks. Another war rocks the Eastern Shelf, and there are whispers, with the weapons they bring to bear, that it might be the last. I am told the world is ending, and I'm told of a witch who would be the one to shepherd it in."

There it was, out in the open. Fucking *prophecy*. She'd seen enough of history not to trust prophets. Even the good ones weren't more accurate than a coin toss. Throw enough shit at the wall, and some of it would stick. She'd refused to sleep with one ratty man five hundred years ago and was still paying for it. *Woe is me, my dick goeth unsucked, it must be the actual end of the world.*

"And what do you want me to do about it?" she spat.

"Nothing," said Razakat. "You are to do nothing. You are to cease your ritual at the great tree. Your ship will be provisioned, then leave port and never return. Orders have been given to fire on any vessel flying your colors that comes north of the Sawhead Reef. The council of wise masters has met and decided that you are more trouble than you're worth. You and any"—he cast an eye at Ajat and sneered—"'associates' are exiled and stripped of title. We have rather outgrown the need for an empress. It is time for us to decide our own fate."

"At least we agree on that," Sibbi spat, though inside she was reeling. It had already been too long since the last ritual: another ten years and the damage would be irreversible. She could feel the tree's great red roots in the mine shafts that honeycombed under the islands and under the channels between them: septic, poisoning the earth. They would strangle the life out of Dawgar. The council had voted on suicide. Not just their own, but that of everybody in the nation. Sibbi realized she was breathing heavily, that heat was moving up her arms, that her head was spinning. Her next words came out as a hiss.

"You can't stop me," she said. She reached into the vines around the palace and tugged.

The room shook, then twisted violently. Pandemonium erupted. The councilors scrambled to keep their footing. A man in an ermine robe crashed to the floor, weighed down and taken off-balance by his own chains of office.

Razakat's laugh was a roar. He slumped back into his throne as the room spun. He fucking *clapped*. "*There* she is!" he said. He grinned, his eyes filled with victory and malice. "There's the witch from the stories, the little mort de la terre."

The councilors were shaken, but not as much as she'd expected. *Gods, they're used to this. The growth is out of control, so it's just normal now. The carpets are padding. Their world is dying, and they're investing in better palliatives.*

"Fuck your stories," said Ajat. It was the first time she'd spoken in hours, and her words came out in a panicked yell. "You're all mad. She's trying to *help*!"

"Her help is not needed," said Razakat.

"According to who? A man in a rickety tower? When was the last time you were on the ground? This place is falling to pieces—sooner or later, that ground will rise to meet you."

"I am a king," said Razakat, "and I do not take counsel from degenerates. I do not take counsel from foolish men who fear their own manhood."

Then Sibbi saw it, written in every crevice of his mind. The faith had reached this place, too. He didn't even know it: he saw himself as beyond the priesthood, more evolved. They'd gotten to him anyway. There'd always been pockets of the faithful, but pirates were impossible to govern or unite and had been happy to leave folks as folks. They'd laughed at anything that told them what to do or whom to love. And yet there it was, plain as day: *degenerate*. The word stung worse than *witch*. A witch was frightening, but a degenerate was disposable, something to be washed away with the rain. She wanted very much to pull the life out of him, to grab ahold of the cord of his soul and yank it out and eat it, make herself strong again. But she couldn't, because she'd seen his backup plan. More than that, when she'd linked threads with him, he'd seen her looking. He grinned again.

"I knew there was nothing I could do to stop you killing me," said Razakat. "If you wanted to come in, you would. Can you say the same for your crew? No spotters on deck, *tsk tsk*. The explosives provided by our wonderful friends in Radovan really are miraculous: impossible to locate, until they're absolutely everywhere. You'll never find all of them before my men set them off. You will leave here at once, or your crew will feed the little fish. Take your freak husband and go."

"My *wife*," said Sibbi, "and I will go without incident. We will go, but I leave you with a warning: the next time I stand in this room, you will die. I will bring this tower down on every single one of you. You will choke on your own blackened tongues. Be warned, King: the next time I stand here, I will break heaven and bring down the fucking sky."

It felt good to say; it felt good to spit venom. It meant nothing. That was the woman she'd left behind in another time. It was a woman who'd emerged shrieking in a fisherman's net. A woman who'd burned more fields than she dared to count. She wasn't that woman anymore.

"And then," she said, "I'm going to save this place. I'm going to find a way to help my people thrive. I'm going to make a world without people like you."

"Bold words for a woman who holds no cards," he said. "But my tongue will remain unblackened and my towers intact."

He was truly lost, but he was right. She tried to search his mind to find where the bombs were, but she knew it was hopeless: he'd given an order to somebody who'd given an order to somebody who'd given an order to somebody else, and by the time she followed the chain, it would be too late.

"I have another home to save," said Sibbi. "But I'm coming back, and when I do, you are going to die."

"That makes two of us," said Razakat. "Now go."

She hadn't felt so powerless in a long time. She turned to Ajat, put a hand around the back of her neck, then pulled her face down and kissed her deeply. It was more a performance than a kiss, but they both slipped into the role quickly enough. When they broke apart, Sibbi turned to King Razakat, stared right into his eyes, and spat on his pretty carpet. An attendant—a boy no more than fourteen—tugged at her sleeve, leading her toward the exit. She didn't fight him.

在找你死党吗？我就是另外那个, *ya cunt. I've been trying to reach the cop, but she's too busy taking terrible advice from herself to listen to anybody else, so I guess you'll have to do. To misquote somebody who used to be a friend, we dig our own fuckin' graves and build our own* fuckin' prisons. That girl, I swear, she's barely even got dial-up and you're in the control room, fiber-optic, gigabit uplink, 4k all day, baby.

It's a metaphor. Ask your missus about it.

Look, Snake ate his own tail. I don't like it any more than you do. I tried to stop him. I said, "You idiot, you fucker, you absolute 废材," but he did it anyway.

That one's only sort of a metaphor. The whole thing loops in on itself, a sort of short-circuit reality. Everybody thinks a short circuit is just when your lights stop working, but that's like saying getting shot is when the skull opens up. Everything has happened before. Snake eats his own tail; history eats itself. The end is coming, a real end, not just sparks from amps dancing in janky circles but the whole rotten house burning down and you're fucking around with boats. I don't love your old mate's plan to alchemy everything, but at least it's going places. "Places" being abso-fucking-lute hell, but at least that's a destination. I'll take it over the killing Quiet any day. The edges are coming apart; things keep happening that have already happened. Empire, revolution, kids playing with grenades. Old mate can't stop them, but at least he's trying.

Ah, you're not listening. **Why can't you hear me?** If I didn't know better, I'd swear the Quiet had gotten to you. There's a hole in the world, and the wind screams through it. You must've cut that part out of yourself. Yeah, yeah, something something input ≠ output, but come the fuck on. You rewired something important, and I regret to inform you that your hack sucks. I tried to wrap my head around it, and all I came away with was the reek of burning fur. I keep thinking about the word channel, what it used to mean; nothing ever fuckin' changes.

Doesn't matter. You'll forget I said anything. You've already forgotten. 去死啦你. Or, well, don't.

We both know that's not how this works.

TWENTY-ONE

Y at stared out to sea and the setting sun. They'd turned the ship around two days ago and were heading back toward Hainak with the easterly behind them—whatever business they'd done in Dawgar was long complete, and most of the crew had been told to remain in the galley during that trip.

Yat couldn't shake the unease she'd felt when she'd entered the mast: she could feel the vast weight of the sea beneath her. She'd thought it was empty, but maybe what she'd really been feeling was the *pull*—all magic going downward through the bottom of the sea and out to the world of the dead. Sibbi was at the helm, steering them back from the faraway islands toward home. Yat was smoking a cigarette: the woman with red hair had offered, and they smoked together in silence. The ship's prow cut through the waves, carving apart the soft white crests, rising and falling with the satisfying slap of wood on water. It had become a familiar drumbeat over the last few days, and it calmed Yat: it felt like an echo of her own heart.

The woman beside her was deathly pale, her skin heavily tattooed. The tattoos moved—some sort of living ink. Yat had never met a real Northerner before. In the stories, they were more a force of nature than anything else, ferocious cannibals who came to loot and burn. The Iron Cult had turned the place into a wasteland in their endless search for more fuel for their great furnaces. Only a few cities remained up there, mostly those like Crow Hearth, protected by stout walls and electric fields. Varazzo liked to play up his Northman credentials when he wanted to seem tough, even though he was from the Eastern Shelf. Accenza was in the northeast and dealt with the occasional raid, but there were juicier targets closer to the tundra, and poorly protected. Accenza had ports and merchants and books and peace. They mostly just fought themselves. The real North didn't even get a name—it was a place beyond words, where the Old Iron roamed.

The woman's name was Cannath, and she was the ship's bosun. That was all Yat had been able to get out of her. She was a broad woman, she looked strong. Her threads were hard to read, less bright. Some of her tattoos ran over scars on her face—whether she was hiding them or painting them deeper was hard to say.

"You fight?" she said. It was the first time she'd spoken since offering her name.

"Sure," said Yat. "We did hand-to-hand at the academy."

"So you fight like a cop," she said, smirking. "Meaning you don't fight."

"I fight fine," said Yat. She'd excelled at drills: her small size made it easier to get under the guard of the larger officers. They had a habit of underestimating her, and she had a habit of punishing them for it. She'd never been able to beat Sen, but nobody could do that. He told everybody he'd taught himself to fight from a penny manual. She wasn't sure if she believed him, but she'd never seen the man lose a fight. She wished she'd paid more attention.

"Show me," said Cannath. She stubbed out her cigarette on the gunnel and tucked it behind her ear. Yat took a deep breath and lowered herself into first defensive stance, with her legs bent and her arms—

The first blow hit her in the stomach while she was still squaring up. Yat saw it coming in the threads before she saw it in Cannath's body: they suddenly flared red-hot, concentrated together in her hips and shoulders, and sent a braid of power down her arm and right into her fist. Yat realized a second too late that the threads weren't dull, their glow was concealed. It was like being hit by a train. Yat doubled over, and a knee caught her in the chin. Her teeth crunched against each other, and she crashed back against the deck. She lay on the boards in agony, tasting the copper in her own blood. "Not fair," she said between gritted teeth. "You didn't let me—"

"I didn't let you, no," she said. "And I'm your friend. Think on that."

A lot of folks on this boat wanted to be her friend, but they had a funny way of showing it. Cannath offered her hand. Yat wasn't sure how she felt about this, but she took it and let the Northerner pull her to her feet. Their threads came together, and Yat felt the tension and a concentration to her threads: they were packed together tightly, ready to explode.

"I'm going to hit you," said Cannath, "and your job is to stop me. You ready?"

Yat didn't have time to answer before the second blow came at her: the magic concentrated in Cannath's hip again, and Yat blocked high, ready for another punch. The knee caught her in her side. She saw the threads shift a half second too late and didn't have time to stop the blow. She turned her body with the impact and let the worst of it go nowhere, but it still hurt like hell as it scraped across her ribs.

"Better," said Cannath. "The first time I died, it was because I expected him to fight fair; I never made that mistake again. The next time, I took the motherfucker with me. Use knees, use elbows, use teeth. You had a cigarette, didn't you? Put that in my eye if you have to. Fuck, kill me; I'll be back. I died in Hainak, and I'll be back here for another lesson faster'n you can spit. The only people who talk about honor are those who are already ahead—they want you to fight fair because that's how they win."

Yat didn't need to read threads to see the woman's rage, but she did anyway: they were incandescent inside her, so dense and tightly tangled that it was impossible to make out one from the next. There was something else in there, too, something fragile: a butterfly trapped inside the furnace. For a moment, as Yat looked, she heard something inside her head: the soft tearing of paper, or boots through fresh snow. *Where have I heard that before?* Something else, too: the sound of machinery, a pressure on her shoulders, a single nail, not flush with the wall.

Cannath paced back and forth across the deck. Her tattoos writhed. She stood up very straight, arched her head back, then took a deep breath of sea air. She looked like she was about to say something else, but Sibbi cut her off.

"Easy, tiger," she said.

Cannath shot her what could only charitably be described as a glare. "Yes, *Captain*," she said. She stormed off, and Sibbi shook her head. She beckoned Yat to her, beside the steering wheel. They stood together, with Dawgar behind them and Hainak somewhere in the unseen distance.

"It's easy to become obsessed with death," said Sibbi. She shifted her hands on the wheel, and her rings clattered against the wood. "Just because you *can* die doesn't mean you should. You know what a hero is, Yat?"

Her mind flashed back to Wajet, walking along the docks with her. *What if the taniwha's nice?* He'd been getting at something.

"A hero," she said, "is somebody who does what's right, no matter the cost."

"Try again," said Sibbi, whose sweet little-old-lady smile was infuriating.

"Okay," said Yat, "a hero is somebody who fights against the darkness."

"Ooh," said Sibbi, "'fights against the darkness.' I like that. Shadows are well-known for their vulnerability to punching. Very poetic. Closer, but no."

"Well then," said Yat, "why don't you tell me?" More damned riddles. Why couldn't people ever just say what they meant?

Sibbi grinned. "A hero," she said, "is a young man—and it *is* usually a man, though not always—who wishes to die loudly. They want everybody to look and say, 'What a hero!' and to be remembered. They read too many stories and get this idea in their heads that death is noble and beautiful and glorious. A hero is impatient to die, and in their impatience, they have a habit of taking ordinary folks down with them—after all, death is *glorious*, and that means killing is, too. Whether they succeed or fail, a hero is defined by death, and that's why I don't let heroes on my ship. I'd rather teach my people how to live."

Cannath was on the foredeck, checking some ropes. Yat tried not to look at her, but the quiet storm of swearing was hard to fully ignore.

"The wound is still raw; she lost the god who sent her back," said Sibbi, "and Tiger was more of a mother than most. She liked to pick up kids in bad spots and give them a second chance, a third chance, a fourth, you get it. Many of the gods are opaque, indifferent, unreadable. They're operating on a logic so sideways it seems cruel and random. Why do they pick who they pick? Who knows. But Tiger? I always got the sense she actually cared. That's probably what got her, in the end. Nobody expects virtue to bite them in the ass, but it always does. Cannath lost her mother and her lifeline. She's a cat on her ninth life—she can still weave, but she's got nobody left to stitch her back together."

Yat started. *Of course she knew who I was thinking about. Magic, or just intuition? What* doesn't *she know?*

"She's an old friend, and I break the rules for my friends, though I never break them for myself. That girl needs all the friends she can get: Tiger Weaving is a lonely art. Ajat and I have the art of flight, but Cannath has the art of silence. It's not invisibility, but something better— unless you're looking right at her, she makes herself not matter. Good for keeping secrets, but not exactly social. She can stop doing it, of course, but as the years drag on, such things become habits."

A flash of silver memory tore through Yat's head again, but it was slippery and evasive, and as soon as she tried to catch it, it was gone.

"Well," Sibbi continued, then paused and cocked her head, "she's a *relatively* old friend."

"Just how old *are* you?" said Yat. The question had been bothering her for a while, and it seemed none of her thoughts were private anyway.

"That's not a question you ask a lady," said Sibbi, "but you wouldn't believe me if I told you."

She tried to read the woman's threads, but she wasn't getting anything—she could see a stroke of emotion, but nothing revealing. More damned mysteries. She didn't know how much of all this she believed, but the crew definitely believed it: they treated Sibbi more like a shaman than a captain. Once Yat had seen it, it was hard not to. They kept their gaze low around her, never raised their voices, and followed her orders with fervor.

Her face still stung. There was blood between her teeth and beneath her tongue. She hated how they treated her: poking and prodding with little questions, shuffling around the edges. Everything was sideways, in metaphor and innuendo—gods and magic and song. She was definitely more willing to believe than she had been a week ago, but there was something else going on: a tangible threat with spies and guns and missing ships. She didn't know magic, but she'd thought she knew, at least, how to fight. The pain in her jaw seemed desperate to prove her wrong. She needed to shut it up. She swallowed some blood and started to walk toward Cannath.

Sibbi didn't move, but some of the threads of the ship turned toward Yat. They were tense and bunching together.

"Hey," shouted Yat, "hey, you!"

It wasn't just the ship paying attention now: the crew were backing up, some of them looking concerned. That was fine: an audience would be good. Her heart hammered in her chest. This was a risk, but her last one had worked out.

Yat stopped right in front of Cannath, who looked bored, leaning against the railing. But her threads told a different story: she was coiled like a spring, about to go off.

"You taught me a trick," said Yat, louder than she needed to be. Maybe for the sake of performance, but most of it was nerves. "Let me teach you one."

The crew was moving closer now—far enough to avoid getting caught up in a fight, but close enough to jump in if need be. The ship itself—seeming to reflect Sibbi, curious but cautious—turned entirely toward them. A row of snapdragons grew out of the gunnel beside her, and Yat reached down and touched one. She focused on it and pushed its threads upward, through the deck and through the mast. She gritted her teeth and hauled a tiny piece of energy from the mast into one of the rigging vines and felt—far above—a flower bloom. The effort set off a stabbing pain somewhere between her eyes and behind her nose. She took a deep breath and turned to Cannath.

"Can you climb?" she said.

The crew's laughter was so loud and sudden that she almost jumped. It didn't help with her headache at all.

"Climb?" said Cannath. "This *is* your first time at sea, huh?"

Yat pointed to the flower.

"Five gold ox says I can get that before you can."

That shut them up. Cannath stuck out a calloused hand. "You're on," she said. Yat didn't wait to shake it. She took off. The main-mast was secured to the gunnels on either side by a dense mycelium shroud, the same stuff they used to brace construction in Hainak. She leapt onto the underside of it and began to climb. The mycelia connected with the mast somewhere above the pub roof, and she realized why so many of the crew hated the mast placement: short of climbing up on top of the pub, this was the only way up.

A sudden weight on the shroud almost threw her off. She didn't turn around. The trick to climbing was momentum: you didn't stop, just kept using your movement into more movement. The mast had climbing pegs jutting out every few feet, but that wouldn't be fast enough—she knew Cannath was already gaining. The woman was faster than she looked, and there was something implacable about her. For the second time in as many minutes, Yat pictured her as a train and wondered whether she was about to be run down. At the connection point between mast and shroud, she leapt. She snatched at a peg, wrapped a loose grip around it, kicked out hard with both feet, and let her body swing pendulum-like out over the deck. At the farthest point of her swing, she pulled down hard on the peg, hauling herself upward—and let go.

For a moment, she hung in the air. She could see her goal: two pegs up, a solid nine feet. She reached out for it and—

The whole mast swung toward her as the ship crested a wave. She smashed into it face-first. Her nose and her eye sockets and all the bones in her face went white-hot with pain, and for an awful second, the world went black. She felt herself falling backward and could hear the shouts and groans of the crew below. She pistoned both arms outward and managed to wrap them around the mast. Another lurch of the ship swung her around it, and the wet wood filled her forearms with splinters. She cried out and felt her grip break. She was falling, falling. . . .

But in that place beyond sense, she knew the ship was alive, and alive for a *reason*. The mainmast thrummed with power: it had a direct line to the heart of the ship. The darkness suddenly cleared, and she was in midair, a good six feet from the mast and falling. She reached out into empty air, and . . .

A vine snapped out toward her like a striking snake. She grabbed it and swung. Cannath was almost at the top: she grinned, as though she could already taste victory. Yat had been in free fall, but the vine used that momentum, taking her down a little before swinging on its axis and pitching her up through the air. The maneuver wouldn't buy her much time: as the vine wrapped itself around the mast, there was less of it for her to use. She swore and—at the apex of her swing—let go. She threw her legs behind the swing and hurtled through the warm sea air. Cannath was reaching for the flower now. Yat was again too far from the mast to grab it, but she knew it could grab *her*. She pulled at its threads, and the flower itself grew as it blossomed through the air toward her. She plucked it from the air in front of her, tried to grab its vine, and . . .

Missed. She tried to make it grow, but she was falling too fast, and out of control. She screamed as she plunged toward the deck and . . .

Hit softness. She looked down and saw a flower bed, suspended in the air by a series of vines. It lowered her down, then sent her stumbling as it disappeared into the deck timbers. She didn't know who'd made the flowers, but she had a sneaking suspicion that if she turned around, she'd see Sibbi looking smug again. Yat stood up and staggered out in front of the crew.

"L-lesson," she said, "lesson one. Momentum. Momentum is, uh, important. Don't stop moving—you can turn a little swing into a big one. Use your hips, knees, feet to keep making the little swings. That's how you keep moving."

She put the flower behind her ear. Her ears were still ringing, but it seemed like something a winner would do. She bowed.

Cannath was climbing down now, muttering furiously to herself. She let herself down onto the roof of the pub, then sat on the edge, legs dangling.

"I'd call you a cheater," she said, "but I guess I had that one coming. Sailors don't swing around; I hope you've figured out why."

She nodded. "Yep," she said, "but also, you owe me five ox."

And with that, the tension lifted. Yat could feel the ship tugging at her, its threads whirling around on the wind. She reached out with her own and linked herself to it. The wave hit her, but she was ready for it. Her anxiety wasn't in her way now: the rush of energy made her strong. She was drawing from the ship, letting it support her. She could feel the flowers and the vines and the ants. She could feel tea leaves resting in the bottoms of cups and beetles chewing their way through the wood.

The warm evening air blew through her hair, and she smiled. Cannath had gone back to dealing with the ship's ropes, but she seemed calm now. She whistled as she walked among the stays, taking them one by one in a clenched fist, then giving each a small tug and a slight smile when it held true. To reach Dawgar, they'd jumped into the wind, which was still blowing a howling easterly. They'd managed to turn at port, and with luck, they'd have it behind them all the way to Hainak. As they sailed into the setting sun, for the first time in a long time, Yat felt a stirring of hope.

TWENTY-TWO

As the days onboard flew by, Yat spent more time in the crow's nest. The mainmast had a strong connection to the rest of the ship, so she practiced moving magic up and down it. At least once, she'd startled a sailor by causing a flower to bloom right in front of him. The one with the bull ring had seen and proceeded to laugh so hard they almost fell overboard—Yat learned that their name was Rikaza, and they were neither a man nor a woman. Several of the crew were the same: some through alchemy, some through dress or custom. Rikaza was older than Yat had first assumed, as well—small with age, but cheerful and easy company. They were the strongest of the crew and tended to get the heavy-lifting work. Yat watched as the magic moved through them, big thick lances of energy that were less like threads and more like scaffolding.

They had a special nose flute with notches carved into it so they could play it with their ring in, and they'd play on deck at night after their shift to keep the others company. The instrument made a haunting sound like the wind rolling through a hole in the world.

Another sailor would sometimes play the viol: a very tall, very thin Easterner named Iacci, with large hands and bags under his eyes. He'd played first chair in the Orchestra Fenatza before the city had been destroyed by an ancient buried ferro bomb. Fenatza was a crater now, and Iacci refused to call anywhere else home, so he'd taken to the sea. It was a story with which Yat would become familiar: over the last decade, Sibbi had been collecting strays. Before that, it was hard to tell what she had been doing, but it didn't sound like charity.

After lunch one day, Yat caught Iacci kneeling over a crack in the wall, his lanky frame bent triple. She'd gotten herself two black eyes from her stunt on the mast and looked a little like a panda. He turned to her and frowned.

"Mousy," he said. His voice was rich, deep, and heavily accented. "There is a little mousy here. We cannot have the mousy, for he will eat the food."

He shook his head, then straightened up as far as the roof would let him. "Tell the captain we must have a cat," he said. "I tell her this, and she does not listen. A cat is good luck, and he will eat only the food we want him to eat."

Yat held back a laugh. She'd known enough cats to cast doubt on that. She thought back to the tomcat who'd come to her house— always hungry, even when she'd just fed him.

"You go to Sibbi," he said, and waved one of his pale, spiderlike hands at her. "I will watch for a mousy."

Some of the crew wouldn't talk to her, but many would, and Rikaza was happy to grease the wheel a bit. They took Yat throughout the ship, introducing her to Xidaj, the deep-voiced Tangata man she'd seen speaking to Sibbi on her first night; Ken Set-Xor, a tiny woman she vaguely recognized as another ex–roof rat; Hestos and Hestas, twin sisters from Dawgar who used to work in the pirate king's private dance troupe; and dozens of others. Very few of them had started out as sailors, and their stories started to blend together: they'd hit rock bottom, and the crew of the *Kopek* had found them and hauled them to safety. Xidaj was on the foredeck when they found him, checking the sight of an immense rifle. The barrel was almost nine feet long, and he rested it on the gunnel while he worked. He took out a small knife and twiddled with something behind one of the lenses—he didn't notice them until Rikaza cleared their throat.

"Mornin', Xid," they said. "Got a minute for a greenhorn?"

He looked up from his gun. "Ah, yes," he said. "The newest friend in our little community of exiles. It is good to see you in the light of day. You wouldn't happen to have brought a glass cutter and a spare photo cathode aboard, would you, e hoa?"

She shook her head: nobody in Hainak used glass anymore, if they could help it. Membranes were tougher and easier to grow.

"Shame," he said. "I suppose I'll have to make do. It's become impossible to get new parts since we lost Auntie Tori's Forge, and nobody on this ship ever has tools for glass, not since the captain started to upgrade. But do be welcome. That was a good trick with the vines. I haven't seen anybody beat Cannath on the masts in years; she's the best climber on the ship. We all thought you were done for, like you'd challenged a camel to see who could go without water for the longest. You fit right in here, you know."

She didn't know how to respond to that. She'd been tolerated on occasion, but rarely seemed to be a part of the pack. The last time she'd had a close friend was Kiada, and she'd learned some hard lessons from that.

"You too," she said, then quietly cursed herself. Of *course* he fit in—he lived here.

He laughed: a trio of quick, smoky retorts. "Well, that's good to hear," he said. "You have to be a special sort of strange to fit in here. Stay safe, Jyn Yat-Hok."

Xid went back to his tinkering. She'd later learn he'd been a slave in Ladowain, taken as a child and made to work in a factory producing guns for their armies. Between his capture and escape, he hadn't seen sunlight for eight years. He wore glasses because his eyes couldn't properly adjust to light anymore, but he hated being indoors. He slept on a hammock on the deck, ate outside, and only went belowdecks if he needed something from the carpenter's workshop. He kept his model ships there, an armada in miniature stuck with sealing wax to any surface that would take them. Rikaza told this to Yat while they shared a cup of tea in the workshop, waiting for Ken Set-Xor. Xid only shared the story when he was drunk, because it hurt too much to say otherwise, but did not mind it being told, so long as he didn't have to hear.

They crossed paths with Wajet, carrying a sack under his arm. He kept his eyes low and pushed past them. Yat almost challenged him but thought better of it. She didn't want to have to deal with the whole over-the-top shifty copper act she knew he'd pull. She knew it was covering for something, that he acted like a crooked cop to hide the fact that he was something else. She just didn't trust the *something else*—you didn't succeed at looking like a scumbag without being, on some level, a scumbag. Nobody was that good an actor, and whatever secret work he'd been given, he was going to come back and hurt them all. He had his own agenda, or he and Sibbi had their own agenda, and either way, Yat didn't like it. She hadn't heard their whole conversation that night, and that troubled her.

Wajet disappeared around a corner, heading for the heart. Yat sighed and followed Rikaza to the top deck.

TWENTY-THREE

Yat saw Iacci on deck a few hours later, playing a familiar tune on his viol: the vocal line from the aria Kiada used to sing. She sat with him, closed her eyes, and let the music roll over her. She didn't cry, though she could feel a tightness in her throat that let her know the tears were buried within her, waiting to erupt. When he finished, he turned to her.

"I did not catch a mousy," he said. "Did you speak to the captain?"

She nodded. Sibbi had been evasive but good-natured, so no change there.

"She says she'll think about it," said Yat.

"This is good," said Iacci. "It is good that the captain thinks on her choices. Meanwhile, we must be vigilanti for the mousy. Vigiliance? Is this the word?"

"Vigilant," she said.

"Yes," said Iacci, "we must be vigilant."

The question burned her up, but she couldn't bring herself to ask it. She let him take up his viol again and play another song: a sad, slow, lilting piece. When he put down his bow, she turned to him again.

"What's it about?" she said. She meant the first piece but couldn't bring herself to say it out loud. Iacci considered her question for a moment and screwed up his lip.

"They are from the second act," he said. "The girl is lost, truly lost. It is night, and she wanders the street and she is alone. She sits by the river and she weeps, and the night eats her. Is this right? Eats her? She goes into the night, and it is not kind. She sings three pieces: a song for dusk, a song for midnight, a song for dawn. The world is cruel to her. This makes her strong, but it does not make the world less cruel."

"How does it end?" said Yat. The tightness in her throat pressed in, making her voice crack.

"Ah," said Iacci. "The girl does not let the night take her. She says these words: *tonight, we live.* It is not much, but it carries her to the dawn. Then it ends with a kiss. It is not a good opera if it does not end in a kiss."

That caught her off guard: it was such an abrupt shift in tone that it knocked her out of her memories.

"What if there's nobody to kiss?" she asked.

Iacci shrugged. "There is always somebody to kiss," he said. "That's how you know it's a good opera."

"Isn't that a bit simple?" said Yat. "Love saves the day?"

"Love is not simple," said Iacci. "You take two of problems, and you put them together and you hope you don't get five of problems. You must be open, and it is frightful to be open. I do not say this right, and I know I do not—it sounds better in Featta. It is music in my tongue, but I do not have the words, and my city does not have enough mouths left to speak them for me. I love Fenatza, my city; I love Featta, my tongue; I love violi, my art. These are the things I love, and they make me weep sometime, but I do not stop my love, because it is not a sack of rice I can throw off the dock. While I love these things, they remain."

"Isn't that sad?" said Yat.

Iacci picked up his bow.

"Yes," he said, with a smile, "very much so."

He played the third piece as the ship rolled on through the night. It opened strong and fast, but then went soft. There was still an intensity beneath it, though, an electric undertow that made the quiet notes ring out like bells at dawn. Yat sat with her eyes closed and let the music wash over her. It made the hairs on her arms stand up. When it was done, Iacci sighed and inspected the strings on his bow.

"This squeak is unacceptable," he said. "I cannot escape the mousy, even when I play. I must buy more rosin. The captain took my block and melted it down to fix this ant house, you know? She does not know how expensive it is."

"That was beautiful," said Yat.

Iacci shook his head. "It is adequate," he said.

"Oi, Iacci, you being maudlin again?" shouted Rikaza. They clambered down from the starboard shroud, dropped onto the deck, and clapped Iacci on the waist, unable to reach his shoulder. They bumped a friendly elbow against Yat's ribs, and she grimaced; she still wasn't entirely recovered from the beating Cannath had given her.

"Anyway," they said, "I need this one." They put a firm hand against Yat's shoulder and gently walked her over to the helm. Sibbi was asleep, so Ajat was at the wheel. She had bags under her eyes and darkness on her jaw. She frowned as they approached.

"Yep," said Rikaza.

"How many?" said Ajat.

"Six," said Rikaza, "with the bulk of the larger ships about two days behind us, headed for Hainak. The corvettes took off ahead and they're really hauling ass."

"Wait a minute," said Yat. "What are you talking about?"

"Oh, right," said Rikaza. "Greenhorn."

They squeezed Yat's shoulder, and Yat realized that her threads were running together with theirs, and suddenly she was inside a memory. She knew the feeling well: she could taste copper and smell kiro, as though she were stepping into a smoker's dream. It crossed her mind that maybe she had always heard the call of magic, but she just hadn't known what she was hearing. As though whatever had been awoken in her was always there, it just hadn't had the chance to catch fire. The world had taught her she was defective, and she'd agreed—made herself numb to her own soul.

She pushed the thoughts away and tuned in on the voices rushing through her.

—*up in the crow's nest, six low, dark shapes moving at speed, not even trying to conceal themselves*—

—*wooden ships, biowork visible even at range*—

—*the vanguard of the Hainak war fleet, coming home*—

Inside the memory, they moved together from the crow's nest to one of the ships, which seethed with magic. Through the night watchmen, the cook, up to the captain and into *his* memories.

—*another day maintaining the endless Ladowain blockade when the call came in*—

—*"must've slipped the net somehow"*—

—*eat eat EAT EAT EAT*—

—ringing the bells, sounding the alarms, rousing every sailor in the fleet—

—orders coming in tinny, garbled with distance, making no sense—

—burning hard south, nobody knew exactly what they were walking into, but every crewman eager for blood—

"Fleet's coming home," said Rikaza.

"Y-yeah," said Yat, "I got that." She could still taste the last meal the captain had eaten and hear the manic echo of the cannon-grub's shrieking thoughts.

"Okay, you got it," said Ajat. "Tell me how many we're looking at."

Yat searched the memory. They'd gone through the ship so fast and it was hard to tell.

Focus. The word made its way into her head unbidden. She took a deep breath.

Focus, go deeper. They'd been on a corvette when the alarm sounded: confusion, chaos, and every soul very much awake. The sailors felt different from the ship, their threads more tightly packed. Their agitation made their threads light up like a sea of marching torches.

"About forty crew per ship," she said, "and twenty marines. The crew aren't soldiers, but they're armed and know how to fight. They might run if they were on land, but they know there's nowhere to go. The big guns aren't on the vanguard ships, but they've still got more than enough cannons to knock us out of the water. Even one of those large-bore grubs gets through the hull, and we're done for."

"So, about three hundred and fifty men," said Rikaza. "They're distracted, but their instruments will still pick us up if we come anywhere near them. We try to fight and we're done for, but waiting isn't an option. We need to jump."

"No," said Ajat. "Out of the question. Sibbi is too weak right now, and there's no way I can get us close enough without phasing the *Kopek* into the docks. Plus, every other Crane Weaver in a thousand leagues is mad as a shithouse rat. You wanna be the one who jumps? You wanna make an ox fly?"

An infectious thought flared up between Rikaza and Ajat, on the edge of being spoken, coming from both at once: *If you can't jump, then what the* fuck *are you good for?*

Rikaza looked shocked with themselves and hung their head.

"I'm sorry, ma'am," they said. "I didn't . . . I—"

"You know," said Sibbi, "you three are thinking loudly enough to wake the dead."

They all turned in surprise. Even Ajat—facing the deck—hadn't seen her come up, and her shock ran through their threads.

"I am going back to bed," said Sibbi. "It has been five days. I am not so infirm that I can't do another jump after almost a week. We will go in the morning, when I am rested, if you three haven't eaten each other alive before then."

"But tahu, you'll hurt yourself," protested Ajat.

"We'll drain the planters," she said, waving it off. "We'll have to restock if we want to do it again anytime soon, and I'm sure the crew will miss the greenery, but it'll get us where we need to be. I love you, but you need to trust that I know what I'm doing."

Ajat looked mollified. "I love you, too," she muttered. "Now please, tahu, go to bed."

Sibbi didn't appear to need telling twice. She turned on the balls of her feet, and her nightgown swirled around her as she stormed back to the bar.

TWENTY-FOUR

*C*ome here, little shipwreck.

    I remember the first time you drowned. I remember the second, the third, the thousandth. I chose you, and I cannot leave your side: I am bound to you, was bound, will be bound. The sun will turn in on itself before I can leave, the stars will lose sight of each other, darkness will blanket the sky, and there will be silence in the world of men before I can leave.

    I remember your fall, as though you were a needle being woven through the fabric of the bottomless night, pulling the world behind you. I remember the man who found you and what you did to him. Tangled in a net, you lashed out and you hurt without end. It is burned into the city now, etched into its nerves.

    I remember the end of the world. I remember staring out across the fields and jungles and oceans and hearing only wind. I remember all these things so you'll never have to; I was like you once, until I became me. You'll forget I said this, but you'll remember it when you need to.

    There is a tree at the roof of the world, and its roots drink from a deep well of poisoned water. There is a splinter in its heart, a madness that hollows and makes anew. It sings in its sleep, and the world shakes with its music and tears itself down and starts over. There is a lion with no teeth, a spider with no legs, an ox with no tail. One of these is not the same as the others, but I cannot tell you which.

There is, as always, love.

You will forget this until the moment it matters, and then you will never forget it again.

TWENTY-FIVE

Rikaza had left to go to bed, but Ajat stayed at the wheel. Yat stood with her, letting the rhythmic slap of the hull bring her heartbeat back down.

"Rikaza's all right," said Ajat after a while. "They were one of the first we picked up. Hard life, that one, more so than almost anybody aboard. That makes you either very kind or very cruel, and we're lucky they fell on the side they did."

"You both . . . well, you know," said Yat. "I'm sure you get on."

Ajat rolled her eyes and laughed, just a little. "Riz introduced me to their fleshsmith a while back," she said. "Got a bunch of dermal implants put in from cuttlefish to make me change color. Didn't work, but it seemed like a fun idea at the time. Fascinating animal, the cuttlefish. Its camouflage uses electricity. Sometimes I wake up with all my hair standing on end. Not quite the changes Riz thought I'd get, ay? They were fine with it—just surprised, I guess. I'm happy with those parts of my body as is. Well, shaving's a pain, but I'm used to it. I've got living hair, but the new recruits always want to talk about the other stuff."

She shrugged, then looked to the place where Rikaza had been standing. "Riz'll come around. Rather have them at my back than a thousand Hainak marines. That's coming from a place of authority on both—I actually served, when I was a different me. My first time on a ship. The ocean was the only part that really stuck. Guess there's a little taniwha in me somewhere."

"You think you're part sea monster?"

Ajat laughed, though it was streaked with bitterness. "Funny how it's monstrous to protect what's yours, but only if a hero decides they want it. Funny who gets to call themselves a hero, too. Sure, why not, but for what it's worth, I'm *all* sea monster. I certainly used to be. You ever seen what a thermite charge does to a steel hull? No Lion set foot in Auntie's Forge, not while I was guarding it. All good luck runs out, though. When the Forge went dark, we started to run low on ammo and needed to mount more and more boarding actions. I took a chain shot to the waist and got thrown overboard. Ship went down, but I didn't. Sibbi picked me straight up out of the water. That's where all this started, you know. We fell in love after that. Things have changed, but we stayed in love. You know what *Kopek* means?"

Yat had heard rumors: *hound, fang, hunt.* She didn't want to say that, so she shook her head.

"It means 'pack' in Dawgae," said Ajat. "Like a pack of dogs. We're all lost pups here, together on the edge of things. We stick together, and that's how we survive."

"Is that it, then?" said Yat. "Survival?"

For a moment their eyes met, and Ajat seemed lost. She shook her head.

"I'm Tangata, you know," she said. "'The people,' like that means anything. Everybody's people—names matter. No, we're Ngā Tāngata o te Pātengi Raraunga. 'The people of the database.' Our atua, Tori, re-corded our entire culture in one place, and we built our lives around it, learned how to add to it for those who came after. Ladowain took her books and gave them to Siviss, but only for a while, took her spade and her trowel and turned them into a pickaxe, took her pā and turned them into fucking caves, gave her a new name and a coat of paint and a shitty statue outside their temples. My ancestor is not some taipō from the damned dark. She's not bent-backed and broken, she's proud and tall and never got her damned books back; if I ever meet her, I plan to change that. I was the kaitiaki raraunga, which I like a lot better than 'database administrator.' I feel like half my life is lost in translation. You could call me a sort of priestess, I guess. The war was bad for us—we lost the Vault and our islands and got scat-tered to the winds. The Vault's a Radovan puppet state now, no matter what folks tell you. When it became obvious the end was near, I did the only thing I could and made a backup." She slapped one of her tat-toos. "Thirty petabytes' worth. Had to get help from the kai-tā. He's gone now, and I'll never be as good as he was with a needle, but I like to think I'm all right. One day I'll find somewhere to upload all this, but until then, I'm the last record of a thousand years of our history. The guardian of our entire whakapapa. So I have to stay alive. And I hope it will be about more than just survival for us one day."

"Me too," said Yat. She closed her eyes and let the sea air throw her hair around. It felt like flying. She opened her eyes again, then patted Ajat on the arm. She'd never been good at comfort, but it seemed to work. They stood there looking out at the ocean for an-other few moments.

"Go to bed," said Ajat. She'd seemed on the edge of adding *Constable* but stopped herself.

"Yeah," said Yat. "Bed sounds good."

She stuck around for a bit longer, then turned and left. She could hear Ajat humming at the wheel: an old song she barely recognized, maybe something from the war. As the song faded behind her, she descended out of the night and into the warm belly of the ship.

TWENTY-SIX

The jump looked different from up on deck. There was more preparation this time around—the crew spent all morning bringing up planters and placing them around the wheel. Yat hadn't noticed it before, but there was some sort of circle burned into the wood there, with nodes for each planter. It had taken about an hour to set up. Sibbi kept ordering the sailors: *No, put the toadstool closest to me; no, the cactus goes in beside the rune that looks like a little house.*

The plants in each node were rooted with magic to the ship—contact points in one giant ceremonial battery. The sheer flow of energy made Yat's teeth hum.

Sibbi stood in the center, hands on the wheel. Ajat stood nearby, not looking overjoyed, but she didn't say anything.

Yat didn't notice the mist until it was coming up over the gunnels. It flowed over the sides of the ship and spread across the deck. It was up to her ankles, then her waist, then she couldn't see a damn thing. The ship kept moving forward until . . .

It finally carved out of the mist and the city lay spread out before them. Somewhere out in the old southern docks ward: mostly abandoned these days, since the shipyards had slowed production. A few drifters on the dock watched them approach and didn't say anything. Xidaj stood at the front of the ship, looking through his gunsight and shouting back at the crew, who sprang up and prepared for a hard turn. The gangplank went down fast, skittering across the boards as the ship slowed.

The instant the plank touched the docks, Yat could feel the whole city thrumming with power—wood on wood, one little battery connecting to a massive machine. It was power she'd felt all her life but didn't know what to do with. People and animals and houses and streets, thousands on thousands on thousands of threads. It used to make her anxious knowing how big the city was, but now it made her feel strong. In the grips of the great gray emptiness that spanned the days between panic attacks, she used to believe that she was uniquely and powerfully alone. Touching the city like this, it struck her how many other souls felt the same—how many threads in this great tapestry thought they weren't a part of anything that mattered. They were an ecosystem, their essences working together and empowering each other. Frayed and knotted sometimes, but still very much alive.

The gangplank was down for barely more than a few seconds when Wajet sashayed down to the docks. He gave a little mock bow as the ship pulled away, and the crew pulled up the plank with practiced ease. Yat ran along the ship's railing, as if to follow him; she sprinted up the stairs of the aftcastle and peered over at the disappearing dot behind them. She'd expected a *stop*, an actual docking, a time to slip out. She'd barely even had time to wave, and now they were tearing back across the water, mist rising once again over the sides.

They were leaving. Something big was happening at home, and they were about to fuck off into the ocean and leave Wajet—big, loud, sledgehammer Wajet—to figure it out himself. When she'd reached out into the city, she'd felt something sinister moving. A disruption in the fabric, a rot beneath its gentle contours. She'd known it before they'd gotten here, but it only hit her in full force as she watched the docks fall away: they had a chance to stop something terrifying, and they were about to entrust it to the least trustworthy man on the whole *Kopek*. She couldn't let the man do it alone; she couldn't depend on his allegiance, his courage, even if his heart were true. And his lack of capacity to do anything but shout and bluster almost always meant a bigger mess than he'd started with. She had *died* that night because of him. Her people were going to get hurt, because Sibbi was sending the wrong man. A man with no magic, no wits, nothing but very noticeable volume issues. Yat knew these streets and these people. They should've sent the whole crew, but failing that, they should've at least sent the good cop instead of the bumbling one. She knew his mission: she knew where to go. She would help him, whether he wanted it or not. She could protect Hainak and the *Kopek*, these beautiful people. She didn't care for all the riddles: Hainak needed a damned hero.

She could still feel the city, an afterimage burned into her soul. If Sibbi could use the ship to jump itself, surely she could use the city to jump *herself*. She'd been there inside the woman's magic when she cast a golden needle out across the ocean and pulled herself tight behind it. She had no idea how, but the water was already lost beneath them and the city was vanishing and she pushed past Xidaj and *reached out—*

Her memory cast back to Dad's protein broth. She knew it made people big and strong, and she wanted so badly to be strong, so she'd poured a little into her cupped hand, and it had burned more than anything she'd ever felt. She'd find out later that it was heavily diluted before anybody was allowed to drink it: that the solution wasn't even safe to touch unless it was mixed to 1:1000 parts with water. The scar still itched on humid nights. Which is to say, *a body can only take so much good.*

Yat died—blew open like a single bulb taking a century's worth of power at once. She was *falling, falling,* falling through the void of death, torn open and spread impossibly thin while massive hands grabbed at her and frantically stitched, hearing whispers and screams and and—

—emerging from the water, bursting up into the world, gasping at every precious breath of oxygen. In the distance, to the south, she saw a ship shrouded in mist. She could feel the anger and confusion on deck even from here. And then, empty sea. The mist collapsed, spread thin, then melted away into the muggy air. She bobbed in the water and, for the first time in several days, noticed its acrid reek of salt and fish and decay. She was in the doorway to another world, and that world pulled at her. She grabbed ahold of one of the dock timbers and hauled herself painfully up. She knew this place, of course: the place she'd died. There were no cops here this time, nor any blanks.

The window of a nearby shop had been blown out, and glass lay all over the ground. Somebody had put warning signs around it, but nobody had bothered to sweep it up. Either it was recent, or uniforms were busy with other parts of the city: cleaning up potential evidence made the detectives furious since it made their jobs harder, but she certainly didn't see any detectives around. Her clothes were already starting to dry—the same warmth that had woven her back together was still inside her, curled up like a fist and radiating a terrifying heat. She reached out into the nearby buildings and found rats, roaches, cats, grass, weeds, birds—*birds*—an old cellulose wall covering a broken piece of wood . . . but not one single man or woman or anything even close. Not even a squatter, and gods knew the city was packed with those.

She wanted to pretend she didn't know about them like she'd done for years, because she needed to say it was all okay in order to stop herself from breaking. Easier to call it a one-off, a temporary twitch from normalcy. But this wasn't new; it was the old, casting off its mask. She'd buried each little piece of evidence, not seeing that it was a blizzard of it, crushing her and Kiada and Hainak and everybody. A crescendo of voices flowing together, fists beating on locked doors while the city shouted back, *This is how it's always been. This is how it's* always *been. Sure, times are changing, but for the better. We used to just kill folks, and now we take their humanity first—see? It's more humane! The city eats them, and they don't feel a thing.* It was all just new tricks for old evil, and she'd made herself blind to it because confronting it hurt too much. Her throat burned, and the nausea rose from her spine into her head, raising the short hairs on her crown. She tried to push it down, but it wouldn't let her. The lump sat in her throat, choking her, forcing her to acknowledge it. She had *known*. She hadn't put the pieces together, but it wouldn't have been hard. Evil like rain: a million droplets, together a flood. She just put it off for another day and then another day and then another. She'd become a cop to fix it, but she'd only made it worse, packed the miseries tighter. She'd known and told herself, *This is how it's always been.* She stood in the street and let the broken city lights play across her face. She didn't know how long she stood there; it could've been a minute or an age. She wanted to stay there forever, but a thought cut through the noise: *Now that you've seen it, you need to stop it.*

But how? You could fight a monster, but you couldn't fight a storm—you just closed the windows and prayed for it to stop. One person couldn't stand against that. She was lost and had no plan, but something Ajat had said was nagging at her: *Every other Crane Weaver in a thousand leagues is mad as a shithouse rat. You wanna be the one who jumps? You wanna make an ox fly?* Crane Weaver. It made sense: Rikaza was strong like an ox, Cannath was fierce like a tiger, and Sibbi and Ajat could practically fly like cranes. In a sense. She had no idea what monkeys were good for. Stealing fruit? But Ajat had covered that one, too: *Monkey is quick and clever and the only one still fighting, and sometimes that's enough.*

She wandered away from the docks and found an empty building to sit down and rest in—she didn't want to risk being seen if the *Kopek* came back. She needed to catch her breath and clear her head. They had been kind to her, but the ship wasn't her home. They were good people, and good people who got too close to Yat got hurt. She didn't know if it was her fault, but it happened every time, and there was nothing she could do about it. Besides, she could protect them better from here: do the necessary work, make sure whatever was tearing through the city didn't burn their strange floating home down.

The empty building had a single open window, and she climbed up a decorative wall covering and hauled herself inside. She had to tear away an overgrown membrane, but it was malnourished and came away easily in her hand. She dropped down onto a rusted iron walkway above a factory floor. The conveyor belts had gathered dust, and she didn't recognize any of the other machines. The red brick walls made it hard to sense threads: she put her hand against them and tried to cast down, but got nothing. Something tap-tapped across the skylight above, and she saw a pair of pigeons roosting on an intersection between the beams. They'd replaced all the glass with membrane, but everything else here was ferro. The old iron roller door was heavy with rust—probably never a very successful business, if they couldn't replace a door like that. She wouldn't be bothered by anybody in here.

The pigeons were concerning. She kept an eye on them, although they didn't seem to be watching her, but *seeming* that could be a long way from the truth. The threat would find a way in eventually, and besides, she had work to do. She hauled herself to her feet, body aching and veins humming with strange power, and set out.

TWENTY-SEVEN

Sen wasn't under house arrest, he just wasn't allowed to leave the house. It had been a rough few days. There were bin chickens watching the place. He'd stepped out for five minutes to grab a rice ball and come back to find a dead rat pinned to the door. The other two cops were no help: they wouldn't believe him about the Sparrows, and they seemed fine with all the soldiers.

The bloody *soldiers*! More of them every day, coming in by train and by boat until they outnumbered the cops. Taking orders from *somebody* about *something* and getting very aggressive when asked about it by some two-bit sergeant with a shitty leg. He'd been praying to Siviss, but things were only getting worse. He poured himself another whisky from the homeowner's "hidden" stash and shotted it down. Might get him in trouble, but he figured it was a lesser evil.

"Wasn't your mum a teetotaler?" said Wajet.

Sen whirled around, forgetting about his leg, stumbled, and collapsed right into a comfy chair.

223

"How in the ever-loving fuck did you get in here?" he said.

Wajet grinned at him. "Amazing how quietly you can move when everybody thinks you're noisy," he said with the finger-wiggling mystique of a mountaintop sage.

"That sounds very convincing, but it doesn't mean a bloody thing, mate," said Sen. "I've got no time for blokes who speak in knots. Say it plain."

Wajet sighed. "My husband and I used to break in here to fuck sometimes," he said. "Nice beds. Anyway, Sen, got a gift for you. Heard you got given one of them gods-awful department-issue canes for your leg, so I went out and got you a replacement."

"You crossed the wall and broke into what is technically a police department to give me a new cane? Are you mad?"

"Exceptionally. Have you met me, Sergeant?"

You had to give it to Wajet: he was very good at failing to answer the primary question. He was canny behind all the bluster: big words hiding little lies. He would've made a good politician. Sen took the cane, gently, as though it might explode. It rattled as he tested it. He stared at Wajet.

"This is a sword-stick," he said. "You're being all coy, but you broke in here to give me a sword." He twisted the head of the cane and pulled. It rattled again but didn't come free. Something in Wajet's eyes betrayed him for a second: he hadn't expected it not to come free. To his credit, he recovered quickly.

"Of course not, Sergeant," he said. "That would be illegal."

Sen handed it back and shook his head. The last time he'd seen Wajet, the man had been leaving with Yat, the night everything went wrong. The last time he'd seen *her*, she'd been talking about Wajet, raving that he was coming for her. This was a trap.

"You want to help out, get me the fuck out of here and get me my bloody rookie back."

Wajet rebuffed the cane, pushing it gently back.

"If I can do the first, will you trust me to work on the second?"

Sen cocked his eyebrow. He liked to think he was good at reading people, and that had almost seemed sincere.

"Go on," he said.

"The owner of this house had a series of trysts with an alchemist on the other side of the wall. He had a tunnel built that leads from the wine cellar under the river, under the wall, and all the way to a hotel on the Grand Canal. There's a fake wine barrel you need to roll out of the way. I can show you which."

"And Yat?" growled Sen.

"I can tell you, beyond a shadow of a doubt, that I left her in *awful* company," said Wajet.

"Good people, though?"

Wajet nodded. "Good people," he said in a low growl. Not making eye contact, but not because he was hiding something—because it was hard for the man to be sincere. He was a joker who used humor to deflect when things got difficult. Sen could relate.

"You'll get her back?" said Sen.

"Hold on to that cane, and she'll come to you," said Wajet.

Couldn't be worse than the one he was using. He tested the grip a few times. It was comfortable. It was just the right length, too: no more leaning over on a cane made for a shorter man. The metal inside rattled around.

"You're crooked," said Sen.

"As a corkscrew, my good man," said Wajet. "And as honest an officer as you'll ever meet. The barrel you want is Carnili Del Piacco, with a chalk mark on it, back against the wall. And now, I must go. I suspect it's going to be a busy night for both of us."

Sen nodded. He gripped the handle of his new cane like a lifeline. He'd prayed for deliverance, and here it was in its strangest bloody form. He'd been wounded and pushed around long enough. It was time to raise bloody hell.

Sen slipped into the cellar when the two other officers—the two he'd taken to calling his wardens—weren't looking. The barrel was huge but weighed almost nothing: it was made out of cork and painted to look like hardwood.

They must've bored out the tunnel with some sort of chemical reagent: an astringent oxide reek hung in the air and stained an oily rainbow all over the bare stone. Little bits of mycelium broke through here and there: the place was well made but hadn't undergone maintenance in a long time.

The new cane helped immensely. He still couldn't figure out how to get the blade out, but he was sure it was there. The thing was weighted well: he guessed there was a layer of lead shot in it to keep things balanced. It was amazing how much of a difference it made to have something built for his body.

He emerged from the tunnel into an empty sauna. It clearly hadn't been used in years, based on the green mold growing in the pools. A chipped fresco on the walls showed jungle beasts cavorting with nymphs. Up the stairs, through the changing rooms, into the hotel proper. It had seen better days. Nice foyer, tall staircase on either side, heavy railings. Good cover—move some of the couches around, and you'd have a decent start on fortifications. He made a mental note of the location, then set out.

TWENTY-EIGHT

As Yat worked her way through town, something pulled at her, a titanic weight in the distance. It was like a lead ball on a rubber sheet, bending the city's threads around it. She crept toward the disturbance, checking her corners and keeping her back to the walls. The noise hit her first: cheering, shouting, the crackle of gunpowder discharge. Then the smoke, acrid and chemical and low to the ground. At first it sounded like a fight, but as she got closer, she realized what she was approaching: a party.

Trust Hainak, of all places, to throw a party while on the brink of war. She'd seen fireworks earlier from out at sea, but it was different from inside the city: they shook the streets like an artillery barrage and thickened the air. This was why the docks were deserted: the siren songs of wine, fireworks, and good company had drawn all the sailors away from the water. A group of men went by under one long ox costume while a little girl ran alongside them, collecting donations. An Erzau priest watched the men go by: Yat could make out his scowl beneath his mask, even at a distance. A band must've figured out how to hook up their instruments to the horn network. It was tinny and hard to make out, but the audience was too drunk to mind. Some instrument she didn't recognize, like pan pipes but low and liquid. It sounded like water running through bamboo, pushing the air out ahead of it.

Something was moving toward Yat. She took a step back and narrowly avoided collision with a drunken reveler, his threads strange and frayed. He saw her, started to smile, then stopped and tried to salute. But his legs were incommunicado with the rest of him, and he tripped and fell.

"'vnin', 'nstable," he said, his cheek scraping the cobblestones.

Constable? She knew she'd ditched the uniform back on the *Kopek*, but then she looked down and realized she was back in her uniform.

The same as when you died.

There was something wrong with him, but she couldn't place it. Folks had gotten drunk back on the ship, but their threads hadn't looked like this. To be fair, none of them had been *this* drunk. She knelt down. His nostrils were red and snotty, his breathing heavy and liquid.

"Are you all right, sir?" she said.

He smiled, not seeming to notice he was horizontal.

"'ys, 'fficer," he said. "Jst'adafew."

She could hardly arrest him, since she'd end up in a cell herself if she went near the station.

"There you are, Bantar," somebody said. "Not giving this nice lady any trouble, are you?"

The new arrival pushed another beer into Bantar's hand and winked. Yat tried her best to look casual while she sized him up. Tall, stocky, uniformed. Not police—army. Extensive scarring on his

228

hands, a telltale sign of combat enhancement. Walked with a slight limp, which meant he was no longer active service. Probably lost the leg and the fleshsmiths couldn't get it to grow back right; depending on whether he was a weathered thirty or a surprisingly well-kept forty, it could've been a pre-alchemy injury where things had been allowed to sit too long. Handsome once, perhaps, but his ears and face had a chewed-up look to them.

"C'mon," he said, picking the man up by his armpits, "let's get you back to your friends, ay?"

She should've stayed quiet. It would've been the smart thing to do, but courage had been serving her better than silence for, well, about a week. She was willing to accept that it was a new experiment with inconclusive results, but she wasn't about to let this go unchallenged.

"You sure he should keep drinking?" she said. "I think he's done for the night."

The big man laughed. "Nah, miss, he's just getting started, aren't ya, Bantar?"

He started to haul, and the hobnails in Bantar's boots clattered along the cobblestones.

"Br?" he mumbled.

"Yes," said the big man, "beer!"

The policeman had a wide smile on, but Yat didn't believe it—it was all teeth, no joy. He looked like he was working. She knew she should leave it alone, but she couldn't. It was time to stop ignoring the little things that were wrong.

"Who's your commanding officer?" she said. Sure, he was army, but they had no jurisdiction in Hainak; whenever they got called in, they worked under police supervision. It had happened a few times when Yat had been a cop, riots and whatnot where they needed backup. The soldiers did what the cops told them, then hopped on a train and went back to being soldiers . . . somewhere else. Somewhere ordinary citizens never mentioned. She swore she'd known once, but the memory just wasn't there.

He stopped and eyed the stripes on her uniform. "None of your business, *Constable*," he said. He let the last word fall out of his mouth like it didn't matter at all. With almost sarcastic care, he lowered Bantar to the pavement, then stepped over him. He was rubbing his right thumb between his left thumb and his forefinger. It was an oddly gentle movement for such a large man. "But you can call me Mr. Źao," he said, taking another step forward.

Her hand flew to her hip, and she felt the weight of her cnida, her thumb moved to the button and—

She felt a steel blade pressed against her neck, not quite hard enough to draw blood, but hard enough to send a message.

"This is my colleague," said Źao. "Mr. Źu."

She didn't turn, but somehow she knew what the man behind her would look like: wiry frame, sharp teeth, probably concealing a lion-head revolver somewhere on his person. *A big one and a small one.*

"Oh," she said.

"Yes," said that familiar, soothing voice. "Oh *indeed*. Pleasure to see you again, Constable. I see you've befriended our old friend."

They'd caught her unawares twice now: she'd been too busy watching the big man to notice the little one creeping up behind her. The difference was, she wasn't powerless this time. She wasn't scared, or high. And he *didn't* have the element of surprise: Źu had blown it to gloat. That was his first mistake.

The blade was metal, so that was no good: she tried to move her power along it, but it was totally inert. The ground was stone. She reached down anyway. In a nicer part of town it would've been granite, and she would've been screwed. Down in the Shambles, they laid whatever stone they could get their hands on, and the whole of Hainak was built on a bed of limestone. Thousands on thousands on thousands of tiny skeletons, all pressed together by enormous geological pressure. Creatures that had lived eons ago, unrecognizable to her even if she could see them, but creatures nonetheless. *Bone.* It wasn't great as living material, but it did the trick.

She pushed the button on her cnida, let the vine roll out and hit the ground. Touching the world was like grabbing ahold of a bundle of live wires—it burned, and that burn let you know you were still alive.

Yat heard a scream behind her, felt the blade fall away, jumped to the side, and saw the earth erupting with dozens of vines wrapping around Żu, stinging and stinging and stinging, leaving purple welts on his skin as his tongue swelled up and the muscles in his neck went far too tight. The cnida was running into the ground, branching out, feeding on the energy from the limestone, and growing larger. She tried to read Żu's threads, and that was the mistake.

He glowed like her. He'd been concealing it somehow, but in the throes of agony he couldn't hold it back anymore. She had reached out to read him, and in doing so connected in a braid of lightning. It was rushing into her, hollowing him out. She couldn't stop it: the connection between them was coring him, draining him, emptying him. Something vital ran down through the blaze into her, and she felt the golden fist inside herself curl and uncurl. She couldn't stop the flow: she was drinking him like she drank the parrot, but magnified a thousandfold. He was like her, and she was killing him—*really* killing him. It only took a fraction of a second to unfold.

She couldn't focus on anything but their connection, and that was when Żao hit her. She'd expected him to fight stupid, all shoves and haymakers. He certainly hit hard, but it was also precise—in exactly the place that would've ordinarily laid her out cold. She staggered and felt the connection between her and Żu begin to tear. He was still stuck in the vines, and she tried to refocus on them, to get them back under control.

The cracking of stone rang out from somewhere nearby, then a cacophony of shouts that quickly gave way to screams. She sensed a new network of threads emerging and realized with horror that the vines were spreading, radiating out through the limestone and bursting up through the ground. Judging from what she could hear, right in the middle of a group of revelers. It wasn't random: the cnida was hungry. She tasted copper and felt her hands start to shake.

Then Żao hit her again. He wasn't trying to knock her out now: his huge scarred fist went for her throat. She managed to lower her chin just in time, but the impact sent her staggering back into Żu. The tentacles brushed against her but didn't sting: she was still the heart to their network, and they recognized their mother.

Footsteps, heavy boots. *Lots* of them. She grabbed Żu by the shoulder—a little dying ember, almost empty—and tried to reach into him like she'd done before. There was so little left, but she grabbed it and pulled.

He went.

There were no other words for it. He'd been in a bad way and fading fast, but he'd been very much alive. When she pulled, she took *everything*. The change was so small and so total—he was alive, then he wasn't. She took his spark, pushed it into the vines, and watched as the street around her exploded into a sea of stinging tentacles.

Żao disappeared, and she couldn't sense him among the new forest of life she'd created. There was something else, though: many some-things, close to the ground. They'd been so similar to the limestone that she hadn't noticed them: millions of tiny, tiny somethings all packed together inside drunken Bantar's mouth and esophagus, and stomach. Millions of little spores, barely alive, that had been tearing through his body and eating from the inside out, yet still starving and starving until *here's the food*.

She didn't see what happened, but she felt it: an eruption from somewhere inside the strange anemone she'd summoned. Those little spores, moving along the network she'd created. She tried to shut them out, turning the dense cnidocyte inward; she managed to keep them away from her, but she couldn't stop them racing through the rest of her vines, erupting out among the stragglers from the party, among the approaching reinforcements, jumping high into the air and moving on the wind. The screams stopped, but that did noth-ing to calm her. Her heart pounded; her head and her back hurt. Żu's carcass was trapped in here with her. She wanted to spit on him, to scream and hit him, but she couldn't bring herself to touch him. His skin—which had been purple when he died—was quickly turning black. His tongue lolled madly in his open mouth. His knife lay on the ground, and his lion-head revolver was still strapped to his hip.

From somewhere outside her terrible new sanctuary, she heard the same heavy boots, but not stomping now: shuffling, clicking to-gether. Something forced its way through two thick vines: a leering face with milk-white eyes. A blank, but not. It lunged at her, teeth gnashing. The stings didn't seem to hurt it, and there was nowhere for her to go. She stepped back and brushed against Żu, whose body was still warm. Her hand touched metal, and she knew instantly what it was. She grabbed the gun, hands shaking, then raised the barrel and fired.

She had expected it to be loud, but not *this* loud. She had expected it to buck in her hand, but the concussion nearly broke her wrist. She felt her bones grind together as the revolver smashed backward into her hand. She'd been aiming for the middle of the blank's head—there was no torso visible, just a welt-covered face intruding into the anemone of vines—but the bullet caught his right temple and tore open half his skull. She only saw a second of it; the shot sent the man twisting away and out of sight. She could sense more of them, dozens of them, converging on the point, filled with a monstrous alien hunger.

She had to get out of here. The longer she stayed, the worse this would get. Her hands were still shaking from what she'd just done, and she felt a familiar panic rising in her. There was too much life around her: millions and millions of threads, all interlinked, and she knew that if she grabbed them, they'd blow her to pieces. She didn't want to die—she couldn't, not now. She knew it was an option, that it wouldn't *really* be the end, but she still wanted to run.

In the human soul, there is a little voice that screams at the thought of death. It did not, in that moment, matter that it would be temporary: it only mattered that she was going to die. It was the fear that had always made her lock up: *Tomorrow I might not be here, and I love this all so much—even when it hurts. I can't just leave. I don't want to die.*

She adjusted her grip on the cnida and felt its tendrils reaching out through the limestone. She could pull the magic from it, but then it would have to go somewhere, and she didn't know if she could take it back into herself without breaking. She scanned desperately for other life, but it was hopeless. There was only the cnida and the ravening blanks—everything else had either fled or been killed. Even the limestone wasn't giving anything up, the cnida having drained it of whatever bits of tiny power it had held. Each little crush of bone was empty for good, unable to be refilled.

She couldn't put it into a blank. It could break them open, but it could also make things much, much worse. Her mind went shrieking back to the art exhibit: blanks could survive things that normal humans couldn't. Lending one that kind of power could make it unstoppable. She had no choice but to take the energy into herself and hope it didn't kill her. She thought back to Ajat: there'd been an intent and direction to the way she'd worked magic back on the ship.

Focus, focus.

There was a glowing core of magic in everybody, and Yat's had been sitting perched in her chest like a hot coal, all fiery potential. She took a deep breath and felt it turn inside her like it was its own entity, sniffing at something on the air. She concentrated on it, and its warmth filled her. She unspooled it and reached down into the earth, grabbing at the central cluster of threads holding the giant cnidocyte together. The instant she made contact, the heat in her chest went from warmth to an all-consuming burn. The coal, the fist, the twisted ball of thread and fire—it threatened to explode inside her, and it was all she could do not to cry out. She could see her hands, which looked normal, completely at odds with how they felt: like they were being destroyed, the skin crackling and peeling away, the fat beneath boiling and running.

Focus.

She pulled on the threads, spun them, fed them into the new furnace in her chest. The cnida writhed, and its tentacles retreated into the earth—slowly at first, then in a wave moving out from her. Through the haze of pain, she saw chunks of shattered street and welt-covered purple bodies. The fire was the worst pain she'd ever felt, but it was exhilarating, too. Her father had once told her that *panic* was a moment of realizing that you were alive, and how perfect and fragile all was. Panic—for better or worse—meant you were touching the world. This was the purest panic: an energy she could barely contain, a flame that wouldn't go out.

And then it was gone. The cnida had retreated entirely into the device in her hand, and she was alone, standing in the remains of the shattered city street. Just her, the limestone, and the blanks—no sign of Źu or Źao. The bodies of the revelers lay cold and empty, dark smudges almost entirely without thread, except for the bacteria still churning in their stomachs, the occasional louse in their hair.

They turned toward her with milk-white eyes, and she ran. She couldn't untangle herself from the city's threads, and as she ran, she felt energy jackknife off her, springing from soul to soul, street to street. She didn't stop until she didn't recognize any of the buildings. There were no footsteps behind her, no slobbering animal hunger. It didn't matter; she could feel the city coming apart. She ran until she got lost, then kept going a bit more for good measure until her veins burned and her lungs seemed to push themselves flat against her ribs. She passed cleaners and stevedores and priests, and none of them seemed to want to bother a cop who had places to be. They looked like they had more pressing problems on their minds. She passed other officers, hands on their weapons, blowing whistles, running toward the hell she'd just made. Some of them tried to stop her, but she was moving too fast and none of them gave chase.

She couldn't get the moment of Żu's death out of her head. She'd hated him more than she'd known was possible, but it was another thing entirely to have taken his life, to be connected to him as his soul was pulled from his body. To break a person open and watch the pieces come out. It had never been like that in her books: the hero cut off the dragon's head, and it just . . . ended. It didn't go down discolored and covered in welts or fall, lopsided, with its skull torn open.

Whether they succeed or fail, a hero is defined by death.

As she ran, she could sense the birds in the air following behind, peering down at her. Dozens of them, hundreds, darkening the sky. Yat ran while the panic spread and the city came to life around her.

TWENTY-NINE

I want to show you this; you need to understand. I know it hurts, little bird, but you need to know what the stakes are. You need to know what happens when you fail.

The most skilled botanist in Hainak lives in Kecak Alley and darns socks for a living. Her name is Nelat-Kar. She was driven out of the academy for the sin of being a woman. They didn't expel her, they just made every little thing a little harder until she collapsed under the weight of it all and left on her own. She does not love her work, but the world makes it easier for her. She lives with her husband, Janek. He is not the handsome prince she'd hoped for, but he is kind and knows how to make her laugh.

They are at home when the first spore burst goes off. It shrouds their home in white powder that looks like flour. She is pregnant, but they don't know that yet. She is scared, but she makes a joke about it. Janek does not laugh.

Nelat-Kar doesn't know the specifics, but she's clever and she knows spores when she sees them. She and Janek seal the doors and *windows with wax and take an accounting of all their food and clean water. There isn't much—their work does not pay well enough for that.*

They are clever and responsible and so very brave. Even when the leering demons, these beasts of new flesh, appear out of the strange white mist, they do everything in their power to survive.

They do not. By morning, their house will be empty. The door will be scattered pieces of timber on the ground. Their flesh will be re-molded and repurposed; they would not even recognize each other, if they were able. This is the story of one house, little bird. There are a million houses in Hainak, the greatest city in the southern sea.

Night is coming for us.

It is not enough to be brave.

It is not enough to be clever.

It is not enough.

THIRTY

The constable couldn't've been older than eighteen. A borer had gotten him in the side, not enough to kill straightaway but enough to make sure he wasn't getting out of it. He couldn't stop crying. Sen held him while the neurotoxin hit his brain stem, while the first wave of convulsions swept through him and he began to foam at the mouth. Just some dumb kid who believed the stories. Sen felt the kid die in his arms. On a better day, he'd have brushed it aside, told himself he'd seen worse. Not today. Sen dragged the kid's body out of the street, said a short prayer, shut the boy's eyes, and laid a half-yan on each of them.

His skin was already blackening and peeling off when Sen left him. Stray round from one of the soldiers, junior officer in the wrong place at the wrong time. It was hard to tell what they were even fighting; everybody was being given conflicting orders. Nobody had even stopped to look after the kid—they'd just left him there and moved on. No point trying to chase down the shooter, who was half a league away on a rooftop somewhere. There was a trick to it that came when called: if you'd seen enough suffering, you learned to turn yourself to stone for a while. You did *that* enough, and you learned to make the statue walk.

There was something very wrong with the blanks. Sen had seen a man banging on a high window, shouting down at him. The blank had grabbed him, pushed against him, and . . .

Melted around him, merged with him, made his features run together. Turned his face into a jumble of parts. Sen barely had time to register what he was looking at; it ducked back out of sight, and he moved on as quickly as he could.

He found two officers in a restaurant cowering behind the bar. Gave them directions to the hotel and told them where to set up fortifications. Instructed them to hold position until he came back. Moved on.

A man with three arms, twitching in the street. A second face splitting off from the first, slightly above it. Two sets of teeth overlaid onto each other, melted together and forked like a snake's tongue. Two irises in his left eye, whirling madly and running together like egg yolks in a frying pan. Sen's hands shook, but everything had been shaking for days.

More cops, locked in a bank vault. They'd received orders to fire on the bank staff, but some had refused. The soldiers did it anyway: the place was a charnel house. The cops who hadn't had any qualms with it had left with the soldiers, expecting their friends to die. Instead, after those cops were locked in the vault, the creatures had moved on. Sen pointed them toward the hotel and continued down the block.

Somewhere out near the Shambles, a dog with a man's face cried out in pain. Its mouth had been remade into a snout like a dog's, but of puckered pink human flesh. It tried to bite Sen until he walloped it with the cane and sent it running off into the rats' nest of alleyways, shrieking in the voice of a child. Sen kept going.

Two dead soldiers in the shattered ruins of a florists' shop. One had a strange mottling around his eyes and an extra finger on each hand. Dozens of severed fingers lay on the ground around them. Must've been growing faster than he could cut them off. They'd shot each other at close range. Their bodies, leaning against each other, had begun to flow together. They weren't up and moving, but Sen had a suspicion it wouldn't take long. He hurried on.

At the docks ward, a mess of charred bodies at the base of a hastily assembled barricade. It was hard to tell how many of them had been infected. Medics pulled him inside, checked every inch of him, gave him a drink of something that burned his throat, and pointed him toward the station.

New banners on the facade. Or rather, old banners brought back: revolutionary colors, Crane symbols. The bin chickens still considered themselves heroes in all this. They'd helped, after all, hadn't they? They'd helped the ruling powers for five centuries, then helped the revolution when it looked like it might go a different way than expected.

Sen sighed to himself. Hell had come to earth, and he'd come to the bloody office. The building was designed to scare the shit out of anybody who thought of disobeying the law, and it certainly scared the ever-loving shit out of Sen.

The doors stood open.

There was nothing else to do: Sen went to work.

THIRTY-ONE

There was only one thing for it: Yat went home. Fugitives always did. She'd thought, in another life so little time ago but so very far away, that they were stupid or sentimental or weak. But she understood it now; when your whole world was shaken to pieces, you needed something familiar, just one thing that was the same as it had always been. She had another home now, somewhere out at sea, but that was out of reach and too new to really call home yet. She wanted to fall asleep in her own bed and wake up, realizing it had all been a dream. She wanted to have a cup of tea and read Dad's old book and pet that damned cat.

She watched her house from a nearby alley. Nobody came and went, though the door had obviously been kicked down: it lay twisted off its hinges. She tried to look inside, but it was still nighttime and the lights were off—she couldn't make anything out. After an hour or so, when the bleed of dawn was starting to make itself known over the horizon, she crept up to her front door and went inside.

They'd turned over every inch of the place. Her mattress lay on the floor, the sheets still half wrapped around it. All the drawers on her bedside table hung open like yawning mouths, and their contents were all gone. She felt a pang for her dad's book, which was probably somewhere in an evidence locker on the other side of town. They'd destroy it after everything got processed; old-world stories were illegal, after all. As if there hadn't already been enough evidence for the brass that she'd been a lost cause all along. *Yes, it's about a cat stealing a golden peanut from the gods. It's got little notes in the margins. "Squeaky voice here" for the talking peanut, surely the sign of a deranged mind.*

They'd always been looking for defects in her, as if women were defective men, and women who loved women were defective women who loved men. As if anybody who loved both wasn't a part of the equation and could be sorted into one or the other without their consultation. She would never be good enough, because she wasn't the person they wanted her to be. The *Kopek* had never asked her to be anything except herself.

They'd taken what little was left of her kiro stash, too. Some officer was probably very proud of the tiny bag of roots and stems he'd found. She hadn't been thinking about her next hit, but seeing the empty drawer made her hands shake and her teeth ache and her head hurt. She'd been shot in the head and nearly knocked senseless by a ship's mast, but those were ant bites compared to the pain that was threatening to split her skull in half. It was as if every cell in her body had a fishhook in it. She wanted to throw up, fall down, and sleep forever.

She made her bed. She didn't know why, but there was something horrible about the way they'd just left it there, scattered all over the place. She put the door back on its hinges and let the connective tissue start to regrow. After that, she went into the kitchen and found her teapot. They'd taken the tea bags—*perhaps that's where she's hiding the rest of the drugs!*—but left the pot. It still had some loose leaves in the bottom, so she filled it with hot water and let it stew while she sat on the bed with her head in her hands and tried not to cry.

When she'd grabbed Żu, the power had been so total that she couldn't possibly begin to resist it. It had carved through her heart like a river through stone. She'd wanted to hurt him, but things had gone so much further than she'd expected. Every time she got close to somebody now, she could feel the pull of their threads, as though their soul were saying *take me, take me with you*.

She couldn't control it. She couldn't jump, she couldn't make things grow—she could only kill. She'd probably killed the blank, the reinforcements, and Mr. Żao. She'd definitely killed the parrot and she'd killed Mr. Żu and she'd killed herself. She was a wicked thing, as dangerous as a knife, a bomb, a bullet. She was the villain from an old book: a queer little witch who stole from the living to make herself strong. Somebody who was on the outside because they deserved to be.

She cried until her throat burned, like she was purging herself of the unearthly fire she'd devoured from inside Żu's chest. She sat on the bed, rocking back and forth, unable to stop the tears.

The mattress depressed beside her, just a little, and she froze. For a moment she thought somebody had sat down next to her, but even with her eyes shut, she could sense it was too small to be human. She reached out for its threads and grabbed.

The cat yowled and tried to jump off the bed, but she was draining it now, and it could barely move. They were connected, and she couldn't break them apart. Its energy was flowing into her, and there was nothing she could do to stop it. The cat cried out in panic and confusion: she could feel its last embers dying.

Nonono, please, she thought, *not this, please, anything but this.* Nothing had been the same since that night at the docks, but this was a step too far. This was her *home*. She would not be made a killer here.

A river of fire ran between them. She wanted to save this stupid beautiful animal whose company meant the world to her. She couldn't stop the flow of magic, but she could change it. The river smashed into something hard, two words: *no more.*

One hand on the cat, one hand on the mattress. Specially treated cellulose on a wooden frame, attached to a fungal house. She let the energy from the cat run through her into the house, then—aching, with gritted teeth—she turned the flow around. The cat wasn't moving: its legs had been kicking, but they'd stopped and curled up under it. She knew if it died like this, there would be no bringing it back. She searched for the light inside it and found the tiniest spark. It was enough.

The magic resisted, pushing back: it wanted to be part of her. There was so much of it, a million strands of light flowing together. She fought it. She fought for Kiada, who was lost; for her father, who'd never had enough time; for empty stomachs and broken locks and sleepless nights. For Hainak and the *Kopek* and the bar with the white door and the goddamn squeaky peanut. And something changed. Something tiny but seismic; a single tremor, rolling beneath the earth, breaking open veins of molten soul, ready to set off an eruption.

She couldn't send it all to the cat; that would break apart its little body. The glow was moving back into it now, picking up speed. Its rear legs twitched and its chest heaved in and out. *Just a little more.*

She stood against the flow and pushed, just a little. The cat's eyes opened, and it yowled in pain. Crying out was good—that meant it was conscious, could feel something and express it.

"Shhh," she said. "Good cat, nice cat."

The house's threads kept pushing at her. She wasn't letting any more magic through, so it was building inside her, and she started to feel the same hellish heat as when she'd tried to pull back the cnida earlier. She pulled her hand away from the cat: though nothing was holding it there, it was as if her arm was made of lead. She stood and wrenched her other hand off the mattress.

Their connection severed, and she fell to her knees. She was almost spent.

Almost. A treacherous little word—*very nearly*, but also *not quite*.

The cat rubbed against her, purring. Strange creatures, cats. They would run away from kitchen implements but stare calmly at a passing train. You would never know how close this one had just come to death. She ran a tentative hand over its fur and didn't feel its threads catch. They twitched and seemed to seek out her heat, but it was under control.

She had never given the cat a name, because she'd been afraid of establishing the connection. She'd kept herself at arm's length from the world because she'd been afraid her touch would break it—that she was too different to fit, that she was poison. It was strange, then, that now that she could actually break it, she felt less scared. Maybe it was that she finally had *control*. An imperfect control, but better than she'd ever had. Though the wind would have its way, she was the one setting the course.

The cat purred, and she stroked its fur again. Its beat-up ginger coat reminded her of Fea, the cat from the book who'd stolen the golden peanut—*Fea*, an old-kingdom word for *red*.

"Fea," she said. "Red the Cat."

Red turned his head toward her. "Mrow?" he said. His threads seemed to hum like the strings of a harp waiting to be played. She took one thread—just one—and spun it around her finger. A trickle of energy moved along it, but she halted it and turned it back around. For a moment, it seemed to hang at the end of her finger, then it flipped back onto itself and floated back to Red. She realized that one of her own threads was twined with it. A small amount of herself was moving down into the cat, too. She was calm now, and she saw that calm reflected in her own threads. When her thread touched the cat, she saw it spread. *Calm.* Red rolled onto his back and purred.

She took her hand off Red and put it on the floor. The house's threads immediately sprang up and wrapped around her hand. They held the same impossible fire as before but didn't burn her. *Focus. Calm.*

The sentiment caught and spread down into the house. Some part of her wanted to merge with it fully, to take in all the energy at once. It was the same thing that always made her panic: the realization of just how *much* there was. How much skyline, how much ocean, how much could go wrong. The flip side of the coin from fear was *hunger*. It was the same voice she tried to numb with drugs: the mechanism that processed everything at once, then shut down screaming at the weight of it all.

Focus, calm.

The threads around her hand went loose, and she pulled away slowly. They let her go.

"Mrrrrp?" said Red. He'd rolled back onto his feet and was rubbing against her side. She picked him up and went over to the window. The warmth radiating from him helped her to stay calm. She scratched the top of his head and played with his threads: *calm, calm, happy*. To her surprise, the emotions hit the cat, magnified, and looped back to her, spreading up her arms and into her chest. She smiled and stared out at the city coming to life in the morning light.

"Nice cat," she said.

She'd become a cop because she'd wanted to do right. Instead, she'd done paperwork and turned her head the other way while her colleagues did wrong. She'd taken people in and never seen them again and been *proud* of it. Just assumed that because she'd filled out the right forms, they were going to the right places. She'd been a good cop because she did what she was told and never asked why. She'd had to leave home and come back for her to see it properly, the cruelty and indifference feeding one another. When everybody knows a certain part of town needs a heavier hand, that hand becomes a fist, and then everybody acts surprised when shit gets broken. This was *her* city, *her* home, and she couldn't keep being the same person if she wanted to make things right. Her agitation ran down the threads, and Red's tail began to whip back and forth. She shushed him and moved her hand over the top of his head, pressing his ears flat against his skull.

Hainak burned with a million souls fighting to live. They'd built walls to contain that life and systems to keep it in line, but it kept finding new ways to spill out, to live loudly in the quiet places. She didn't need to touch the threads or even see them to know they were there and that they mattered to her. She'd become a cop to do right, but right by whom? Not her beautiful city—some higher ideal that existed in stories but fell apart when it hit the street.

She put Red down and opened the window for him. He didn't move. She thought *home* at him, but that didn't change anything; he remained curled up on the bed. *Home, not here,* she thought, but Red didn't budge. She sighed, picked him up, and hoisted him onto the window ledge. He meowed in protest, then jumped across onto a nearby rooftop and sat there looking expectantly at her. She poked her head out after him.

"I'm not going t—"

Something changed in the threads of the house. They whipped reflexively toward something outside, and she followed them. The figure glowed blowtorch-hot. It was human in shape, but seemed impossibly *condensed*, like she'd been told gunpowder got when they packed it up for transport. One spark in a firework factory was enough to cause a catastrophe, since each barrel was enough to level a building. This spark-bomb of an entity was reaching out to the house, and she heard a familiar voice.

"Constable Hok," said Mr. Żao. "I know you're in there."

She hadn't sensed him before, but she hadn't sensed it in Żu either: he'd hidden his power until the moment he needed to use it. As Żao tied himself into the threads of the house, she felt a flash of a memory that wasn't her own.

—*two brothers playing in the sand while their mother brings in a basket of seaweed—*

—*huts at the mouth of a river that Yat recognized yet didn't—*

—*their father was a spear fisher with kind eyes who sang them the old songs—*

—*a fire that came down from the sky and cracked the earth, Mother grabbing the boys and diving beneath the water and realizing too late that the ocean was boiling—*

—looking up from the gallows at an invader's flag, always hungry to add more stars—

—wings unfolding, and kind eyes, and the softness of falling onto feathers—

—two brothers, a thousand years and a thousand more—

—as they traveled the ocean and slew the gray wyrm and left new cities in their wake—

—as they chased the crows all the way to the roof of the world—

—as Crane went mad and they went mad with her—

—as they filed their knives and teeth to points—

—and never forgot their mother—

—and love—

—and rage as the earth erupted and his brother's light went out forever—

—and fear, for there was work to do and a home to protect—

—and rage rage rage at the girl who ended the brotherhood of an eon—

"*Connnstable*," he said. "This hunt is over. It is a solemn time, and you should be kneeling." He dragged the last word out like he was chewing on it with his long, sharp teeth. The house spasmed, and a root shot out and wrapped around her ankle. She kicked her left foot free, but the tendrils around her right foot pierced into her ankle and began to drink. They split skin, tore between muscle, forced apart bone as they expanded and grew. A convulsion racked her body, and her withdrawal hit her all at once: she realized that her magic had been keeping the worst of it away, and that magic was now being torn out of her. Blood ran down her forehead into her eye, and she realized she was bleeding from the exact point where she'd been shot.

"I'm going to empty you, Constable," said the voice. "Won't that be nice? All that energy, all that movement, don't they shake you? I'm going to take them away and weave them together and get my brother back. I'm going to take your soul and use it to tear a hole in the heavens. I know you've been empty before—I can see your little thoughts, see what you did when your father died. I know where you got your scars, Constable. I'm going to finish the job."

The door creaked open. He stepped inside and closed it calmly behind him. He looked perfectly ordinary, and that was the worst part. He was wearing soldier's leathers, but she swore she'd seen him on patrol or in the mess hall or handing out infractions. She might've helped him fill out paperwork or helped him keep an eye on an unruly drunk while waiting for the wagon. His smile was wide and rigid, all teeth. As she watched, they grew and sharpened. Not orderly fangs like a cat's, but irregular spurs like an anglerfish's, pushed forward and interlocking in an ugly mess of bone in front of his mouth. It wasn't that hard to make dental implants, but these were biotech— no Lion operative would have access.

Stop assessing the goddamn tech. We're dying. We're dying. You don't want to die, remember? You only thought you did. Now run, girl, run.

He was coming closer, and she couldn't move. Her whole body ached, and she could feel the life fleeing from it. The pain came in waves. Blood coated half her face, and her vision blurred.

RUN.

A jolt went through her. She didn't know where it had come from. It lasted only a second, but she tore her feet from the floor— tearing flesh and muscle, cracking bone—turned on her heels, shrieking through the pain, and hurled herself out the window. It was only half-open from when she'd let Red out; she slammed into the frame, twisted in the air, landed awkwardly on the next-door roof, and felt something in her arm shatter. The cat yowled and jumped out of the way. She tried to stand, but the pain tore at every muscle and joint.

RUN.

She tried to pull magic from the neighbor's house, but it was long abandoned and hadn't eaten in months—there was enough there to stop the bleeding, but not much more. She ran her sense along the house's root system. There was hunger there; it had been empty for a long time. There was a tea shop below, but the apartment's owner was an old man who lived alone, and the house was built for a family. In its hunger, it had reached out a tendril and linked up with her own house. She could still feel Żao inside her room, trying to find a way to get to her. Bone spurs had grown out of his arms now, piercing through his uniform.

And coming up the stairs from behind Żao was an ordinary little human light. It was her turn to think it now: *Run, you idiot, run! Whoever you are, run.* It wasn't listening—it was picking up speed. Żao sensed it, too. The figure hit the door with a bang, and it flew open: light spilling into the house, throwing Żao's shadow over the window box. He spun and thrust his arm toward the door. With a tearing of flesh, a bone spur ripped its way out of his forearm and hurtled through the air.

It hit nothing.

She could feel her own heart thudding against her ribs and she could taste her own blood. She didn't know how much power she had left, but she sensed that if she pushed it, she'd come apart at the seams. She couldn't save the person about to come through, but she needed to try. She sent her threads through the house, searching, and found the teapot. Leaves in the bottom, basically dead, but still with the tiniest spark. She grabbed it and pulled. They grew so quickly that the teapot jumped into the air and clattered against the wall. Żao turned, only for an instant. . . .

And Wajet came through the door shooting. Big, heavy revolver, another Lion firearm. She could sense Żao's shock. He reached out to take control of the gun, but it wasn't Hainak tech, and he couldn't manipulate steel. The first two shots took him in the chest, soaking the window box in blood. The third took him right between the eyes. The back of his skull detonated with a sick, wet crack. For a moment, she didn't understand what she was seeing: his head was the wrong shape, all bone splinters and weeping gray matter. In that curious moment, she dissociated and saw congee. The congee inside his head was spilling everywhere. How could he be so clumsy?

He lurched back and fell across the window frame, almost as if he were leaning out to relax in the sun. She laughed; she couldn't help it. It was such a silly thing, to see the congee man enjoying a lovely day. Then his neck rolled back with a series of concussive cracks and his brains spilled out the window, across the window box, down the wall, and reality reasserted itself.

The magic block cleared; Yat didn't realize how totally he'd cut her off from the weave, but energy flowed back into her. The bones in her shoulder clicked painfully back into place, and she cried out as a carpal spasm wrenched her hand into a claw. In the window, Żao's body was slumped out of sight. Wajet stood in the doorway, breathing heavily. He holstered his gun, then walked to the window. No casual saunter now, but a quick, efficient march.

"Constable Yat," he said.

"Sergeant," she said. She brought her hand lazily up to her forehead and gave a weak salute. Bile burned her throat, and she retched once, twice. She tried to stand up, but the muscles in her legs responded with spasms of pain, and she collapsed. She tried to reach into the house, then gave up and lay stiff on her back.

"Sergeant," she said, "it's something a.m., and all's not well."

He sighed. "Come on," he said, "we've got shit to do."

Red rubbed against her legs. She nodded weakly at Wajet and tried not to faint.

THIRTY-TWO

Sen had been to war. He'd been a young man during the revolution, seen brother strike down brother, cavalry charging into protesters, folk go house to house to burn anybody who spoke the wrong words. He'd been at Syalong Cherta, seen ten thousand Ladowain soldiers throw themselves against the bastion's impossible walls, the bleeding-edge splices killing half the men they were meant to enhance. He'd seen a lot of ugly things. They tended to be spontaneous, a sudden fire in the brain that made somebody haul off and do evil and attempt to justify it to themselves in the morning. This evil in front of him today was an entirely different color, the sort of thing he'd seen in the bunkers *beneath* Syalong Cherta and been ordered to forget; ancient, hermetically preserved corpses in prison jumpsuits staring up sightlessly from behind smash-proof glass, men in lab coats, whose bodies had turned dark and hard as oak instead of rotting away, lined up against a wall.

This was premeditated.

At first, he'd thought the station at the docks was abandoned.

There was nobody in the foyer waiting for their shift to end. There were no signs of disturbance or flight. It was exactly the same foyer, just . . . empty. Pushing aside the wrongness of it, he made his way to the little staff kitchenette. Somebody had raided the coffee tin, but there was enough clinging to the bottom for a cup, so he put the kettle on and—for the first time in what was probably an hour or two but felt like a thousand years—he sat down and was alone with his thoughts. Just him and his heartbeat, and the rising whistle of steam. He tried not to think about the dying kid, then he thought about the dying kid, until the kettle pinged and brought him back to the quiet beige-walled world of the station. His hands shook while he poured boiling water into the cup, and he had to fight to avoid spilling it as he set off deeper, into the guts of the station, and that was when he saw them.

The fucking bin chickens.

Dozens of them, wandering the halls, shepherding the officers toward the main conference room. He was taken gently but firmly by the arm and guided along with the rest of the force. The room was packed. Somebody had taken the table out and placed a lectern at the front. Captain Trezet stood at it, adjusting the little Tinker's Horn they'd installed. He'd never been good with tech. He tapped it, then blew on it.

The last week of the dry season was hell, and everybody knew it, the humidity building up and building up until walking down the street took the same effort as swimming. People always went mad in that week: killed their families, killed themselves. It was invisible but inescapable: the crushing pressure of storms to come. Sen felt it acutely in this room, potential energy packed too tight, ready to burst. Light in the eyes of the officers, the resolve on Trezet's jaw. Every man in the room knew what was coming and had already resolved to say yes. The specifics didn't matter: Trezet would speak about order and how he hated to use force but it was necessary to protect the city. He'd speak about his friends in the priesthood and their concerns, and then an institutional scythe would whirl out and not stop until somebody stopped it or it ran out of things to reap.

Motherfucking *cops*.

Many of them had been on the wrong side of the revolution, and everybody had agreed to forget about it because they did their jobs and didn't bother the wrong class of person. There were men in the office wearing traitors' colors who openly flouted the law, and that was okay, because they were cops, but gods forbid they found you walking home after curfew. Gods forbid you didn't have enough cash in hand to pay a bribe or didn't look like you did. Everybody broke the law: it was just a matter of who you wanted to hurt for it.

Most of the officers in the room weren't bad sorts. He couldn't see Varazzo, for one. These were the middle-of-the-road guys, the smilers, the ones who looked after their kids. There were just enough of the other sort of officer to matter, almost as though it weren't an accident. You put a nice cheery middle-of-the-road lad next to a screaming madman, and he'd eventually smile and nod and start saying, "Hmm, yes," to each scream and never think to stop it.

"Some of you," said Trezet, "are aware of the unfolding situation. For those who aren't, there has been another major incident, which is currently unresolved. The city has been placed under martial law; we're following orders from the army moving forward. I will not ask any of you to stay tonight, but those who leave will not be asked to return in the morning. Our city has been rotting from the inside, and we've let it happen. We let criminals flout the law. In their bars, in their enclaves—"

—in their manicured streets, Sen thought, *in their gardens, in their proprietary houses—*

"—in alleyways and brothels—"

—in churches and banks—

"—right beneath our very noses."

—right above our heads.

Sen knew what came next. He knew there wouldn't be many who'd refuse, and those who stayed would have themselves a very bad night. They hadn't warmed themselves up to evil yet, and Sen wasn't sticking around to watch it happen. An arsenal of loose cannons, each one thinking he needed to kill for the good of the city. Sen nudged the priest beside him.

"I gotta take a piss," he said, then pushed past and slipped out through the door. His bin chicken paused, then moved to follow him. New convert, most likely. Still hadn't picked up the bulletproof righteous authority of a proper clergyman. That was good, that was usable. Sen shot him a withering look.

"I know the way, mate," he said. He tried to sound formidable, but he just sounded tired. It seemed to work anyway. The priest went back into the conference room. The door shut, then Sen heard the unmistakable sound of the latch sliding home. Locked in. He immediately turned and made for the exit.

Sen hobbled out into the entrance foyer. Each step sent a lance of pain up his leg. The doors were wide open. He could see smoke rising in the distance and hear shouting. It was chaos, but it was better than whatever was happening with his former colleagues. There were people out there willing to help, which he couldn't say of anybody inside the precinct. He took another step forward, and Varazzo stepped out into the light. He had his hand on the hilt of his sword.

Totally against regulations, but it seemed like the place was going to the dogs anyway.

"You leaving?" said Varazzo.

"Yeah, mate," said Sen. "Just hitting the clock, ay. You wouldn't believe the day I've had." He put his coffee down on one of the side tables and pulled out his punch card. He slotted it in and waited for the *ka-chunk* and the hiss of the enzymes activating. It never came. He shrugged and left it in the machine, then picked his coffee back up and took a sip.

Varazzo drew his sword. It was practically soundless: the sheath must've cost a mint. This was the first time Sen got a good look at the blade—long and thin, but with a slicing edge. Espada ropera: he'd seen mercs carrying them while he was stationed up near the border. They could do incredible damage. Primitive, but highly effective. *It'd be great*, thought Sen, *if Wajet had given me a bloody sword.*

"You're funny, Sen," said Varazzo. "It's a pity you chose the wrong side. I'll say a few zingers at your funeral."

"Better start writing 'em now," said Sen. "I reckon it might take you a while."

Varazzo lunged. He held his sword high in one hand, point forward. Sen had one bung leg, a cane, and a cup of coffee. He could barely stand up straight. He was also the dirtiest fighter on the fucking force. He pushed off with his cane, pivoted on his good leg, torqued his body around and flicked his wrist. Scalding-hot coffee hit Varazzo in the face. He screamed. His thrust kept on its path, but Sen was no longer there, and the blade clattered off the wall. Still blinded, Varazzo swung haphazardly. Sen kicked forward with his bad leg, balanced on his good one, and let his whole body float backward. The blade sailed over his chest as the same moment his foot crashed into Varazzo's cock. His leg hurt like hell, but the movement seemed to hurt Varazzo worse.

They broke apart, Sen leaning against the wall to stay upright and Varazzo blinking through coffee, a little bow-legged but still clutching his sword.

"You could've been one of us, Kanq-Sen," spat Varazzo. "You could've been *somebody*. Instead, you stand with *them*. And you're gonna die with them."

He raised his rapier, blade pointed at Sen's throat. He pulled back his elbow and struck. Sen twisted as much as he could but knew it wouldn't be enough. With the last of his strength, he flicked his wrist again and brought the cup in front of the blade. It smashed through the cheap tin, but the shock of hitting metal twisted it just enough. It cut across Sen's jaw and went deep, hitting bone. Through a haze of pain, he twisted the coffee cup, snatched up his cane, and brought it down on the sword, right at the point where the blade met the hilt. The blade shattered with a wrenching of steel, and Sen brought the cane up into Varazzo's chin. He swore he could hear teeth splintering. The big man went over backward and cracked his head against the polished marble of the foyer.

"Yeah, nah," said Sen, "I'm good. Tell Trezet I quit."

Varazzo looked like he was ready to say something else, but Sen hit him in the face with the tip of the cane. He went still. Sen stepped over him and left the station.

THIRTY-THREE

Wajet paced the room. He was talking, but not to Yat—more like talking at the air while she nodded and gave the occasional supportive *mhm*. Her body was still reknitting itself together, a painful process. They'd relocated to the foreman's office on the top floor of a warehouse a few precincts away, with windows overlooking the Grand Canal. The building had its own small tributary built into the bottom floor, with a decrepit rowboat bobbing up and down in it. She barely remembered the trip. There was a broken sink in the bathroom, and Yat had tried to clean the blood off her face there but only succeeded in spreading it around. She was leaning against a wall now, making sure all her pieces were still there. Red hadn't left her side, and the gentle music of his purr helped calm her down. It wasn't entirely succeeding, but it was better than nothing. She gave him a pat and winced as her nerves sent another shriek of pain through her arm.

"I went to the university. No one there is talking," said Wajet. He twirled his hand for a moment as he sought out his next thought. "They sent a man out to speak to me, but once he saw my face, he clammed up and left. They opened the gate for a uniform, which tells us something."

"Mhm," she thought she said aloud, though the word didn't feel like her own. It was like hearing an echo of herself. Somebody blew a whistle outside, and the beggar's trumpets responded. The sound moved away from them, and they stood in silence until it was gone.

"So," Wajet carried on, "they're not talking to just *anybody*. Our two gents had army uniforms. If they were following protocol, that would put them under police jurisdiction within city walls, but I haven't heard a thing about either of them. Might just be above my head, but we should mark it down as suspicious."

"Two of them," she muttered.

"Yeah," he said. "Haven't seen the little guy all day, which means he's somewhere around."

"You know them," she said. She wished now that she'd asked him earlier; maybe they wouldn't have been able to get the jump on her if she'd known about them before.

"By reputation," he said. "I was under the impression they'd fallen foul of, well, something very much like this. Sibbi said they've been out of action for almost a thousand years, which raises the question of exactly what they've been *doing* this whole time. She thought they were dead, but I can only assume they were making plans."

Wajet sighed and slumped down beside her. "This magic thing isn't exactly my wheelhouse, so take everything with a grain of salt, but here's my understanding: you've been told what happens if you come back once too often, and that's it," he said. "They're splintered men. But they were heroes once, you know. Used to be the Brothers Tikmanak, although they dropped that name a long time ago. They take new ones every time they come back. I'm told they killed a taniwha, a terrible thing to do. No wise man kills a guardian. They must've been desperate to find out what it was guarding."

Even with all the impossibilities she'd had to deal with, this was too far. She shook her head. "That would make them tens of thousands of years old," she said.

It wasn't impossible, though. She'd felt it while she'd been inside Żao. So many lives, the force of millennia bearing down and chipping away at his soul like the wind turning a mountain to dust. There was something else: he thought he was protecting the city. It had made no sense. Her body ached. *Focus. Work with the data you've got.* She didn't trust Wajet, but he was her only immediate lifeline, and he might have pieces of the puzzle that she was missing. If he'd wanted her dead, he would've let Żao kill her. She took a deep breath.

"They were putting spores in the beer," she said. "I walked in on it. They were plying people with booze at the parade. That's how this started. There were spores on the missing ship, right? Something dangerous. This fits the bill."

"That's half of it," said Wajet. "The other half is . . ."

He stared at her, then shook his head and sighed. "They're the Sparrows," he said. "I didn't know it was *them* until recently, but I knew they existed. It's hard to get promoted above a certain rank without hearing about them. You can't hide that sort of thing, so you don't. You just say it like it's a joke over and over again, and it gets picked up and nobody can talk about it seriously. The un-secret police, what a laugh. If they're involved in this, then the force are, too. That's why the university sent a man out to see me: they know, and they know we know. I've never mentioned this to anyone outside the *Kopek*—anybody who talks ends up a blank in a heartbeat. That's the other half of how they've kept it under wraps for so long."

"The Sparrows," she spat. "Great. You got any more folktales for me? 'Cause two feels like enough for today."

She didn't mean to sound so bitter. He'd been more open with her than she'd expected, though it could still all be a lie. But if the last few days had changed her in any way, they'd opened her up to trust.

He was still staring at her, his expression filled with concern.

"If we make it through this," she said, "and there's any city left in the morning, I'm going to shout about the Sparrows to anyone who will listen. I won't mention you, but if this falls back on you, there's nothing I can do about it."

His face went card-player stoic, but his strings stirred, agitated.

"I can live with that," he said.

"What I don't understand," she said, "is what the brass gets out of this. They're hurting people. They're hurting *themselves*—how many men are they going to lose tonight? Even if the men at street level don't know, somebody must."

"Isn't it obvious?" said Wajet. "To scare people."

Then it hit her. The revolution had been all sorts of folks: students and bakers and sweepers and streetwalkers and cops and chemists. In the ten years since, a strange peace had held between the authorities and the people: Parliament. Sure, they fought and argued, but the city moved forward. The police played only a small role in the system, and she knew many officers resented that fact; they thought things would be better if *they* were both the voices and the enforcers of law. Cops were *heroes*, after all, and who opposed heroes? A poisonous thought curled itself around her mind, seductive in its simplicity. If you were on the side of the law, then anybody who said *no* was on the side of evil. You didn't negotiate with evil, you beat it. You did so with force or with cunning, but either way, you beat it until it stopped moving. All the storybooks said so.

"Oh *gods*," she moaned. "This was about the election."

"The election," he said, nodding. "Provisional government, right? Meant to be temporary. It's a wonder it's lasted this long at all. Say you're part of a fragile coalition, a dozen small quarreling parties, barely holding on to power. You want to break it apart and remake something more amenable to your goals. People get scared, and whose star rises? The cops, the church. Folks rally around the flag. That's why Ladowain hasn't attacked: it was never going to. It was about making people think they *could* attack at any moment. Syalong Cherta made everybody feel safe—no army was getting past it, and the naval blockade had kept them from going via the sea, but commandos slipping through the cracks? Sure, and that's what they needed us to think. If there are bad guys *over there*, you send your men there, but if there could be bad guys *anywhere*, then—"

"Cops everywhere," finished Yat. "More patrols, more churches, more money."

He was pacing back and forth, which made her anxious, but she continued, keeping a select few suspicions hidden.

"More seats in Parliament," she said. "So you hire two very special men and have them make a mess. They do it again and again, and you keep escalating until people are mad with fear. Then you walk in and tell them you can make it stop, if only they give you all the little things that don't matter, and you take all those little things and you crush them. What I don't understand is what the brothers get out of it. I suspect Sibbi and I need to have a conversation when this is over."

They sat in silence for a while. She stood by the window and

watched the city. They were in an odd part of town: the middle of the
north side, along the canal. Foreign merchants used to stay here on
trips, before the revolution and the apparently endless civil wars on
the Eastern Shelf had made things too difficult.

The warehouse was part of a long chain of them running the
length of the canal, but directly across from them were cafés, sweet-
shops, a run-down hotel in the old Ladowain style. A rough barricade had been erected at the hotel's main doors, and the windows
were boarded over. She could see figures moving around inside. A
broad, well-made bridge crossed the water between, wide enough for
market stalls to be set up along the sides. The mechanisms to lift
the bridge had long since jammed, and nobody had a reason to fix
them. The stalls lay abandoned, their produce strewn over the bridge.
Beyond it in front of the hotel was a small square with a statue of
the Brothers Tikmanak bedecked in flowers. They looked different in
copper, both tall, broad, and handsome, but she doubted the sculptor
had based them off the real thing—nobody knew what they actually
looked like, after all. They were just a myth.

"We can stay here for now," said Wajet. "It's safe. Sibbi's swinging around in about three hours. We can take the rowboat up the
canal to the docks, but I don't think we'll want to linger there. We
jumped ahead of the navy, but the vanguard'll be in the harbor
before midnight, and then we're fucked. Another jump would be
suicide."

Yat reached out into the city and felt a numbness spreading from
the point where she'd ruined the brothers' party. Everywhere else
was alive with threads, energy, and emotion, but there was something metastasizing, swallowing the city block by block, soul by soul.
It was far enough away, at least for now.

A little girl peered out at her from between the slats over the hotel window and waved. Yat waved back, but the girl had already disappeared.

The warehouse was made of brick, which made it hard to reach out into the city. Even overgrown with vines, it seemed to dull any threads on the other side. Wajet paced back and forth, hand on his gun. Yat sat down in a small clutch of weeds that had spread up through the floor and let her consciousness seep out into the city.

There was nothing at first: little fits and starts, but there was still an overall order to things. Lots of anxiety but no panic. As the afternoon wore on, that changed.

—gods, it's just chairs and tables, what sort of a barricade is this—

—Wajet got him the stick, we can trace it—

—oh gods oh gods oh gods, Vara, please, it's me—

—somewhere off the Grand Canal, haven't got a lock—

—can't even get into the docks now, they've pulled the bridges—

—unknown. They blew early—

—please, I don't want to die in here—

She pulled back. The flurry of voices was disorienting and difficult to navigate, but she thought back to her time with Ajat and the heart.

Focus.

One voice was different, still with a hint of panic, but not blind. She turned to it and dove.

—"moving ahead as planned," said Varazzo. The officer in front of him had no uniform, but there was something about his manner that said he was accustomed to being obeyed. Built like a brick shithouse, with chemical burns all over his hands and face. Another little man followed him around, taking notes. Dr. Jakuda, on assignment from

the university. There were bags under his eyes, but he was smiling and bobbing up and down.

Despite all the chaos, Varazzo wasn't nervous; he was excited. The city was a mess, but they'd always refused to let him help—that was gonna change. They'd look at him and beg for his help, and he'd magnanimously offer it, and they'd be fucking grateful for once. They'd always treated him like a joke because he saw what a degenerate mess it all was. That godsdamned cripple wouldn't be laughing for long. Varazzo's face was still raw from the steaming coffee, and his teeth ached from the whack he'd been given. But now more than ever, Hainak needed courage and strength; it needed heroes, and it was gonna get some. He was grateful to the Sparrows and the brass and even that little degenerate rat whore who'd almost gotten him killed. Sabotaged the borer nest somehow: must've planted something on him. Still, that stay in the infirmary had set him up to meet a very important benefactor and be given a crucial mission. They'd given him a few enhancements to get him back on his feet: toughened him up with a few special injections and infusions. The burns on his face were half-healed already.

"It is imperative that no spores cross the wall," said Jakuda. "Containment is our number one priority. If the wind changes, we'll need to move the launch site. Are your officers ready?"

They were, but the hyperactive shit could hang a little. He wasn't the one giving orders, Žao was, and he should know better than to question the force like that. Civilians didn't know what it was like and always tried to push cops around. He chewed on the thought for a moment, and Mr. Žao cleared his throat.

"Sergeant Varazzo," he said. *Sergeant. Varazzo smiled. One day, it would be Commissioner Varazzo, President Varazzo.*

"Yes, sir, they're ready. We already shut off the docks and all the main gates out of the city. Anybody slips the net, we've got riflemen waiting for them on the roads. Anybody who tries to leave will be borer food."

"And the wall?"

"We've got a man tracking the wind, and I'll alert you if anything changes."

"No mistakes, Sergeant Varazzo," he said. "This could be big for you. If you do well today, I'll make sure they hear about it upstairs. But if you do poorly, I'll make damn sure they know."

"Yes, sir," he said again. Mr. Żao was a good man who knew that a good cop couldn't work effectively with all that paperwork and oversight—that you needed to break the rules sometimes in order to enforce them. A single trained officer was clever, but in general, people were stupid and panicky and needed a firm hand. Sheep needed shepherds, lest they fall to the wolves. The brass didn't see that yet, but they would. Tonight was the nigh—

Something hauled Yat out of Varazzo's mind. Wajet was standing over her, shouting, shaking her by the collar. A bang of flesh on metal rang out, and the warehouse's main door buckled.

Yat jerked to her feet. Red hissed and leapt out of her lap as she drew the lion revolver and pointed it. It made her wrist ache just thinking about firing it. She tried to reach out with her threads and see what was behind the door, but its iron wouldn't let her through.

She didn't need to wait long: a second impact punched a hole through the door, and a canine snout shoved itself through, snarling. It snapped its jaw and pushed, and the metal bent around it—sightless eyes, missing patches of fur, and patches of white fungus growing on its exposed skin.

Wajet got to the trigger before she did, and his shot smashed into the metal in a shower of sparks. "*Pokokōhua*," he swore. The head withdrew, a third impact hit the door, and the whole thing came down.

The dog wasn't the worst of it; the *dog* was somewhere just above the creature's waist, which was a head and a single broken foreleg jutting out uselessly. The beast stood on its hind legs like a man, though those legs were large, powerful, and hooved. A muscular tail whipped across the ground, and Yat realized in horror that it was a cnidocyte. The top half was even more terrifying, a mess of flesh and fur from a dozen different animals. Screeching faces—cats, dogs, birds, horses—stared blindly out from it. The bulk of it appeared to be two men, merged at the collarbone. One's head was twisted at an awful angle, and the top of his skull merged with the other head's jaw. One arm was monstrous and clawed, while the other was withered and bent back. The whole creature was blanketed by patches of white fungus that seemed to warp and grow as she watched. It yowled and brayed and shrieked in a dozen voices as it took a jerking step toward them, bracing against the ruins of the door with its good hand while its tail slammed against the ground.

She tried to reach into it, but its threads were impossible to grasp: dozens of different creatures all tangled together in a knot. She pulled at them anyway, but their resistance made her stumble, and she could taste blood—she was only making the knot tighter.

The concussive blast of Wajet's gun made her ears ring. This bullet found its mark: it smashed into the beast's chest and sent it reeling backward. As the bullet sank in, an eruption of spores spurted out toward them. They came out as loose powder, floating in the air, but coalesced immediately into a whiplike tentacle over the bullet hole. The new growth pushed the creature's upper body back, and its vertebrae played an awful clicking melody. It took another step into the room, and the tentacle lashed out toward Yat. She jumped back, and it swept through the air in front of her face, leaving a trail of spores hanging in the air behind it. The movement threw the beast off-balance, and it staggered toward them, pulled along by its tail.

Wajet fired again and again, filling the air with spores. Yat could feel their threads: minuscule little creatures, millions and millions of them—a city in miniature. They were reaching out to her, calling to her, but there was a hunger to them—they wanted to consume her, to take away everything that made her *her* and replace it with numbness and calm. They were close now, so close, following the pull of her breath toward her mouth and nose. She clamped her hand over her face and stepped back, but moved too fast, and her feet tangled together. She fell, and her head cracked against the cold warehouse floor. Floating lights exploded into her vision, and she had a moment of blind panic as her mind screamed, *They're in your eyes, the spores are in your eyes*. She rolled along the ground and heard Wajet fire off his last three shots.

The air was still filled with spores, searching. She grabbed at just one and pulled at its thread; it went out, and she felt its energy join her own—small, but so much larger than expected. They were packed with life. Her head cleared, and she sprang to her feet using old roof-rat reflexes she didn't even know she still had.

She backed up, fired, and struck the beast in the side below a mangled human leg. It staggered, and she fired twice more at the same spot. The spore expulsions roiled outward and warped back around onto the wound, but the impact had knocked the creature sideways. Its heads shrieked in awful harmony, and it toppled and fell, landing on its muscular hand. Its bones cracked as fungus filled the bullet holes and warped its body. It twisted over backward, and one of its flailing human legs found the ground. It was bent backward—if it did have a front and back—on all fours: two horse legs, one human leg, and its monstrous arm. Its twin heads screeched at her, their foreheads scraping the ground and their hair dragging behind them. The cnida whipped around and wove back and forth over its back in tight, quick, powerful movements like a scorpion's stinger. It struck at Yat, and she jumped backward, her back hitting the wall as the cnida hit her face.

The pain was worse than anything she'd ever felt: worse than being shot, worse than taking in the whole city's threads at once. Every nerve ending shrieked, and she felt her legs collapse beneath her. Felt herself sliding along the wall, the spores rushing toward her, all hunger hunger hunger. She reached out for something—anything—to stop them from getting in and . . .

She jumped.

THIRTY-FOUR

See me, creature, see me through the glitch; I am the place where it begins. See me as I spread my broken arms wide like wings and the world falls beneath their shadow. I am chapel and tree, I am the shattered roof of heaven as it leaks black blood, I am the smell of distant snowmelt, I am twelve iron spears that clash in the dripping dark, and you, you, hurtling through endless night, but not dead this time, no, not dead, just taking a little shortcut through the back roads, the roads you can't see unless you knew they were there, unless you'd been there before, unless you were broken and stitched back together, unless you were—

Hello, little monkey.

Do you see me?

I see you.

THIRTY-FIVE

Her back slid down the wall, but not brick this time—just safe, comforting wood. When Sibbi had jumped, there'd been a profound sense of direction and intent. With Monkey, it was like slipping through an unknown door in the back of the universe. That was Monkey Weaving, the way of secret roads. That was how he stayed alive: even *he* didn't know where he was going, so nobody else could predict it.

She braced a hand against the wall and felt its energy flow into her, invigorating her. She couldn't stop the flow, but she didn't want to. Her cheek burned where the cnida had touched her, but the warmth flooding into her kept the worst of it from reaching her core; it didn't numb the pain, simply overwhelmed it with its own fire. She reached out into her environment—no spores, thankfully. The room had a water heater and not much else: it was only by sheer luck she hadn't ended up inside the thing. She could hear water running through the pipes.

She needed to go back—Wajet was still fighting that creature. She had no love for the man, but she couldn't let him die like that. Or, *die* didn't seem like the right word—she couldn't let him become part of that mess. All of this was her fault: she'd unleashed something on Hainak when she'd killed Źu. It might have been an accident, but somebody else was trying to do it on purpose, and this was just the beginning. When she'd reached out, what she'd seen deep beneath the creature's boundless hunger was intent. This wasn't mindless consumption: it was building something.

She tried to remember what it was but felt like she was grabbing at fog. It was something that went up above the wall and the sun and reached out with febrile tendrils into the heavens. Something whose shadow would darken the world. But what? A tree, a lake, a child . . . random images that meant nothing.

She needed to figure out where she was. She opened the door of the water-heater room and found herself in what looked like a hotel. Nice carpets, but covered in muddy boot prints. A tall woman in uniform pushed past her, not paying her any mind; she recognized her from the canteen back at the dock ward station, though they'd never really spoken. Another officer pushed past, then a third. They weren't running, but they had their hands on their weapons and their eyes firmly forward. Yat kept her helmet's brim low over her face and let them pass. The fourth officer was Sen.

He walked with a cane, swinging his left leg stiffly. He had bags under his eyes, and she could've sworn he had more gray hair than when she'd last seen him. She kept her brim low as he passed. His cane rattled as it struck the carpet. She leaned against the wall and nodded at him as he passed, trying to look casual. The door directly across from her was open; the room inside was sumptuous, full of red silks and intricate biowork. A large window cut across the far wall, and an officer in a gas mask looked down on the street below and took notes. He opened the window and peered out at something. She could hear shouts from the street.

"You," said Sen, "with me."

It took Yat a moment to realize he was talking to her, and she looked up. Recognition dawned in Sen's eyes, and she felt his threads light up with surprise, confusion, rage. She tried to reach out and pacify him, but her own heart was racing. She didn't trust her magic not to hurt him, so she reached out the normal way and grabbed his wrist. Despite his injuries, he'd retained a wiry strength. But she held him there, sinking her chewed-up nails into his arm. She looked him in the eye and saw his fear. He wanted to hurt her before she hurt him again. A week ago, she would've felt the same. But he'd had faith in her, even then—when she hadn't had faith in herself.

The other officers had stopped and were staring at her. They were all wearing their uniform, but none were wearing badges. Sen's uniform had a small tear where the pin had been. She could see snatches of his thoughts: *chaos in the streets, uniforms shooting uniforms, survivors regrouping and trying to do the jobs they no longer had. The last of the good cops, united in accidental rebellion. Something in the powder, something terrible in the fucking powder.* He was open to her now, and she let herself be open to him too, showing him her death, her dreams, the bottomless strangeness of the last few days.

She let him go and took a step back.

"Do you trust me?" she said.

"Sure," he said, though she could swear his voice had just gone up an octave.

"Good," she said. "You're learning, fuckwit."

He slouched over his cane. The other officers were still staring at him, and he waved a lazy hand at them. They took their hands off their weapons and went back to work. He smiled at Yat, though his eyes weren't entirely behind it. Wounds didn't heal so quickly.

"Today has stretched the limits of believability pretty far," he said, "so I want you to understand, Constable Hok, that when I tell you that what happened just now was weird, it was weird even by the standards of a very, very weird day. Gods above and below, here's hoping we've hit the roof on strangeness." He paused for a moment. "It's good to see you, kid."

The man at the window was shouting something to muffled voices down below. A few officers with rifles pushed past them and threw open the windows. Their borers opened up with a series of wet thumps, and she heard a ghastly, inhuman shriek from the street below, followed by a familiar voice.

"GODSDAMNED JELLY-ARSED MISMATCHED GALLOWS-BIRD," boomed Wajet. "COWARD! WEAKLING! ARISTOCRAT! I'M NOT DONE WITH YOU, SIR."

She didn't hesitate; she was halfway to the window by the time Sen had time to react. Judging from what she could see, she was about three floors up. No way to hit the ground from that height without hurting. No plan, just muscle and instinct—just the panicky animal that she'd spent half her life trying to silence. She hadn't meant to run away, and she'd made a promise earlier: no more running. The distance disappeared beneath her. There was a space between the two riflemen, not much, but enough. She twisted to her side and leapt.

All the voices in her head—all the incessant piping neurotic jabs— fell away. She was in the air, three floors up. The bridge stretched out across the Grand Canal. Wajet was on the far end, up against the warehouse wall. The fungus covered most of its body—it was almost unrecognizable but for the awful harmonic shrieking of its twin heads, hidden somewhere within its undulating mass of spores and flesh. Wajet's left arm hung limp and swollen at his side. His gun lay on the ground, and the monster stood in front of it.

She closed her eyes. The city was alive with the energy of people and animals and plants. It was everywhere; that had always been the problem. Too many roads, too many souls, too many songs, too much damned *life*. So many decisions she couldn't make, which ended with her doing nothing. She reached out.

—*Wajet, fading, screaming, insensate*—

—*Red, curled in a corner*—

—*a bird, somewhere in the distance, seeking, seeking*—

—*Sen, somewhere behind*—

—*houses, houses, houses*—

She grabbed a house by its threads and pulled. Wood and stone shattered as a tendril thick as a tree trunk shot out toward her. She locked onto it, and it bent with her momentum but resisted just enough to slow her fall. She could feel its fibers tearing, felt its pain inside her own body. She hit the cobblestones on her shoulder, rolled, snatched up Wajet's gun, and rose up firing.

The shots knocked the creature off-balance again, and it swung around to face her. It no longer had human eyes; instead, a monstrous pustule in the center of its chest leered at her. There was something cancerous about its pale, soft flesh. She'd lost too much already. She didn't trust Wajet, but she liked him despite herself. Maybe that was enough. She'd spent her whole life not trusting anyone; she'd spent it being scared. It was a defense mechanism, and not one without its reasons, but it had outlived its godsdamned welcome.

"This is *my* city," she roared, "and you can get the fuck out."

Her magic was still connected with the house's, and the houses were connected by a network of thick hyphae belowground—wispy strands that grew through every crack in the rock. She reached out to all of them and pulled.

The city came to life, the houses in the square twisting and breaking their bonds. Some shriveled, and others grew. The street shattered, and a hundred arm-thick mycelia burst up and wrapped around the beast wherever they could find purchase. It toppled and tried to rise, but the vines held it fast to the ground. She was linked to it now. She didn't have the strength to pry its knotted threads apart, but she didn't need to: the city itself had a hold on it, and she had the city.

The thing wasn't done, though. She could feel its malice pulsing white-hot. It heaved against the bonds, and tensed, and readied itself, and shot a massive cloud of spores into the air. The white plume rose, hit its apex, and fountained outward. She reached out to their threads, but there were millions of them, each bursting with power. She felt her skin crackle again, her eyes melting, her body cooking from the inside as a torrent of magical power flowed through her. She was on her knees with her hands pressed hard against the ground. She could see the burn manifesting on her skin, a rash of red welts breaking out at her wrist and swiftly flowing up her arm, crisscrossed like streets on some vile map. She was losing control of the houses.

Somebody grabbed her. She screamed in pain and surprise. It wasn't the beast, though. One of Wajet's arms was limp at his side, but the other was wrapped around her shoulder. She didn't know what he was doing at first, but then she felt it: the magic dividing itself between them, diffusing through multiple bodies. She hadn't lost her connection to the city yet, so she reached into the hotel and found Sen. He seemed to sense her somehow, and he began to absorb the power too, splitting it again so the burn inside her guttered out. There were still red weals along her forearms, following the path of her veins and scars. The thing on the bridge lay still, but she was alive.

She turned to Wajet.

"Did it work?" he said. She realized he couldn't see the threads like her, that he'd just sensed distress and grabbed her—he'd known exactly the right thing to do, though he was the last man in the world she'd expected it from.

She nodded, and he grinned.

"Sibbi told me about that trick," he said. "Some things, you can't do alone."

She stood and brushed herself off, then turned back to the hotel. Sen stood in the window, holding a protective mask up to his mouth. He gave her a tentative thumbs-up, and she waved at him. He started to return the gesture, then froze. The men in the windows raised their weapons, pointing at something in the distance, and prepared their long guns. Yat followed the arc of their fire and saw it.

Across the canal, coming out of the mist, were a hundred more beasts, a thousand. An army of twisted flesh tearing down the street. How many people had the spores taken? How much work had it been to fight just one? As they charged down the street, a cloud of white spores trailed behind, so thick it left an oily sheen in the air. A shudder rolled through her, and she sensed it again: *a bird, seeking*.

Wait . . . mist. It roiled up over the canal walls, so thick she couldn't see her own hands. Across the canal, the shapes of the advancing flesh were lost in it: just lumbering, gibbering silhouettes.

285

Another dark shape, closer now, carving through the air. A wall, a mountain, a beast of masts and rigging with a dogheaded mermaid beneath the bowsprit. The *Kopek* filled the entire width of the canal. Its boards scraped against the sides with a splintering of wood. Displaced water rushed over the canal walls, spilling into the street. Yat didn't have time to brace for it, and the wave washed over her. Through a mouthful of filthy canal water, she saw the bowsprit clear the bridge, and for an impossible, illogical moment, she thought the ship was flying, that it was going to go right overhead. Then the figurehead hit the bridge railing, wood on wood, and she was part of the circuit: Sibbi, Ajat, the heart, the crew were all together with her, spreading the magical load. Through the haze of pain, she could feel their panic.

—we've come out the wrong side, what the fuck are those?—

—the keel's too low, we're taking on water—

—PORT BATTERY, FIRE—

She heard a ripple of a half-dozen gunpowder roars. The first of the creatures was outside the cannons' arc and already crossing the bridge, leaping over the body of its fallen comrade. Yat's magic was still inside the houses. At once, she let them go and pushed everything she had into the figurehead. The dog's face warped, split, and spread roots through the cracks the impact had made in the bridge. They expanded, forcing the tortured wood apart. The thing tried to lunge at her but lost its balance as the bridge groaned, twisted, and shattered in an explosion of wood and stone beneath its feet. The figurehead had exploded outward into a bushel of wooden lances, and the impaled monster hit the water with a crash. Yat let go of its threads. Some of the creatures were still standing, but a burst of disciplined fire from the *Kopek* sent them scattering off into the alleyways and out of sight. Giving chase didn't seem high on the priority list.

For just a moment, there was perfect silence. Sound came back to the world in pieces—creaking wood, rustling sails. Yat exhaled and let the tension go from her shoulders. Ajat poked her head over the gunnel. She looked like she was about to say something, but she pulled her head back out of sight.

Across the canal, she could barely see. The air was thick with spores, mingling with the mist. The creatures weren't moving; some of them twitched and pulsed, but they did not rise. It was hard to tell where one ended and the next began. The one in the water wasn't moving, either, and she wondered for a moment whether the salt had done something, if it had some purifying effect that stopped spore growth. It was a thought out of nowhere, but she was her father's daughter.

"Ma'am?" shouted Sen. Yat turned to face him.

"You don't need to call me th—"

Sibbi's slap wasn't particularly hard, but the rings gave it a tooth-loosening weight. Yat's head snapped to the side as she reeled back. Mist danced between them. In a moment of rage, Sibbi was doing nothing to conceal her power, and Yat *saw*—

—a thousand years and a thousand years and a thousand more and—

—the wind wearing a mountain down—

—frayed threads barely holding together—

—seismic power, measured in magnitude, threatening to tear her body apart—

—powerful—

—fragile—

"We're done, you and I," said Sibbi. "Do you know how many people died today? How many are going to die? That's on you, hero. Come near my ship, and I'll have you dragged across the keel."

She drew back her hand for another slap. Yat cringed away from it, but it never connected; Wajet pushed his not-inconsiderable bulk between them and let the slap bounce off his chest. The *Kopek*'s gangplank came down, and Ajat was the first across it. She put one hand on her wife's shoulder and another on her waist.

"She didn't know."

"When was that ever an excuse?" spat Sibbi. "Ignorance doesn't raise the dead. If you started counting the fallen now, you'd be gray before you finished. I wanted you to be better than that; I wanted you to be better than—"

Me. Better than me.

The thought floated free, and Yat caught it without meaning to. She stared at Sibbi. She didn't know what to say.

"I'm sorry," she said. That didn't even begin to cover it.

"Sorry for what?"

She didn't have the words. Sibbi took control of Yat's threads and pushed them out into the city. Where there had been life, there was silence. A bottomless, mountainous silence. It was the silence from her father's bedroom the night he stopped breathing, an emptiness that pulled you all the way down. An emptiness she'd courted in the dead of night, staring at her roof and wondering if things would ever get better. The killing cold she'd almost let in the night her father had died.

"Sorry for . . . all of this," she finished.

Sen and his officers came out of the hotel at a brisk trot. Yat didn't know how much he'd heard or how much he knew. She didn't have the strength to reach into his mind; she felt hollow. The pirates on deck raised their weapons, and the advancing cops stopped dead. Sen raised his hands.

"Ma'am?" he said to Sibbi, who turned and glared at him.

He canted his chin down and lowered his gaze. "Ma'am," he said, "we need to talk."

THIRTY-SIX

The whole ugly story came out. They'd already had an idea, and between Sen and Wajet, they pieced together the rest. The brothers were operating out of a mansion in Heron Hill. They'd brought two divisions of the army with them and taken control of the force, including the watch. Soldiers were on the wall and the gates out of the city; cops were in the streets. They'd been given clear, strict orders: containment, nothing more. They were to lock down the infected district, shoot anybody who tried to leave, and wait for the plague to burn itself out. Some had refused to follow orders, which was how they'd ended up stuck here in a forsaken district.

Nine officers in all. There had been more to start with, mostly newer recruits. Maybe fifty civilians in the hotel, though none in any condition to fight. Yat recognized Mr. Ot, who sold soup in Janekhai Street, the one she'd nearly run into during a chase that evening that seemed so long ago. He must've gotten free from the paddy wagon somehow. She didn't ask.

A little girl peered out from behind his legs—Yat had seen her in

291

the upstairs window earlier. Her name was Bykra. She was nine and very talkative: she thought Yat had pretty hair; her dad was really nice and made the best soup; she'd stubbed her toe; she could count to a thousand. She didn't say anything about the monsters, but her blazing thread of fear was unmissable. *It's not there if you don't talk about it, if you talk about anything else.*

The *Kopek* was a wreck. It wasn't going anywhere today or tomorrow or for months. The water pressure and canal walls had torn open the hull. The collision with the bridge had turned the prow into matchsticks. One of the starboard shrouds had gotten wrapped around a lamppost and brought the whole mizzen down with it. The ship listed hard to the right, the broadside having knocked it off its axis and managed to get the old girl jammed into the canal like a cork in a bottle. It would take an army of carpenters a year to even get it seaworthy again.

Most of the district was clear of infection, at least for now. There weren't enough of them to try for another push for the time being, but if a group of the creatures broke the barricades, it would get bad very quickly. They hunted in packs. They'd merge with each other to overcome obstacles, getting larger and larger. The smaller ones followed the bigger ones, sometimes clinging to their bodies and trying to graft themselves on. In the distance in every direction, they could see towering, lumbering forms, some terrifyingly close. The *Kopek* had gotten them a reprieve, but it wasn't going to last. Ajat set up sentries. Yat watched, numb, as she ordered pirates to move in fire teams, covering all the entrances into the square. Xidaj was in the hotel window; he'd glued a ring to the sill and put the barrel through it to keep stable. Iacci was unarmed, tending to the civilians. Rikaza and Set-Xor were off somewhere on the rooftops. Wajet sat on a bench with Red in his lap. One of his arms was clearly broken, but he didn't seem too bothered: he patted the cat and seemed very content to still be alive.

Sibbi fidgeted as she listened to Sen's plan. She took the thumb and forefinger of her left hand and squeezed each knuckle on the right, one by one, until they clicked. She would tent her fingers, click them all, then go back to the knuckles. She hadn't quite managed to regain her full composure. Her threads writhed around her like a halo of snakes. They were so bright, Yat could barely look at them.

She sat down and spread her consciousness through the city. The emptiness burned, but she was looking for something specific, and she found it.

Varazzo was walking alongside a blank. He was nervous: he'd been assured these blanks were safe, but he wasn't willing to take that on faith. The blank was a woman, perhaps twenty years old. She was carrying a crate up a ramp. Mr. Żao had assured him the gunpowder was safe, but that didn't assuage his fears: he'd seen them add something to it, and they'd been very sure to check the seals. Żao had locked himself in one of the offices with a fancy ventilation and filter system. They'd given Varazzo a gun, and he liked the weight of it. He had orders to put a bullet in any blank acting strangely. He liked the thought of shooting somebody—it felt good to have that power. The woman stumbled and lost her grip on the crate. It fell, and the lid sprang off. They were meant to be sealed tighter than a virgin asshole, but it just came clean off. Glass tubes rolled everywhere, and one tilted off the ramp and fell. Varazzo didn't even have time to cry out before it hit the ground and . . .

. . . didn't break. He breathed a sigh of relief. Then he noticed the blank. She lay facedown, twitching.

"Aww, hells," he said. He checked the gun's cylinder: two chambers empty, five full. He loaded in two more bullets, just be to safe, then got as close to her as he dared. Pity, she was pretty fuckable—looked good lying on her front. He considered it for a moment, then, shielding his face with one hand, unloaded two bullets into her back. She jerked up, then slumped, and he shot her once more at the point where her neck met her shoulders. She didn't move again. He signaled for another blank to drag her away to the incinerator. At this rate, they wouldn't have any left by sunrise. Not that it mattered.

Yat could feel her grasp slipping. He was too far away, and she was so tired. She tried to pull energy from the city, but too much of it was empty—the more people there were, the easier it was to move threads around. As the city fell to pieces, it became so much harder to hold on to. As she was drawn back to her body, Yat looked around for anything to go on. She could smell chemicals: potassium nitrate, chlorine, ammonia, and . . . kiro? Not the smell of smoke, but the pungent, acrid reek of spent roaches.

She came back to herself to see Sibbi shouting at Sen.

"No, I can't 'just disappear everyone,'" she said, "My godsdamned *ship* would sink in the ocean now; surgeons don't work with their bare hands. I'd have us raining from the heavens if I tried."

Cannath and some of the other crew were standing by. Some mingled with the civilians and cops, but Cannath sat with her legs dangling into the canal, just beyond the ruined bridge. She stared down at the water and hummed a tune Yat could swear she'd heard before.

Mr. Ot raised a hand. He'd been hanging back, and the politeness of the gesture seemed to disrupt the rhythm of the shouting match.

"We're . . . we're not just going to leave, are we? Where are we supposed to go? This is home. This is where my family is."

"Not mine," snapped Sibbi.

Ajat stepped forward.

"Look," she said, "we don't know where our enemies are, we don't know what they're doing, and even if we did, we're surrounded. They're going to come here tomorrow morning to clear out the corpses, and what happens when they find us?"

Yat could still smell Varazzo—his sweat, his rancid breath, the chemical reek of the building. She'd smelled those chemicals before, in her father's lab. Nitrates as fuel and payload, chlorine for an oxidizing agent for those nice blues and greens.

"Fireworks," she said. "They're in a fireworks factory. But why?"

Something in the powder.

It hit her. Midnight. A thousand bottle rockets blazing into the night sky, exploding, spreading their payload over the entire city. Each one stuffed with enough spores to bring down an empire. More spores than there were numbers for, spreading on the wind, settling in every crevice, filling lungs, feasting on mucus and tissue and then exploding out again and again. Even if the city survived, it would be decades before it was habitable again. The infection could survive in the houses alone for at least that long.

But why would Parliament want that? She'd seen something in Żao and reached desperately for the memory.

—wings unfolding—

—a tower of meat, reaching for the sun—

—an onrushing night, stealing names and eating through memory like a worm in an apple . . .

Hello, little monkey.

Crane did not speak—it changed the world, so it had already spoken. A shadow of two great wings fell over Yat, and she saw—

—the rumble before an avalanche—

—a hiss of carbon monoxide and a blocked tailpipe—

A single spark moving with purpose—the overture to an inferno.

A long night falling across the world and the world and the world and the world . . .

She was standing in the snow, her ragged breaths ejecting white plumes into the air. Her fingertips ached with cold, and she didn't know what to do with them. She had never been this cold before, but she knew this place would kill her if she stayed. The city around her was silent: huge plate-glass domes emerging from the ground, lit from the inside but with no promise of warmth. She could see ice forming on the insides, frozen figures wrapped up in blankets, holding each other, staring sightlessly outward. A tree stood in front of her, in the ruins of what might've once been a town square. Its bark was tooth-pale. It was barren of leaves, and its branches twisted at sudden odd angles like a snatching of broken arms.

Then a voice moved across the world and shook her. It wasn't using words she understood: it communicated in ideas, and her mind painted over the rest. It was like seeing her own reflection in a fast-flowing river. The ice water carved through her, channeled and given form by her memories, her anxieties, her loves. The crew behind her still quarreled ten feet away, a thousand miles away, as though they couldn't feel the eternal emptiness of the void pulling at them like fishhooks in their very marrow. They were there, not here.

Hello, little monkey, Crane said. *I have a lesson for you.*

Know this: your father died because he thought that if he worked hard enough, he could logic his lungs back together. If he just found the right combination of elements, he could do it painlessly, and he could save himself and everybody else. He kept working while that work ate him, piece by piece. He did the responsible thing, and it killed him. You don't argue with disease; you burn it away. You cleanse your body with fire and pray that the sickness burns before you burn with it. This world is sick, child. I will burn every soul in it, if I can stop the sickness from spreading.

Know this: you cannot fight me. I have seen the end of this, and you are nowhere in it. You are a bit part in the song of this world, and you will be forgotten. You knew this long before you saw my face, but it seems I must make it clear: you will die by my hand or you will die by your own, and either way, you have no choice. I have seen through you, and this ends with you empty. If you try to stop me, I will make dust of you, and you will thank me for the kindness. At last the pain will stop. The only reason I have not done this yet is because you do not matter and will change nothing. You were nobody, are nobody, will be nobody. Know this.

A powerful vertigo filled Yat. She stumbled, and her hands hit stone. The snow was gone, but she could still feel its chill in her bones. The quarreling stopped, and somebody put a hand on her shoulder.

When she looked up, the shadow was gone, but she could still feel its darkness hanging over her. And, here in the silence, she found the missing piece. She reached for the thought, though it recoiled. There was emptiness in place of a memory, and she felt for it like the space left by a missing tooth.

She didn't know what to do. She could still feel the chill stinging her in a million different places, the emptiness hollowing her out. She had never been so freezing cold before, but she knew the emptiness well. She knew it would be back eventually, pulling her down to the earth, flattening her.

Focus. Go with the data you've got. Yat breathed deeply and felt her heart stop racing. *Slow, methodical.*

"A fireworks factory," she muttered, "near a kiro refinery, one that puts out a lot of ash."

"Anyasz Fireworks," said Wajet. He had on a medicated-looking far-away grin, though she hadn't seen him take anything. That said, if anybody could surreptitiously drink on the job, it was Wajet. "They make the best damned Ahi Reapers on the continent. What about 'em?"

Everybody looked at him, and he shrugged. "Can't a man enjoy a few explosions in the comfort of his own backyard?" he said.

Yat stood up again. She stared down Sibbi, who stood with her arms crossed.

"Mr. Żao is there," said Yat. "With guards and black powder and enough spores to make today's whole mess look like a sunny afternoon at sea. Reach out if you don't believe me—you'll find him."

Sibbi stared her down, then slumped her shoulders. "I can't," she whispered. Her hands were shaking. She took a step back into Ajat's. Their threads ran together—Sibbi's were pale, lifeless. Energy moved between them, but it was going to be a slow recovery. That last jump must have cost her almost everything.

"She's telling the truth," said Cannath. Her eyes were glassy, and the fingers on her left hand were stiff, pushed down hard against the wood on the side of the canal. She cocked her head to the side.

"Ten men, not including Żao," she said. "Maybe fifty condemned."

The word *blank* played across Yat's mind, but she pushed it away. The word held too much pain for her. There was still a memory there, a thorn Yat couldn't bring herself to grasp—she didn't want to face Cannath's wrath, but she could finally see the faint outline of what she'd been reaching for, and somehow it felt even worse than the cold.

"If one brother's there, the other can't be too far," said Ajat.

Yat shook her head. "I killed the other one," she said.

After looking around at each other for a moment in disbelief, Sibbi, Ajat, Wajet, and Cannath each said a different swear word at the same time, and it all came together in a single percussive blast.

"No," said Sibbi, "you didn't. He's like us; he'll be back."

"I know he's like us," said Yat, "I . . . emptied him out."

"No," said Sibbi, "you did *not*. A matchstick can't put out a forest fire. I don't know what you think you did, but L—Żu isn't—"

Her eyes went wide, and then she stormed over to Yat, grabbed her by the chin, and tilted her face upward so they were staring right into each other's eyes. For a moment she was a raging fire, but then it seemed to contract all at once, pulled tight and wrapped around her like a suit of armor. Very carefully, not breaking eye contact, Sibbi said, "I know where she is."

"Who?" said Yat.

Sibbi stared at her, unblinking. The moment went on too long, and folks around them started to mutter. The muscles in Yat's neck had begun to ache.

"Cannath," said Sibbi, "knowing what you know, you trust her?"

Cannath didn't reply; she just sat on the ground running her fingers across the dark metal blade of her knife. She closed her eyes, cocked her head to the side, then looked up at them.

"I do," she said. "He's not a Tiger Weaver, so he can't hide for shit. If he were around, we'd know it. I think she really got him."

"*Vlakas*," said Sibbi, the word seeming to rush out unbidden. It wasn't any language Yat had ever heard, but she knew cursing when she heard it. A momentary flash of emotion ran across Sibbi's face, something akin to sadness. She released Yat.

"That asshole was always so cocky," she said. "Knew it was gonna burn him in the end."

Sen cleared his throat. "As much as I love . . . whatever this is," he said, "we need to get moving. There are guards on every route out of this district. Nice open streets here, big sight lines. You'll never even get close to the barricade."

Yat looked up at the drainpipes, awnings, and rooftops. Despite everything today, she smiled.

"Don't need to," she said. She turned to Cannath. "You know how to climb?"

THIRTY-SEVEN

Mate, woulda been really useful if you'd given me some sort of sword instead of a cane. I mean, I like it fine as a cane, but I really would've liked a sword.

I swear on my mother's grave, Sergeant, it is a sword! You just need to twist it the right way!

I did twist it!

Then you weren't doing it right. Give it here. Hmm. Like, uh. No, clearly not. Mm. Wait, like, no, ah. You know what, Sergeant? It appears I broke the latch. At least the lead was useful? It gave our good captain a target for the jump. We would've been lost without you, old friend.

I, uh—fuck's sake, Wajet. I'm not even going to touch that one.

Contain yourself, Sen. I'm spoken for.

THIRTY-EIGHT

Sibbi couldn't go, and Ajat refused to leave her wife's side. Sen was similarly out: his leg was healing, but there was no way he could climb. The remaining sailors and cops were needed to guard the hotel.

That left Cannath. She'd been thrown against the gunnel in the crash but wasn't too badly hurt. Plus, she healed fast anyway. It was amazing to watch her threads move around her wounds. Yat swore she could see the cuts on her arm closing up as they formulated their plan.

East first, out through the Shambles, then northeast through the merchant quarter. The more built-up parts of town would mean more contiguous buildings, which made it easier to move without touching the ground. It also meant more people, and more meat.

"Stay indoors where possible," said Yat. "Most of the buildings should be abandoned, and we don't want to risk being spotted. Lots of amanita, which should give us more options. Rooftops if we need to—I don't think these things can climb very well, not yet at least. So long as we can't be seen from street level, we're probably safe. We'll need to cross the bridge at Kanajet Canal—I can't see any other way of getting across."

"The closest barricade is about four blocks away, facing south," said Sen. "You should be fine; they're not meant to leave their posts. Just keep an eye out."

Cannath grunted. "We'll be fine," she said. "So long as Little Pig here doesn't start to have second thoughts."

Yat tried to joke it off. "You still owe me five ox," she said.

Cannath fidgeted with an unlit cigarette. Nobody laughed.

THIRTY-NINE

The warehouse had roof access, and from there it was a straight shot east to the edge of the district. The houses they moved through were empty. They did their best to ignore the broken plates, half-packed suitcases, and boundless silence. They found a woman, perhaps seventy, naked on the bed with her wrists open and a photograph on her chest of her younger self, smiling, with a handsome lantern-jawed man at her side. The skin on her shoulders was scale-like with tumorous growths—she'd stopped the spread of the infection the only way she could think of. It wasn't clear how much had grown after her death, but it couldn't have been long since it happened. The spores needed a living organism, even if it was a small one: yeast in beer, tiny cysts that made up cnidocyte walls. The woman's body wasn't free of infection, just full of dormant spores.

Cannath wouldn't leave the house without placing a coin on each of her eyes and muttering a short prayer. Northern didn't sound like Yat thought it would: all clipped vowels and liquid consonants, like bad wine being poured out in an alley. Yat stayed outside the bedroom. She'd been the one who found the woman, but she couldn't bring herself to stay in there. She couldn't look at the scars on the woman's arms without thinking about her own, couldn't stand that close to death without it swallowing her. Instead, she looked out the windows. There was no life outside—no people, no cats, not even any birds in the sky.

After a minute or so, Cannath came out of the bedroom and they kept going. Yat had thought her companion would need help, but she moved smoothly from house to house. She knew her cat leaps pretty well for a sailor. The humidity made it hard to go far— their clothes were quickly slick with sweat. The past week had hardened Yat's muscles, but she still struggled to complete some of the jumps.

They stopped to catch their breath in the apartment above an upscale tailor's shop. They stood in the kitchen together, leaning against the counter. They broke the wax seal on a jug of water: somebody had been preparing for the long haul, but they were gone now.

"You been to Hainak much?" said Yat.

"Grew up here," grunted Cannath. There was something in her voice that was hard to place—maybe annoyance or agitation? Yat didn't push it any further. They drank the water, then kept going.

Sunset bruised the sky in grays and pinks. It was behind them, and they cast long shadows as they broke open windows, picked locks, scurried from room to room. At one point, they saw a large steamship moving down a canal, packed to the hilt with survivors. It was sitting too low in the water: the boat wasn't built for so many people. It scraped along the canal walls, and Yat worried for a moment that its hull would collapse like the *Kopek*'s. They waited for it to drift out of sight, then kept going.

They arrived at last, when the sun had been eaten by the jagged teeth of the Hainak skyline, at Kanajet Canal. It was deep—one of the arterial waterways that connected the ocean routes to the inland train system. The bridge was new. It had a network of vines growing through the canal walls that responded to pressure in the water by opening to let ships through. The organic components would reseal after the split, including the train tracks.

They watched it for a few minutes. They were about to jump down from a rooftop when the bridge split. A dark shape glided through the water. It surfaced, and Yat saw maggot-white puckered flesh, thousands of red, rolling human eyes in two great fly-like clusters, and a human face on the top that opened its toothless mouth in a mock yell to eject a plume of water and spores. So much for her salt theory. Yat knew the reek of an ocean-bloated corpse too well and had to fight back a scream—it smelled like the body at the docks the night this had all begun. As she watched, a roiling mass of fish followed it, eating the dark slick of spores it left behind. She couldn't see them well enough to find out how it was changing them. She didn't want to. The beast descended under the water again, and its awful trail was spreading across the water's surface, making it hard to tell where the creature was. The bridge stayed open for a full minute—the longest minute of Yat's life. The cover sealed last, its vinework interlacing like long, pale fingers. She dropped down onto it, and its surface sank a little beneath her feet. She steadied herself, then signaled for Cannath to follow. The woman was mid-leap when the beast resurfaced.

It must've come up from the very bottom of the canal: the bridge didn't register it until it broke the surface of the water. The vat-wood groaned, and the structure split, an engineered suppuration that dripped clear pus into the water below. Yat grabbed a vine and planted her feet as the bridge lifted her up and back. Cannath, twisting in midair, tried desperately to adjust her landing. She hit the wood and slid. She was muscular and heavy; the whole bridge shuddered with the impact. The angle changed, first going shallow, then jerking back in response and almost bucking Yat off. Cannath slipped back, rolled, and began to fall. In the water below, a titanic mouth opened. It was filled with tens of thousands of human teeth at a riot of angles running down into a deep, pale gullet.

Cannath fell, and Yat—

—reached out for her. A vine shot forth from the bridge, and Cannath snatched at it. It snapped taut, and for an electric, blinding half second, the two women were connected. Yat sent a single panicked thought down the line.

Momentum.

Cannath stuck her legs out as she hit the bottom of her swing. The creature lifted itself out of the water, its grasping pale limbs pushing it up the wooden canal walls. Cannath kept going, and Yat hauled on the vine just as the creature's massive, vile maw snapped shut with a chittering *click-clack* at the spot she had been. With one final push, Cannath let go. She hung in the air for a moment, then reached out and—

—grabbed the other side of the bridge. Her body moved like a pendulum and dumped her on top. She slid down and hit the ground on the other side of the canal. The monstrous whale landed back in the water with a wet slap, and the bridge groaned once again and began to lower. Once it had laced itself back together, Yat scurried across, then dropped down beside Cannath.

The two women stared at each other.

"We good?" said Yat.

The response didn't come straightaway. Cannath had that same energy she'd had when Yat had first met her: wound tight like a spring, about to launch her into the sun.

"Yeah," said Cannath, "we're good. For now."

It would have to do.

"Let's get away from this bloody canal, ay?" said Yat.

Cannath nodded. "Anyasz Fireworks is close," she said. "I can *feel* him, that emptiness. It's like poking a cavity with your tongue, you know? He's all rot now, all poison."

Yat didn't want to say it, but she'd felt it too—a colossal pull on the edge of her senses. The world bent around Żao, like the sheer weight of his magic was pushing down against reality, ready to tear a hole in it. A nearby Tinker's Horn crackled, then blared to life.

"Nine p.m.," it said. "Nine p.m. and all's not well."

"You can say that again," said both Yat and Cannath. They spoke on top of each other, almost in harmony.

Their eyes met. Cannath broke away first; she turned and started to scale a nearby drainpipe. Yat stared after her, furrowing her brow. A thought had moved between them just then, something bright and sweet. She'd reached for it, but pulled back right before grasping it. A feeling stirred on the edge of her memory, but she shook it off, and they kept going.

They smelled Anyasz before they saw it. The Xineng district at the edge of town was home to fertilizer factories, kiro refineries, the dodgier sort of alchemist's shop—anything that belched smoke and fumes. Most of the buildings were stained black with soot. Very little could grow out here, as nobody had managed to engineer cellulose that could withstand this level of industrial pollution. It was the part of the city least changed, trapped in amber on the outskirts. Red brick and smokestacks blanketed the area. Cruel rows of iron spikes surrounding each roof forced the two climbers down to street level.

They stepped over the body of a man who was missing his head. It hadn't been blown off, but rather looked like it had grown down and in, so the neck was a U-bend of shattered and fused vertebrae. One of his arms ended in a series of hooklike claws. He'd been shot in the stomach, the blood long since dry.

The buildings were pressed tightly together, but Anyasz had a wide berth around it. Even with space at a premium, nobody was stupid enough to share a wall with a fireworks factory. Yat realized with a sick jolt that she was staring at the same ramp where Varazzo had shot a woman. It was caked with blood. The factory's impressive iron doors were shut. There were no blanks or soldiers in sight.

Cannath took a step forward when they heard the click behind them. It froze the blood in Yat's veins. She'd last heard the exact same click when a smiling man in a police uniform had put a bullet through her head.

"Ladies," said Varazzo. "Hands up, please." He sounded like he was enjoying himself.

Yat raised her hands. She reached out for Cannath's threads and spoke along them: *No sudden moves, okay? Let him talk.*

There was nothing to draw from the environment here: no life in the buildings, no surviving animals, no other people.

"I see you've brought a friend," said Varazzo. "No problem, I've got enough lead for you both."

He laughed at his own joke. Yat couldn't see him, but she could feel his threads—the same febrile panic from earlier, but twisted into a vicious molten chokecherry. He did a good job of hiding it, but he was scared, and he dealt with it by attacking whatever scared him until it broke. He felt like nothing, so he cut down everything around him to make himself feel like more. At the core of all of it was fear, burning heavy in his chest. She could use that.

He was coming closer, his heavy boots clacking across the stone. Yat thought back to when she'd calmed down Red: *take the threads and push*. She wished she could push back his fear with her own courage, but she was scared, too—scared of everything. Of the city and the spores and Crane's long shadow. So she took that fear, wove it together, and pushed. The fear hit his threads and blossomed outward.

"Don't move," said Varazzo. "Don't you fucking move. I'm warning you."

Run.

Fear flooded his body, overwhelming reason. It didn't take much; he'd been halfway there already. He was a little boy again, terrified of the shadow on his bedroom wall. The women before him were giants, monsters, typhoons. The gun wasn't a comfort, but a burden. His hands shook, and he dropped it. He let out a sick moan.

RUN.

The gun clattered off the cobbles. Yat turned to face him, just in time to see him fall to his knees. He prostrated himself, pushed his forehead against the street, and wrapped his arms around the back of his head.

"Please don't kill me," he said. "Please don't kill me. Please."

Yat took out the lion gun. She had three bullets left. It was tempting, but it would make her somebody she didn't want to be. She hesitated.

"Fuck's sake," said Cannath. She snatched the gun, raised it, and . . .

Varazzo coughed. He pushed himself up, clutching at his throat. His face was white but quickly turning a pallid shade of blue. His neck twisted. At first it was as though he were trying to look at something behind him, but then it kept going with a series of concussive cracks. A bone spur exploded out of his throat, and a lumbar vertebra, swollen and sharp, pierced the back of his neck.

"P-p," he spluttered through bloodless lips, "please."

He fell, and so did Yat. She had no control over her body: somebody else was in charge, and her knees snapped tight and forced her down. She tried to put out her hands to brace herself, but they weren't working, and she hit the stone face-first. Cannath fell beside her, her mouth stuck open in a silent, furious shout.

"I'm getting tired of you, Constable Hok," said Żao. "So very tired."

Mist whipped around his feet and spilled out across the ground. He stepped over Varazzo's body.

"Look at you, hero," he said. He spoke in erratic bursts, as though the words were some creature raging inside him, trying to break out. "Look at you, in league with the hypertrophics, protector of the choking roots. Luckily for us, God made two things: he made wildfire—"

He lunged, and a single bone spike emerged from the base of his palm. Yat rolled out of the way, but he moved with her. It slammed in under her jaw, up through her mouth, through the roof of her mouth, and she felt it begin to *pull*. She knew what was happening, but her limbs were lead. His words slipped through the spreading curtain of numbness.

"—and he made *me*."

As their minds ran together, she saw.

—*a field of ice and stones and rot. A great tree, upward and upward and upward, its bark made of skin, its core made of flesh, its great green heart pumping blood from its deep roots up to its towering peak. Piercing the sky and going farther, until it went so far past the top*

312

that it found itself at the bottom, in the darkness, bridging two worlds. It spanned across the darkness where Monkey dwelt to a place on the other side that she couldn't quite see. Across that bridge, the souls of ten thousand years, lost no longer. An end to suffering. Friends, lovers, family, pouring down, home at last. Żao's mother, smiling, her arms spread wide. Yat's father, whole again, walking hand in hand with a woman she'd seen only in her dreams.

Something grabbed at her from behind and pushed back. Cannath, joining their threads, pushing something toward her: a memory. She reached out, and grabbed it, and—

—sitting on a rooftop over Henhai Lane, watching the crying girl who'd just lost her father—

—dreaming of running her fingers through her hair—

—tentative at first, sharing bread with her, showing her how to pick a lock—

—a whistle, the rough hands of an officer—

—drinking the bitter water, and feeling something vital gush out—

—hearing the technicians wonder whether they'd ever get the reversal tech right, whether she'd be under long enough that they could bring her back, or whether they'd just extend the sentence again—

—silence, silence, but still in there screaming as her body lifted sacks, and pushed carts—

—in a moment of madness, she had control over her shoulders, and she rammed her forehead against a loose nail, not quite flush with the wall—

—waking in the water, where they'd dumped her—

—running, running, a woman with rough hands grabbing her and taking her aside and asking, Can you keep a secret?—

A jolt ran between them, and Yat's muscles screamed as they broke free from Żao's bonds. "Kiada," she whispered. The word was barely audible. There had been ten years, and she'd added a lot of scar tissue and about seventy pounds of muscle since Yat had last seen her, but she couldn't believe she'd missed it. As their gold threads ran together, skin, muscle, and bone expelled Żao in an explosive burst, stitching the hole back together. She was light-headed and every-thing hurt, but that was how she knew she was still alive.

They rose together. Żao wasn't ready for it, and Kiada rammed the heel of her palm into his jaw. For a single moment, her body was illuminated in gold, a clear line running from her hip up her waist into her shoulder and along her arm. Żao staggered backward and tried to grab onto Kiada's threads, but Yat grabbed his elbow and pulled. His chest came down, and Yat smashed her knee into his ribs.

The flesh on his hand yawned open, and a shard of bone slid out. He squeezed it, snapped it off, then slashed out with it like a knife. It sank into Yat's shoulder, and she screamed. The bone was a conduit between them, and he was draining her dry. It was over this time, truly over. She could taste iron. A sudden pressure threatened to split her skull, and she could feel it start to come apart—

The first shot blew through his knee at point-blank range, sev-ering his lower leg entirely. He squawked and pitched back. Their connection tore apart, and Yat screamed again as his pain lanced through her before he broke away.

He lay on the ground, panting. Then he grinned at them, and Yat realized that he was looking over her shoulder. She turned to see something tearing through the night: a tiny, distant, indistinct shape, followed by a billion more. The fireworks reached the apex of their arc and exploded. One bloom of green sparks, then another, and another, and another: dozens, hundreds, thousands. The biggest fireworks display in the city's history, each explosion carrying a deadly payload. Yat staggered, her wound only half-closed. She'd realized she'd been overconfident, that rebuilding a skull wasn't something you did on the fly. And when she tried to inhale, she realized she couldn't breathe.

Źao laughed. "Too late, little firebreak," he said. "This whole rotten forest is coming down."

Kiada shot him in the chest.

"WAIT," shouted Yat, but Kia shot him again. His body jerked, then he slumped and went still. She screamed and pulled the trigger again and again while the firing pin clicked through empty cylinders, each empty metallic ping punctuated by a word.

"Leave—"

—*click*—

"—her—"

—*click*—

"—alone."

She put the gun to her own head, pulled the trigger. Another empty chamber.

"Fuck," she shouted. "*FUCK.*"

She threw the gun to the ground. The sparks from the fireworks were gone, but their afterimage lingered, and in the sky, Yat could sense *them*. She couldn't control that many spores; not half that many spores, or a tenth, or a fraction smaller than she knew. It was billions on billions, each one packed with magic, raining down across the city.

Kiada turned to face her, saw the wound only half-closed, saw her face turning blue. She grabbed her, pulled her close, face wet with tears.

"Not now," she said. "Please. I just got you back."

It was too much, all too much—a blizzard of paper cuts. The world had overwhelmed her every day, but she'd kept going. Yesterday had been too much; today was too much; tomorrow might be too much, or the day after. But she was still standing, if not for much longer. There was no secret to stop her hands from shaking, to stop her chest from burning, her veins pumping, the cold spreading down from her throat. She could feel her lung knitting itself back together, but it was too little, too late.

She was going to die anyway, or face something worse; it couldn't hurt to try something different.

She took as deep a breath as her open throat would allow and let it out. Then, shaking so hard she thought she might fall apart, she reached up toward the sky.

Fire rolled over her and through her. Her cells screamed as the water in her blood boiled away to steam. She couldn't even begin to control it: the power coursing through her was more than she'd ever thought possible. It burned through her faster than it could heal. It rooted her to the ground, paralyzed her, broke down the very bonds holding her together. She couldn't close her eyes or twitch her fingers or breathe. She could smell her flesh cooking, feel her skin begin to slough off and—

She heard a voice on the air, from right beside her, from a thousand miles away. The voice of a girl, lost. The voice of a girl, found. It came from two mouths at once.

"No," it said, in a whisper that could reach between worlds, "tonight, we live."

Kiada kissed her.

She kissed back.

316

They'd kissed only once before: coyly, on the cheek, like they were playing a game. This wasn't that. Through the haze of pain, she felt a hand around her waist, pulling, another hand against the back of her head, a wrist against the nape of her neck, an elbow between her shoulder blades, pushing. She tasted salt, coffee, and tobacco. Yat couldn't let go, and she didn't want to. When their bodies wove together, their threads did, too, the same pain lancing through them, building, threatening to burn them both down.

They kissed as though they needed to fit a whole lifetime into a single second. With death raining down, they kissed for every missed hour, every swollen silence, every thrice-cursed goodbye. Despite the urgent crush of their bodies, Yat stopped inhabiting herself and lived only in that minute. The sky bloomed with fire, a million tiny motes of magical energy tearing downward into them in a great golden fountain only they could see, as they came together in one endless moment.

The fire arced between them, and they closed their bodies around it, crushed it down and down into a fist, then a shard, then a needle of pure concentrated magical energy. They held it between them. Yat had expected it to be vicious, for the thing that had caused so much pain to lash out one last time. But there was no malice there, only hunger. In the absence of that, the spores were just simple, beautiful animals. Tiny, tiny things—curious, innocent, lost, but seeking. She and Kiada took the point of the needle and, without resistance, cast it down into the earth.

It pierced through the soot-stained brickwork, through the foundations, through the silt and clay. A single light tearing down through the darkness, through the crushing pressure of the earth. At the very bottom, it ran out of thread and detonated.

Waves of life rippling out, waking long-dormant seeds, nourishing hungry roots, spreading out through the network of vines and hyphae that linked the city together. Where the lines went dead, it made new ones, growing a whole new ecosystem beneath the earth, bursting through stone, pushing aside great heaving of mineral and hard stone, going through what it could and around what it couldn't.

Yat didn't see any of that. She saw, from inside Kiada's arms, the street erupting with trunks; the houses breaking their bonds and spiraling up and up; on the wall of Arnak-Vonaj, in the distance, vines thickening, tightening, spreading out like seeking fingers, a filigree of green spiderwebs unfurling until it seemed like the implacable iron edifice was transformed into shattered stained glass; a sky filled with sparks; a tearing of metal, a screaming of bolts and joints, a crumbling of masonry; a skyline twisting, growing as she pulled Kiada's head to her shoulder, knowing her warmth as though it were her own; the houses growing tall, the wall crumbling down, rupturing in a thousand places, so thoroughly broken you couldn't even melt down what was left for scrap; Kiada's rough hands on her, and Kiada's soft lips so very close; a world erupting, being destroyed and reborn; the cover of branches and hyphae, the creaking of new wood; a slowing, and finally, a cessation; the warm silence of a city anew.

They stood together and did not speak. When the sky had gone dark and the distant shouting had died down, they stepped apart.

"So," said Yat. "That was, uh, something."

Kiada looked surprisingly sheepish. It was possible that this fell outside her expertise.

"A good something?" she said.

"Yeah," said Yat. "Definitely good."

The Anyasz building had been torn in half by a gigantic amanita cap covered in metallic scales. It twisted in the wind, its thick, pale neck making it look like an old man in a very large hat. It leaned right and knocked some more brickwork loose. If somebody put in the time, the thing could fit a dozen families. There would be more of them, too, though Yat didn't know how many more. Her fingertips were numb and tingled when she rubbed them together. She'd made it through the fire. *They*'d made it through.

Stumbling together arm in arm, Yat and Kiada watched the last fading sparks fall onto a brand-new town.

FORTY

Come here, little bird. I've something to show you.

As the beasts chased your people through the streets of the market district, as the Kopek fell, as the hotel barricade came down, as the sky filled with green fire, something wonderful happened: your girls pulled through.

Faith is rewarded. I know it hurts, but the scars will heal: they always do. You were right, as you always are. That is why you are so very precious to me.

Come closer, let me show you more.

See the new flesh melting like spring snow. See the stumbling naked people looking at their hands, trying to come to terms with their memories. Not all of them got out, nor most, nor many. Tens of thousands rot in gutters, barely recognizable. Some return to their bodies without memory and stumble down streets they do not recognize. Nevertheless, some did escape. A miracle, but I do allow those from time to time when nobody is looking. I have my tricks.

See the people emerging from their houses, tearing down the boards on their windows, venturing outside: first cautious, then observant, then bursting into sobs—sorrow, relief, joy. It differs from soul to soul. They are weeping because your girls pulled though.

See the streets where the crew of the Kopek stand. The soldiers tried to come for them, but they held. They have scars now—or did they always? It's hard to tell with your time; let us say their scars are new again. They bleed, but they still stand, and the city rises around them.

See soldiers sifting through the wreckage of the wall, the police trying to figure out who in all hells took control of their entire department. They know, of course, but it's easier to pretend they don't. Nobody will ask questions, and those who do will be made to stop asking. A few of the guilty will pay, though not nearly enough.

See a little red cat crawling from the wreckage, yowling. It is missing large patches of fur and has lost blood. It will find your girls, and they will love it, and it will heal.

See movement, from north to south and south to north. The soldiers will try to stop it at first, but they are spent and wounded, and no more orders are coming in. They relent. Weeks pass. Pieces of the wall jut forth from the earth like the fingers of a great iron god reaching to heaven. They are a monument to something, though I cannot yet say what.

See the shipwrights marveling at the Kopek, wondering how a warship got itself stuck in the canal. They try to get it out with a crane, but it's stuck fast. The city offers to buy a new ship for you as payment for services rendered. It could never be the same, but you smile and nod and, in the dead of night, have a crew of trustworthy sailors move the heart from one to the other.

See Wajet standing before the politicians. His arm is in a cast, his scars have healed poorly. The men in the seats shout, they roil, but Wajet stands at the lectern with a grin like a cat in a rats' nest. He likes this, you know—he was made for it. You've given him everything you know, and as he stomps up and down the Lords' chamber, jabbing his finger and waving papers, one person at a time, the hall falls silent. When this is done, almost half of them will be in chains. When it is done, he will have a seat with his name on it. I cannot say whether he will use it well.

See the woman put on her caul and step out of the greenroom and onto the stage. The bouncer is new, and there are scorch marks on the walls. It has been a strange and difficult week, and the room in front of her is not as full as it once was. Still, the crowd waits for her—this place is still home, despite it all. She takes a deep breath and begins to sing.

See Kanq-Sen pacing back and forth while the brass tell him that he's a good cop, that he did the right thing, that he'll keep quiet if he knows what's good for him. See him slow, lean on his cane, look so very tired. They've given him his badge back, but it feels too heavy, and the pin keeps jabbing him. "And what if I talk?" he says. They laugh. "Who will believe you?"

He nods, then takes off his badge and puts it on the table.

"Gentlemen," he mutters, "I think we're done here." And he leaves without another word and makes for the last place he felt good.

Come closer, little bird, I've a memory of you.

Near the cliffs, behind the olive groves, in a place far from here, there was a town. When the first boy went missing, they thought it must've been a wolf. They mourned, then got on with things: it wasn't a common occurrence, but not as rare as it should've been. When the second and the third went missing, they sent out search parties into *the night and slew every wolf they could find. When the fourth went missing, they came for you.*

Your mother had died the year before. She lived on the edge of the forest and knew every berry, bark, and leaf. She could ease pain, quicken or extinguish the flame in a woman's belly, send men into strange dreams. They called her "witch," but they dared not move against her, because she kept them healthy.

When the children started to go missing, they blamed her. You'd put her in the ground yourself. She passed in the depths of winter, coughing up phlegm and bits of lung, and nobody in the town would give you the things you needed. They came for her anyway, said she was a spirit, a demon, a revenant come back for the flesh of the innocent. When they couldn't find her, they chased you.

Out of the forest, out onto the plains and through the olive groves, out to the coast where the wind flattened the tough cliffside grasses. You ran for hours, but the hounds did not give up the chase.

That is where it ended; that is where it began. They beat you and burned you and threw you over the cliff. But they did not break you; if there is one thing I have seen throughout time, they cannot break you. Down through the water, all the water, to the bottom, so dark that all time is crushed together by the monstrous pressure. In that darkness, in the nexus of future and past, you hear feathers unfurl.

There is something here even I cannot see, eaten by the Quiet, but no memory comes to us complete.

You rise up through the water, but it's still too deep, and you drown. You drown again and again. You drown for a thousand years until you are shrieking, insensate, knowing only darkness and pressure. You drown until you are caught in a fisherman's net, and he pulls you up and up and the sunlight through the deep water burns you and you ache with power. I have seen a lot of violence, little bird, but I still have no words for how you hurt that man. An eon of suffering, forced outward, filling him with so much pain that his wrists opened on their own and he spilled out across the deck of his own little ship. I do not mean to hurt you with these words, but they must be said: hurt begets hurt. You must understand your enemy if you are to defeat her, and none know her better than you. You will break the cycle, starting with yourself, then the girl, then the gods. It takes a thousand years; it will take a thousand years; it has taken a thousand years.

I saw all this but did not speak: I could not. I alone knew what was coming, but I also knew I would never be believed. That is past now: Crane's eye is off you. She searches the jungles for more of her great enemy. Hainak will stand another day. At last, at the dusk of ages, you come to me.

Little bird, little shipwreck, little Sibbi.

Wise woman, lost girl, eater of days.

Come closer; there is work to be done.

FORTY-ONE

J yn Yat-Hok and Kiada sat together on the dock, looking out at the lighthouse. The heaviest rains had come and gone, but a gentle almost-mist fell around them. It was warm and not unpleasant. Time had passed enough for their hearts to stop fluttering, and now they sat in comfortable silence. Red purred in Kiada's lap. He was stubborn and wouldn't let them heal his scars; he'd scamper away whenever they tried. They'd given up and just let him heal naturally. Sibbi's new ship sat in the drydock across the harbor. She hadn't named it yet; it was bad luck to name a ship before it sailed.

"Iacci almost gave me up," said Kiada. "I told him to keep it a secret, that I didn't want you to know. I told him and Rikaza I'd seen you in town, and we made up a Northern name on the spot just in case you were, well, different from what I remembered. We heard you almost arrested a roof rat, so I thought maybe you'd changed. The crew didn't question it—folk on the ship change their names all the time, and I gave it a little bit of Tiger Weaving just to make sure. Folks don't notice me unless I want them to, and I just . . . wasn't sure I was ready to see you again. I was the one who'd asked Wajet to bring you onboard, but then I couldn't deal with it, so I made up a story about being some Northern girl, and everyone did their best to make you believe it."

"You speak Northern?" said Yat.

"Not a fuckin' word," said Kiada. "Why, do you?"

It occurred to her that she did not speak, as Kiada had said, a fuckin' word.

"You could've just talked to me, you know," said Yat.

Kiada tilted her head back and gave Yat a disbelieving stare.

"Just *talked* to you? You, even more scarred-up than me? You, who was so deep in yourself that you didn't even *recognize* me? My art only works if you aren't looking, and you certainly weren't looking. That made me angry, you know. I put on a mask because I was worried you'd know straightaway, but you didn't, and even after the mask came off, you didn't see me. Even when we ran together, or after that moron Iacci started playing our song. I don't understand that man. He finally caught that fucking mouse, and he put it in a box and let it out in the docks ward station. All that work just so it could get fat on police cheese."

"Wait," said Yat, "*our* song?"

"Yeah," said Kiada, "our song. I sang it once and you liked it, so I kept singing it because I liked seeing you happy. I don't even remember where I first heard it; I was so young when I first came to Hainak. It was during the war, you know—lots of us displaced, stuck in one town or another, waiting for it to blow over. I remember a ship, and somebody singing that song to me. I've been back to Accenza a few times, but it doesn't feel like home—I don't know anybody there. Home is where your family is, you know? Even if you haven't got one, you make a family: folks willing to walk beside you through even the worst times. You put your heads and hearts together, and that's how family happens—that's what makes a place home. You and I were family once. We had a song and everything."

"Were?" said Yat. She caught on the little fishhooks.

Kiada let out a long, slow breath. "Are," she said. "Maybe. I don't know. It's been a big week, you know?"

"Tell me about it," said Yat.

And Kiada did. They had a lot of catching up to do. As the night rolled on, they shouted and sang and kissed there on the dock, daring anybody to stop them. They ran their fingers through Red's gnarled fur, and repeated the steps until the first fingers of dawn came up over the eastern horizon.

A cane clicked against the wood behind them.

"Yep," said Sen, "that's light."

He sat down beside them and pointed at the sunrise. His uniform was a mess, and he smelled faintly of wine. He wasn't wearing his badge.

"Liiiiiight," he said.

One of Kiada's hands instinctively balled into a fist. Yat reached across and gave her forearm a gentle squeeze, an *I'm here*. They'd made a rule not to push thoughts on each other, so the small touch would have to do. She turned to Sen, then knocked out a mock salute with her free hand.

"With respect, Sarge," she said, "go fuck yourself, ya fuckin' fuckwit."

"That's go fuck yourself, *Mr.* Kanq-Sen," he said. "Handed in my papers. I'm a civilian now."

Yat was technically still a cop. She'd received a letter of amnesty that made a big show of how gracious it was, dangling the carrot of her old job back. She'd asked them whether they'd let her run a unit that rehabilitated street kids, that got them off the streets and into good homes, that stopped the other cops from doing them wrong. Not just a token seat, but a change in attitude on the force, a change of heart. There'd been no answer in almost a month, so she'd gone to the station and asked in person. Nobody had come out to see her, so she'd gone home and torn up their letter. She wanted to believe they'd really consider her offer, but she knew deep down they would never. The job wasn't about the people, it was about the *people*; the wretched, the different, the poor didn't count. It was about protecting those who needed the least protection. Her uniform hung in the closet back in her house—a house several stories higher than it had been when she'd moved in, now jutting out over Janekhai Street. It was larger, too, with an improbably huge bed and the glow of an electric lamp stuck in the "on" position, its energy coming from somewhere deep inside the wall. The house made her feel very small, though she and Kiada had spent several nights doing their best to fill it. She didn't fit there anymore: it was just a place they slept sometimes.

She took her flask out of her pocket and turned it over.

"You ever wonder whether you're holding on to the wrong things?" she said. "Struggling to keep memories alive while the people close to you are hurting? Trying to help people but never asking what sort of help they need? I feel like I've been laying down a story over the world, then getting angry when it doesn't fit; I never stopped to ask *why* it didn't fit. I never saw the woman standing next to me, because I hadn't written her there. I became a cop because I wanted to be a hero and help people. And now I don't know who I want to be, except that I want to be with you."

The engravings on the flask were beautiful. The woman who owned it had been a hero; the woman who owned it had died twice.

She barely even knew that woman anymore. She took a deep swig of cold tea. It tasted like its container: steel, tobacco, kiro. She spat it out into the water. Some of it ran down her front. She stood up, cocked her arm back, then threw the open flask as hard as she could. It splashed into the water and sank like a stone.

Kiada stood up, put an arm around her waist, cocked her head so it lay against Yat's shoulder. She was humming the aria: the third part, timid yet brave, filled with quiet strength. She hummed the whole thing, then kissed Yat on the cheek.

"I wonder that all the time," she said. "Now, finding the right things to hold on to, that's the bastard."

They stood there on the dock, making a powerful lack of eye contact.

"You're looking at me, aren't you?" said Yat.

"Yeah, dummy," said Kiada.

"Right."

Sen cleared his throat. Yat had forgotten he was still standing there.

"You gonna join us, miss," he said, "or are you happy with the whole lurking situation?"

Ajat stepped out of the darkness. She looked different, like she had when Yat first met her: no bags under her eyes, no shadow gracing her jaw. She was finely dressed in rich silks, with fresh biowork running up and down her arms: some alchemist-tailor was probably eyeing up a second house. The city had paid a lot to make sure everybody kept things quiet. Rikaza stood with her, dressed in practical leathers, though they'd replaced their old iron bull ring with a silver and sapphire arrangement that made them look like the monarch of some long-forgotten empire.

"We're going north," said Ajat. "Sibbi says there's something in

Dawgar that needs looking into. She also says that if you steal her bosun, she'll hunt you down across every ocean and then make up a few more just to cross to find you."

"She use those exact words?" said Yat.

"She was a bit more . . . emphatic. It doesn't translate well, but I'd take her on her word—the last country that fucked with her doesn't exist anymore."

Yat grimaced. She'd felt at home on the ship, but she wasn't sure whether she was back in Sibbi's good graces. And Hainak was home, too, wasn't it? She'd fought hard for it and made it better. She couldn't just turn and run. She had family here, though she also had family on the *Kopek*. The epiphany crept up on her while she rolled it over in her head: she didn't have to choose one home. It could be with Mr. Ot and his little daughter Bykra, or on the docks with Kiada, or a bar with a white door, or the Sea of Teeth or Ladowain or Suta or the thrice-cursed North, if that was where her family went.

"I'm no sailor," she said. Which didn't even begin to cover it.

"Bullshit," said Kiada. "You're a born sailor. You're quick, you're light, and you even come with your own cat."

"You're a taniwha," said Ajat. "You belong in the water."

"I'm a dragon?" said Yat.

Ajat laughed. "Gods," she said, "I thought we had this conversation already. Not a sea monster, not a dragon. No, a taniwha is first a kaitiaki: a guardian. Second, a taniwha is a fierce and powerful world-spirit, one with sea and soil. Third, it sorta looks like a dragon if you squint. Everybody starts at number three for some reason. Look, you planted your feet in the land and grew a whole damned forest in your home overnight, real taniwha shit. I know you're short on scales, but change takes time. Gods do I know, change takes time."

Kiada held up Red. Most of his belly fur was missing, though it was growing back slowly in patches and clumps. His legs swung back and forth. "Mrrow," he said, looking as disdainful as a cat could.

"I'm just . . ." said Yat. She thought back to that awful night when she'd felt the shadow of Crane's wings fall over her, when she'd looked into Żao's head and seen a vision of a tree going up and up into heaven. It wasn't a metaphor: he'd *seen* something. She tried to think back, but it was all fragments. Freezing cold, a monotone voice on repeat in a language she didn't understand, roots drinking deep and . . .

. . . the smell of fresh snow. Not her own memory. Something she'd stolen along the way, but something painfully, intimately familiar.

"North," she said. "You said north?"

She looked back at Hainak, then to Ajat and Rikaza and Kiada and Red. She'd keep Kiada here and face Sibbi's wrath if she had to, but she knew on some level beyond sense that this business wasn't over. Whatever this looming darkness was, it would be back. Hainak wouldn't leave, and if her family there did, she would find home wherever they went.

"North," said Ajat. "And then? Who knows. I think we've gotten enough of this town for now."

A squeak cut through the night—it sounded like two pieces of soap being rubbed together. Yat turned to see Iacci walking toward them, moving a small dark block along the hair of his viol bow. He grinned as he saw them. He wore the same clothes as always and carried the same viol, but tied to his back was a large hessian sack with the word ROSIN printed in blue across it. After rubbing on another layer, he held up his bow for inspection.

"I have caught the mousy," he said. "It is no more."

He put the rosin cake back in his sack, then placed his hand on his heart and nodded. Yat didn't know what it meant, but he seemed satisfied, and pointed at Red with his bow.

"I have heard Mrs. Sibbi's protestations on the matter," he said, "but I place my vote in the 'yes' for Miss Yat. She has a cat, and this is good on a ship."

"Well, that settles it," said Rikaza. "Can't argue with the votes. You're family now, Jyn Yat-Hok. Report to the *Kopek* by 0700."

Yat sighed and smiled at Kiada. She could do this.

"Sure," she said. "Not like I was doing much else."

Ajat turned to Sen. "You coming, old man?" she said.

"Didn't think you'd want a cop aboard," said Sen.

Ajat grinned at him. "Nah," she said. "You're good luck: pigs float, and I reckon I'll make a friend of you yet. If you're really lucky, maybe I'll even give you a tattoo."

He sighed. "Sure," he said, in a piping imitation of Yat's voice. "Not like I was doing much else."

Yat flicked him a rude hand sign, and he grinned at her. For a moment, she felt cold, and knew she stood in the shadow of a great pair of wings. Crane's words came to her unbidden: *You will die by my hand or you will die by your own, and either way, you have no choice.* She looked to the moon, then to her friends. She could feel the winter chill in her bones, the weight of the sky pushing down. She stood dockside, staring out over the endless dark water, and took a breath that burned her throat and made her voice quaver.

"Maybe," she said, "but not today."

Small words, but the shadow fell back.

Kiada stared at her, eyes wide with worry. "You all right?" she said.

"Yeah," said Yat. "Yes, everything's fine."

They stood in a circle around her, attentive. Rikaza put a hand on her shoulder and squeezed. Ajat did the same, as did Iacci and Kiada and Sen. They embraced in silence. Few words moved between them, but they knew each other in the way of family and knew what to do.

"I'm all right," said Yat, her voice muffled into a shoulder, made rough by pain. "I'm really, really all right."

And she meant it. She thought she'd forgotten how to cry, but it came up now, all at once, and she didn't stop because she didn't need to, and so the rain came. She smiled through her tears, and felt them change course, running through the lines in her face—rivers breaking, merging, weaving across her smile, carving across her cheeks, turning barren earth into fresh soil again. The rain came, and she let it, and they stayed close until it was done and the danger had passed. It was enough, for now. Kiada kissed her on the cheek, then smiled, then kissed her again. They kissed as the rest of the group moved back one by one, chuckling or biting lips or pretending not to look.

"Ah," said Iacci. He drew his bow across the strings and played a bar of their song. When he was done, he lowered his violin and nodded to himself. He was staring out to sea when he spoke next.

"It ends with a kiss," he said. "Very good."

The group turned and stumbled toward the new ship. Kiada and Yat stayed close, leaning on one another, taking turns to hold the cat, taking turns to hold each other. The sun rose over the horizon, and the family went together.

[LOG DBG 43 00:00:00:00—FATAL SYSTEM ERROR]

Źao awoke facedown between the tracks. No, not Źao, Źao was dead. There was a protocol. Meet back at the tree, revise identities, head back south. He'd changed identities so many times it had become a habit, but in the space between faces he always went back to the first one, which fit like an old jumper: Hector. He'd held on to it for generations, seen it shift and change as the world changed around him, collide with other names and change into something he barely recognized. There were only four living souls who remembered Hector, though the integrity of one of those souls was negotiable, and another was . . . out of commission, but hopefully not beyond recovery. Three souls, perhaps: two whole ones and two maybes. He groaned and rolled onto his back. A guttering electric light flickered on the roof above him. His arms were stiff at his sides: he'd been electrocuted more than once by coming back in the wrong position. Hell of a new tether. His own damned fault, but he'd been paying for that mistake for millennia.

Where was everybody? The station intercom gave a distorted ping, and a female voice filled the tunnel. *Message repeats: the 26:15 to Crow Hearth is delayed until [Dunbraig/1.4/7600 00:00:00:00]. Please remain in the terminal: an attendant will see to your needs. Norlink is proud to provide a selection of [panic: runtime error: index out of range].* Her voice changed: harsh, male, different accent. Svensdottir and McCullough, of course. Hard to tell which generation from voice alone, but they were largely coherent, so that meant it wasn't latest gen. Red lights flickered on, and the McCullough blared, *ERROR 458 ERROR 458: Obstruction on the tracks. Staff, please report to platform six.*

Careful not to touch the rails, Hector stood. A faceless stared at him. Well, *stared* was the wrong word: it stood at attention, with its smooth skin-plate facing in his direction. The red light inside its head dulled and turned halogen-yellow, and the Svensdottir returned.

Passengers, we are clearing an obstruction on the tracks. Please stay in your seats. Complimentary refreshments will be brought out to you, but remember: patience is its own reward. Have a nice day, and thank you for choosing Norlink!

He took a careful step over the rail, then hauled himself up onto the platform. A squad of faceless normally had him in the sauna by now. They couldn't hold a conversation like the clones could, but he didn't dare go anywhere near the vat facility these days. What had Luis called it? Some pair of words as sharp and hard as bullets. *Bit rot*, that was it. *Can't store a soul on SSD, no matter what Vic says.* Hector gathered himself, then turned to the faceless.

"News," he said.

Static burbled from inside the faceless's smooth blank domepiece. "Status report: Crow Hearth," he said.

The 26:15 to Crow Hearth is delayed until [Dunbraig/1.4/7600 00:00:00:00]. Please remain in the—

He waved it away and made his way through the terminal. It was a mess. The food inside the automat vending machines had long since turned to slime. Trust goddamned white folks to put hot sausages inside a subway wall and expect them to do anything but rot. The few faceless left weren't working properly: they were stuck in strange loops, walking into doors, babbling nonsense. He made his way to the viewing platform, where happy families would—once upon a time—wait to watch the trains. At first, he thought something was wrong with the window panels, maybe a malfunction that set them to white. Then he realized it was moving: a blizzard the likes of which he'd never seen. He stood there for almost an hour watching the snow fall. A faceless kept trying to bring him an empty jug stained red with traces of old wine. He ignored it and stared out.

For a moment, just one perfect moment, there was a gap in the snow, and Hector saw:

—the great dam at Crow Hearth, towering into the night, a great dark edifice, its lights extinguished—

—an iron hulk on the tracks, with the ruins of a train curled around it: something like a great spider the size of a city, crowned with a dozen chimneys, still letting out a gentle plume of dark smoke staining the sky black—

—beyond the dam, emerging from the heart of the city itself, reaching to heaven, weaving back and forth in the polar wind—

Despite his headache, despite the empty station, despite everything he'd been through, Hekat smiled.

The hunt wasn't over. There was work to be done.

339

ACKNOWLEDGMENTS

First and foremost, Dave Agnew, friend, confidant, accidental publicist, and agent for the first edition. Nothing you're reading now would've happened without Dave, who believed in it from day one and threw himself into getting *The Dawnhounds* on New Zealand bookshelves, who lugged boxes of books around Wellington, who spent far too much time answering emails and queuing in the post office on my behalf. He's also a much better author than he gives himself credit for; dammit, Dave, finish the wizard book, we all believe in you. You're my . . . monorail? I still don't understand *Homestuck*, but I think Dave is my monorail.

To Joy and Wayne, Lucy and Claire, who are all more patient than I deserve.

To Sara and Amara, who took this from small press to world stage without stripping away a single part of its soul. I suppose that's the magic of editing; a good editor can make a book more like itself, and I have a *very* good editor.

To Danny, who helped with the Mandarin translations, who has a much better taste in music than I do, and who wrote a horror-comedy about a precocious corgi that I have been totally unable to forget for over five years now.

To the team at Saga, to Bo for the cover, to the copy editor and proofreader and publicists who have to put up with me constantly trying to smuggle incomprehensible NZ slang in under the wire.

To Hugfest, who were there from the start with honest crit and excellent company, and from whom I have learned many things about centaurs, most of them against my will. For what it's worth, I still think the human bit would need to Naruto run; there's just too much wind resistance otherwise. It's in a published book now so if you roast me in the group chat, just know I have citations.

To Pepper, whose original first-edition cover art is never coming down from my wall.

To Mel, Andi, Eddie, Cass, Marie, Rem, and the whole damn Wellington SFF community. I forget how many of y'all I owe drinks at this point, but you know where to find me. You know what they say: you can't live here by chance.

To you, whoever you are. There is not enough time in the world to list everybody who had a hand in this, but I see you.

To Tamsyn. I am still baffled as to why you took a chance on me but I'm eternally grateful you did. I believe you were one of the first ten people to read the book; I don't think my mum had even gotten around to reading it at that point, and I don't know whether any of this would've been possible without you in my corner.

And finally, to the bizarre found family of authors I stumbled into almost a decade ago, you beautiful mad bastards. I love you all, but I love Crabrock the most. May you wear thunder like a crown.

I said it the first time around, but it's even more true now: it takes a bloody village, aye?